I0603614

PERFECT SEX

ROBIN STOREY

This book is a work of fiction. Any resemblance to any person alive or dead is purely coincidental. The Sunshine Coast is real and apart from some well-known landmarks to provide authenticity, locations within that setting are fictional.

Copyright Robin Storey © 2013

www.storey-lines.com

The right of Robin Storey to be identified as the author of this work has been asserted by her in accordance with the Copyright Act (Australia) 1968.

All rights reserved. No part of this publication may be reproduced in any manner whatsoever without written permission from the copyright owner, except in the case of quotations used for reviews or articles about the book.

Cover design by Judy Bullard

Customebookcovers.com

DEDICATION

For Aaron

TABLE OF CONTENTS

PART ONE

PART TWO

PART THREE

PART ONE

Chapter 1

Body type: average (should I say slim? I'm only slim when I'm wearing my long black skirt and haven't eaten all day)

Eye colour: brown

Hair colour: fair (they don't have a category for nondescript brown)

Smoke: no

Drink: social (don't laugh, I'm very social when I'm drinking)

Have children: yes and I live with them ('co-exist' might be a better word)

Want children: no (can it be retrospective?)

Ethnic background: Australian (should I put something more exotic? I believe my grandmother had a dalliance with a member of the French Foreign Legion)

Religion: none

Occupation: communications (they don't have a category for aspiring gold-digger/bestseller novelist)

Education level: degree/diploma

Political persuasion: swinging voter (I take it that doesn't mean partner-swapping at election time)

Vegetarian: sometimes (on off pay weeks)

Personality type: social

Sign of the zodiac: Gemini

INTERESTS:

Music: I love traditional jazz, Van Morrison, Pink Floyd, Supertramp and Joe Cocker.

Reading: biographies, whodunnits, humour, *Bridget Jones's Diary* is a favourite

Movies: Crime, romantic comedies, anything with Tom Hanks, Billy Crystal, Meg Ryan

Sport: I enjoy walking, bodysurfing and I go to the gym as often as possible (about once a month, but who's to know?)

I'm a freelance writer and mother of two, and enjoy a busy, independent lifestyle. I work from home and I enjoy going to the beach, which is 10 minutes walk from my home, and going to the theatre and movies. I love reading but don't get time to do as much as I would like. My ideal man is over ninety and rich with a nasty cough, but failing that I'll settle for an intelligent, tolerant guy with a good sense of humour, who enjoys music and stimulating conversation.

IDEAL PARTNER:

Between 40 and 55 years old, looking for just a friend, short-term or long-term relationship.

***

Email to: JulesYoung4ever@gmail.com

From: SusieH@gmail.com

Hi Jules. Just enclosing my profile to submit to eMatch. What do you think? If you were an unattached man between 40 and 55 looking for a date (not a one-night stand), would you contact me?

Love,

Susie.

After I've clicked the send button, I log into the website of eMatch to have another browse through the gallery of potential perfect partners. Cara swaggers into the doorway, jeans almost falling off her non-existent hips, her midriff top revealing the smooth expanse of concave adolescent belly inlaid with a twinkling belly button jewel.

I hit the exit button.

'What's for dinner, Mum?' she asks.

Her boyfriend Jay comes up from behind and rests his head on her shoulder. They look like a freak circus act — one body, two heads. If only they were, then I wouldn't have to worry about what the two bodies are doing when I go to the shops.

'Wouldn't have the faintest idea.'

'We're going for a walk.'

I try not to look at Jay's lip. He has two rings through it. I am fascinated and at the same time repelled by body piercings. Just imagining someone putting a needle through my lip sends little arrows of pain shooting through me. And what would kissing Jay be like? Eating paper clips?

The thought of Cara kissing him makes my insides squirm and I expunge the image from my mind before it goes any further. Kids think the idea of their parents having sex is repugnant, with wrinkles and cellulite slapping against each other and things getting lost in folds of skin; but the thought of them banging away with their taut butts, unblemished thighs and flat stomachs makes us sick too. Particularly when it's your sixteen-year-old daughter and a monosyllabic sex maniac with metal lips and God knows what else on other parts of his body.

Stop thinking about sex!

I go into the kitchen and start preparing the sausage casserole. While I'm chopping carrots and thinking about creative things you can do in the kitchen (like the scene in *Nine and a Half Weeks* where Kim Basinger and Mickey Rourke smother each other with honey and whipped cream), Jules phones.

'Are you looking for a carer for Grandma?'

'What?'

'Or a babysitter for the cat?'

'What are you on about?'

'Your profile — the only men you're going to catch with that are some doddery old fart who can't get it up and wants you to spoonfeed him his Viagra, or a poof who minces around quoting Sartre and who's too scared to come out of the closet.'

Never having been great at biology, I haven't the faintest idea where my hackles are, but I can feel them rising all the same.

'What's wrong with it? Anyway, you're hardly one to talk about being too scared to come out of the closet.'

Jules has the misfortune of being bisexual, and apart from Woody Allen's adage that it doubles your chances of a date on a Saturday night, it's had the effect of leaving him in a permanent state of confusion and indecision.

'You know perfectly well I've come out of the closet — it's just that when the big world out there gets too scary, I have to scuttle back in with the brooms and dustpans, and the Australian rugby team. I'll write a profile for you that'll have men queuing up to go out with you.'

My hackles have now risen so high I'm in danger of being spirited away by them. How dare he presume he can write a better profile than I can! So he won a national award for best TV ad, but I like to think I'm a cut above *Snugglepot* disposable nappies. Anyway, do I want men queuing up to go out with me? Or is this just my fear of success sabotaging me?

***

'Of course you want men queuing up to go out with you,' Myf says. 'If this is for journalistic research, you want to date as many men as you can.'

She, Annie and I are having our post-power walk coffee at our favourite cafe, Bee-Jays, on the Mooloolaba Esplanade. Usually the slightest indication of rain, wind or other meteorological irregularities results in the walk being abandoned in favour of the coffee, but the spring weather has been so clear and mild, we've run out of excuses.

'What's this about research?' Annie asks. 'I thought you were just doing this because you're so horny that every male over the age of forty will be in danger of being assaulted if you don't get your rocks off.'

'Yes, I mean, no. Look, I had this brilliant idea to put a profile on the net, see how many replies I get, meet the guys and go out on a date if I like them; and then write a book about my experiences – a sort of guide to internet dating for the over forties. If I happen to find someone I really like along the way, that's an added bonus.'

Annie rolls her eyes. 'You're so full of shit! I've seen you on the beach when the lifesavers are doing their kayaking training with their Speedos pulled right up their bums. It's a competition to see what's hanging out the most — your eyes or your tongue.'

'Hanging out is the operative term,' Myf says. 'Anyway, so what if she's doing it just for the sex? Women are in their prime in their forties.'

'Is that what Jason told you while you were packing his school lunch?' I ask.

'Jealousy is a curse,' Myf says, baring her teeth at me. 'Jason is very mature for a 25-year-old male — he can actually make his own lunch. If we're not at uni at lunchtime, we're usually in bed.'

'I can't remember the last time Richard and I did it during the day,' Annie says. 'We're flat out finding the energy to do it at all.'

'Try phoning him at work and telling him to come home at lunchtime, and then meet him at the door in a see-through negligee,' I say. 'I wrote that once in an article on "Fifty Ways To Spice Up Your Marriage".'

'Did it work for you?' Myf asks.

'I just wrote it; I didn't actually do it myself.'

'That's just it!' Myf slams her coffee cup into her saucer. 'Those articles in women's magazines are all crap — how to seduce your man, rediscover the passion, blah blah. Why is it always the woman's responsibility? Why can't the man rush home from work and cook a three- course meal and then appear at the door in a G-string?'

Annie giggles. 'Bit embarrassing if it happens to be the plumber! If Richard did that, I'd be laughing so hard I'd choke on my dinner. Then I'd plead food poisoning and go to bed with a book.'

It seems to me inevitable that boredom sets in when you've been married for a while. When you're first together, you're at it all the time. Then with time and familiarity, sex becomes a chore — particularly after children. Not one married woman I know admits to enjoying sex with her husband.

I think back over my own marriage. There was no rabbit phase. It was bland from the start. Back then I thought it was normal to lie awake in my husband's arms after sex with a niggling sensation that something was missing. And The Voice was always there in the background, piping up at the most annoying moments.

Well, that was pretty ordinary.

Orgasms aren't everything, I told it. It's just as nice giving pleasure to your partner and lying naked together and being close to each other.

Yeah, right.

Jeremy and I are such good friends, I'd reason. That's more than a lot of couples have. So it's not important if there are no fireworks in our sex life.

Forget the fireworks, you haven't even got a sparkler.

Sometimes I could swear I was schizophrenic and when The Voice wouldn't shut up, I'd get out of bed and sit on the patio with a glass of wine, looking at the moon and wondering if I was being ungrateful and selfish to want more out of my marriage.

'Relationships are so complicated sometimes,' Myf says. 'Thank God for a girl's best friend.'

'Diamonds?' Annie frowns.

Myf looks at both of us, eyebrows raised.

'Oh.' Annie's cheeks glow pink. She looks around then drops her voice to a conspiratorial low.

'I haven't used my vibrator for ages; it's at the back of the cupboard somewhere. But it's so noisy — no wonder it was in the marked-down stock bin.'

'As long as it wasn't in "Preloved Goods",' Myf says.

Annie grimaces. 'Last time I used it was when Richard was away and the guy next door banged on the wall and told me to turn it down!'

'Perhaps you can buy a silencer for it,' I suggest.

'Jason and I use mine during sex,' Myf says. 'He gets really turned on watching me use it. He even takes photos.'

'Anyway, I must be off,' I say, getting up hurriedly before Myf whips out her iPhone and shows us the evidence. 'A sex researcher's work is never done.'

As I walk home along the Esplanade, I'm thinking that I've missed a vital part of my sex education. Since when did a vibrator become a necessary female accessory? It's never been mentioned in any of the magazine articles on fifty things a woman should never be without, along with a little black dress, panty liners and $20 taxi fare. Annie and Myf are obviously old hands with vibrators; and I've never even used one, let alone owned one. I always thought they were for oversexed or desperate women. Hang on, that's me!

I survey the faces of the women sitting in the cafes and restaurants that sprawl along the pavement looking out over the ocean. It's Friday afternoon and there's a vibrant buzz of expectancy as everyone winds down from the week and gears up for the weekend.

How many of them have used a used a vibrator? Those teenage girls flirting with the waiter? They start young these days. That group of middle-aged corporate-suited women sipping on their chardonnays? Or that gorgeous young thing sitting at a table by herself — is the mind beneath that halo of blonde hair racing with images of her last encounter with her favourite sex toy?

Am I the only woman in the Western world who's never used a vibrator?

Chapter 2

'No, you're not.' Jules says. 'My mother's never used one.'

I've managed to wrestle the phone out of Cara's grip and have closeted myself in my bedroom.

'At least not for its intended purpose. She found one while she was staying here, that an old girlfriend had left behind, and she thought it was a back massager. She said she felt heaps better after using it, and I said people usually do.'

'That doesn't cheer me up to think that even your mother's one up on me in the sexual toys department. And which girlfriend was this that left the vibrator behind?'

As Jules's closest friend, I consider I have the right to be a bit proprietary when it comes to his partners, past and present.

'Annaliese. I don't think you met her.'

That's not surprising. She wouldn't have lasted more than a few weeks, and she would have been a knockout, of course. Nothing but the best for Jules, including partners.

'Anyway, I'll have to rectify this glaring gap in my sexual experience. Can you help me buy a vibrator? I don't have a clue where to start.'

'A sex shop would be a logical place. And what makes you think I'm an expert on vibrators?'

'You're more of an expert than I am — at least you've had temporary possession of one.'

'Your flawless logic never fails to astound me. Okay, you name the time and place. Now, check your email. I've done that profile for you.'

***

To: SusieH@gmail.com

From: JulesYoung4ever@gmail.com

Hi Susie,

Here's your new, improved profile. For a writer, your creative skills are sadly lacking in this department — you need to learn the art of shameless self-promotion. I've revamped the second part of your profile, with the emphasis on *vamp*. My comments are in brackets.

INTERESTS:

Music: I love most kinds of music — R'n'B, jazz, Robbie Williams, Macy Gray, The Black Keys, Green Day (forget Supertramp and Pink Floyd, your taste has to be eclectic but modern)

Reading: I do love to read sexy books and when I have a spare afternoon, I love nothing better than to relax in my spa with a glass of champagne and an erotic novel.

Movies: I love the movies! My taste is varied — *The Godfather, Rocky, Lord of the Rings*. I love the old Hollywood classics, foreign films and I adore sci-fi. Can't wait for the next *Aliens* movie. (romantic comedies are a no-no — most men won't admit to liking them even if they do. A woman who likes sc-fi is a definite turn-on)

Sport: I work out at the gym regularly as I like to keep fit, and I also enjoy swimming and jogging on the beach. I think it would be fun to try some indoor sports...

I absolutely LOVE life and don't take myself too seriously. I'm attractive, fit, fun-loving, with a great personality and a bod to match. Now I'll tell you about my good qualities. I love energetic activities, all types of music and dancing, particularly belly dancing, and going to the beach (getting my gear off and feeling the water lap over my body). I love cooking up a storm in the kitchen; anything to please my man. I am a very passionate woman, and I would love to hear from you if you are a passionate guy who wants a real woman.

What do you think?

Love,

Jules.

***

'Why don't I just come right out and say "I'm incredibly horny and I want someone who'll screw my brains out?"'

We're in Jules's car on the way to the sex shop.

'The number one rule of internet dating is never tell the truth,' Jules replies. 'You have to start out on the basic premise that everyone is exaggerating to some degree to make themselves look as attractive as possible. So you have to do the same to put yourself on a level playing field.'

'If that profile puts me on a level playing field, then I'm lying at the goalpost with my legs open yelling, "come on fellas, score a goal!"'

Jules gives an exaggerated sigh. 'Susie, Susie, Susie, let me give you a quick lesson in how men think.'

I glance at him. He's wearing hot pink cargo shorts, a floral shirt with lots of pink in it, and four gold chains around his neck. Barbra Streisand is blaring out of the CD player and in the console, two bottles of nail polish nestle furtively together.

'Okay, tell me how men think.'

'Men's brains are not wired for subtlety. You have to give it to them straight. I'll admit that profile makes you sound like a nymphomaniac, but that's what men want — at least, that's what they think they want. So you use the "If-you're-the-right-guy-for-me-I'll-bonk-you-till-your-eyes-pop-out" approach to lure them in, and when they meet you they'll discover all your other good qualities and fall madly in love with you. And they won't care that your favourite movie is *When Harry Met Sally* and that you don't have a spa.'

'What about the great bod and working out at the gym bit?'

'What about all the guys on eMatch with six packs who supposedly spend two hours at the gym every day and do ninety-five different sports? You can bet the only six packs most of them have seen are the ones they pick up from the bottle shop. Anyway, there's nothing wrong with your body — you look pretty good for your age.'

'I don't want to look pretty good for my age,' I wail. 'I want to look good for a twenty-five-year-old.'

'Exaggeration's fine, but let's not set the bar too high.'

The sex shop is on a busy road in Maroochydore sandwiched between a florist and an electronics store. It's painted in the traditional red and black, and proclaims itself unashamedly in large letters – 'The Love Shack'. A mannequin with a Barbie doll figure in a black see-through negligee, stay-up stockings with lacy tops and shoes that would need a high-rise permit poses in the front window, her vacant gaze resting on a large, furry stuffed cat beside her.

I can't resist the temptation to take a quick look around to see if anyone I know is lurking around waiting to spot me going inside. It's a tribute to progress that trenchcoats, sunglasses and seediness are no longer prerequisites for frequenting a sex shop. I put on my 'woman-of-the-world-we-all-have-needs-that-have-to-be-met' expression as we go inside.

'Don't put on that fake woman-of-the-world look,' Jules says. 'There's nothing to be embarrassed about.'

There are no other customers in the shop. I guess sex is not foremost in most people's minds at nine-thirty on a Saturday morning.

The decor inside is also red with black trimmings. Our feet sink into plush red carpet and Barry White's deep mellifluous tones in *'Can't Get Enough Of Your Love'* are reverberating throughout the store. I remember reading an interview with Barry White in which he claimed that a whole generation of children had been conceived to his music. Everywhere I look there are breasts and phalluses. I stand in the hallowed halls of hedonism, not knowing where to begin.

There's a whole wall devoted to penises, with or without attachments. Interspersed amongst the shelves of edible body paint, fur-lined hand and ankle cuffs, lingerie and latex outfits, penis-shaped bottle openers and adult board games (Strip Scrabble, What's Your Perversion), are rows of simpering women and smug men (and I guess I'd be simpering and smug if I were as well-endowed as they are), leering at me from the covers of boxes and magazines and DVDs. I feel as if I've arrived at an orgy where everybody's started without me.

The young sales assistant with the come-to-bed-and-I'll-show-you-my-new-toys eyes smiles at us and leans over the counter, exposing a cleavage that the average man could disappear into.

'Hiya Jules,' she drawls. 'How'ya going?'

'Great, Lisa. How are you?'

'Not bad. Can't complain.'

'You'd be mad to in your job.' Jules turns to me and whispers, 'She gets to road test all the stock.'

'How come you're on first-name terms with her?' I hiss back.

'I've been here before, a couple of times. A man has needs too, you know.'

He points at the penis wall. 'That's what you want. Have a look and see what takes your fancy.'

That's like asking Peter Pan what sort of condom he prefers. I start at the end and work my way along.

I notice that there are two types of vibrators. There are the clit stimulators, encompassing a thorough representation of the animal kingdom, from dolphins to eagles. Or you can go the whole hog and have the penis attachment as well. The penises are all obviously in the aroused state and look huge. It's been a long time since I saw a real one — are they always that big? Or are they like condoms and only come in large or extra large? They all boast an extraordinary range of titillating movements, and for a moment I have a fantasy about all the vibrators being turned on at once, the wall coming alive as a vibrating, pulsating mass, luring anyone who comes close and subjecting them to eternal orgasms, like a scene from *Alien* meets *Hot Swedish Lesbians*.

I look around for Jules. With relief I notice he's not browsing amongst the detachable double dongs and butt-rammers. He's in the lingerie section, immersed in a sea of fishnet, lace and nylon, thoughtfully fingering a fur-lined G-string.

'I'm thinking of becoming a cross-dresser,' he says. 'Women's lingerie is so sexy — why don't they make lingerie for men?'

'I guess men borrow it from their wives or girlfriends,' I reply. 'But there's an opening for you, if you like.'

'Hmm ... Lingerie for Men — masculine yet soft and sensual. For the man who wants to wear something a little daring under his suit for that important business meeting or just to lounge around at home watching the footy. Yes, I think it could work.'

'Sorry to interrupt your fantasies, but I don't have a clue what to buy. It's not as if there's a money-back guarantee.'

'A friend told me that the Japanese sort are the best,' Jules says. 'Haven't you noticed that Japanese women are always smiling?'

'I thought it was a cultural thing — you know, being polite and courteous.'

'Very deceptive, but no — they're always smiling because they're in a permanent state of sexual satisfaction due to the superior quality of their vibrators. But don't take my word for it, or rather my friend's word. Let's ask Lisa.'

Jules goes over to the penis wall and selects a box inscribed with the words 'Catwoman Vibrator, Product of Japan'. A curvaceous woman in a catsuit almost leaps off the front of the box with the anticipation of what's inside. Jules opens it and slides out a pink plastic penis with a clit stimulator attachment in the shape of a dolphin's beak. The head of the penis is shaped into a woman's head. Why a woman? Considering where she's going to be inserted, wouldn't it be more appropriate for it to be a man's head?

The blurb on the back of the box promises me 'multi-speed rotation and vibration with five exciting rhythms that will make your toes curl'. I'm not sure whether the ecstasy will be worth the agony of a permanent foot affliction. The rhythm bit arouses some apprehension. I've never been good at anything rhythmic; I couldn't even march in time at school. That would be the ultimate ego deflation: my vibrator rejecting me because I can't keep up with it.

Jules takes the vibrator over to the counter where Lisa is rearranging a box of breast-shaped erasers and sharpeners. She's standing upright now and the valley of her cleavage has become two gigantic mountains.

'Can you give us a demo on this?' Jules enquires.

Up until now I think I've managed the cool, nonchalant act quite well. I've casually surveyed shelves of rough rider condoms and flavoured lubricant, strolled past a wall of anal teasers without even a backward glance and studied rows of vibrators with the same care and intensity as if I were considering brands of tuna in the supermarket.

But now I feel the embarrassment rising up my face. I don't need a demo. Surely it comes with an instruction booklet. Let's just buy it and get out of here.

Jules glances at me. 'It's OK,' he says out of the corner of his mouth. 'She's not going to use it on herself.'

Lisa opens up the box and removes the vibrator. 'I'll just put some batteries in,' she says, bending down behind the counter.

She pops up again, breasts quivering like excited jellies, slides open the battery cover at the back of the control panel and inserts the batteries.

She switches it on. The penis lights up to a dusky pink and the dolphin's beak quivers (so fast that it gives a double beak effect) to the accompaniment of a high-pitched humming.

'That's the clit stimulator.'

She must think I'm a total idiot, or just escaped from a nunnery.

'I really don't need...'

'Or you can have the works.' She turns on another switch. The penis flashes green and begins to swing around in a circle, faster and faster, the woman's head lurching crazily around, all the while emitting a throaty whirr as a bass in contrast to the dolphin beak's soprano.

It's like something out of sideshow alley, like one of those gimmicky toys that Zac brings home in his show bag that breaks after two hours. My face is on fire and I daren't look around, in case there's a crowd of curious spectators behind me.

'That's full speed,' Lisa explains. 'You wouldn't start off with that, you'd work up to it.'

'Okay, it looks fine, how much?'

'One hundred and sixty dollars,' she says. She sees the look on my face. 'I'll throw in some new batteries as well. This is top of the range — you won't regret it.'

'Is that a personal testimonial?' Jules asks.

Lisa smiles knowingly and sticks her boobs out even further, something I wouldn't have thought possible. 'You'll be on the ceiling. Guaranteed.'

I thought Jules was joking about her road testing the products. A vision pops into my mind of Lisa at home in the evenings surrounded by erotic goodies, fragrant clouds of incense and massage oil wafting through her neighbourhood, accompanied by the steady hum of battery-operated implements and the sighs and moans from the latest *Confessions of a Pool Cleaner* DVD.

On the way home, brown paper package on my knee, I contemplate Lisa's confidence in my levitating abilities. It's a pity it's not the children's weekend to visit their father. The wall between my bedroom and Cara's is far from soundproof. My options are either to lock the bedroom door and put on Pink Floyd at full volume, or wait until tonight after they're both asleep.

I'm leaning towards option number two. Number one will arouse the children's suspicions and I'm not confident of Zac's ability to restrain himself from breaking into my bedroom if he discovers we're out of ice-cream.

'Do you want a coffee?' I ask Jules as we pull into my driveway.

'Love to but I can't. I've got Max coming round at eleven o'clock to give me some advice about redecorating. '

I think of Jules's immaculate little unit at Alexandra Headland with ocean views. All glass and chrome like something out of *Beautiful Homes and Gardens*, furnished in what decorators call the minimalist style. To my mind it's cold and clinical without any of the personal touches I have in my own decor — a combination of family hand-me-downs, what's on special at A-mart and objets d'art made by the children.

'Your place doesn't need redecorating.' Then the penny drops. 'Oh, I get it. Max is your next conquest.'

When Jules was dating Dan, the architect, he redesigned his whole apartment; with James the chef, he took cordon bleu cooking classes; and with Helen the doctor — let's just say I was never quite brave enough to ask what services she provided. Assuming that Max is an interior decorator, it will be interesting to see what he does with Jules's apartment.

From minimalist you can only add on, unless you go for the warehouse look — bare floor and walls.

'You don't have to put it like that,' Jules says. 'At least I have some conquests. I hope you and your vibrator will be very happy together.'

'I hope so too.'

When I walk in the front door clutching my package under my arm, Cara and Jay are entwined on the couch watching 'Rage Top 40 Hits'. Cara is sitting with her legs draped diagonally over Jay's and his arms are wrapped tightly around her with one hand resting on her breast. As a concession to my presence, he moves his hand fractionally so it's resting just below her breast.

'Hi Sue,' he says, as if it's perfectly acceptable for him to be sitting there on my couch mauling my daughter.

What I really want to say is 'Don't your parents like you? You're never at home because you're always here. Don't you have any other friends or hobbies?'

But instead I say 'Hi Jay'. There are two used bowls on the kitchen bench.

'Put those two bowls in the dishwasher please,' I say to Cara. That will disrupt her cosy little tete-a-tete for a few seconds.

Zac is in his bedroom ensconced in front of his Wii, glassy-eyed with fingers flying in rapid rhythm over the control buttons. It's hard to tell whether there's any direct connection from his brain to the rest of his body.

'Hi Mum.' He lifts his eyes from the screen just long enough to notice my package. 'Did you buy anything for me?'

'No.'

'Oh.' And just as I'm walking away, he says, 'By the way, we're out of ice-cream!'

I go into my study and shut the door. I turn the computer on and log into eMatch. I choose Sunshine Coast area, age category of 45-60 and start browsing.

There are no new ones since yesterday. There's Greenie, a 47-year- old environmental studies student with bushy hair and a beard. He looks very earnest, and I can picture him saving the world while munching on a bean and tofu burger. And Itchy Feet, 49, a free-spirited teacher who has travelled widely and is fluent in many languages. He looks the smooth type who can say 'let's go back to your place' in five languages. Then there's Looking for Love who's 50, divorced, and freely admits to having lots of baggage, 'but only the best quality — Louis Vuitton'. It seems that lugging all that baggage around has caused premature ageing as he looks more like 70 than 50.

I scroll quickly through the rest of them. There's 150 altogether in the category. If I dated all of them, would there be at least one I could connect with? I think of Myf's motto: 'So many men and so little time!' She's doing her best to live up to it. She must be about halfway through the entire under 30 male population at Sunshine Coast University.

I'm going to be a little more discerning. But on the other hand, this is research for my book. The more experiences I have, the more material I have to write about. And the more men I date, the more chance I have of meeting Mr Right — or at the very least, Mr-As-Good-As-It-Gets.

I set up another email account specifically for my eMatch contacts, so I can keep them separate from my everyday business. Then I click on the 'Write profile' option, take a deep metaphorical breath and key in my Jules-created profile — my passionate, belly dancing, skinny dipping, gourmet cooking alter ego. I have decided not to include a photo because I want to meet men who will look beyond the superficial (sensitive), are prepared to take a chance on meeting me sight unseen (brave), want to get to know the real me (adventurous) and discover my inner beauty (patient).

Besides, I'm thinking this profile will have the guys' imaginations so fired up they won't need a photo, and their fantasies are not likely to include anything above the chest.

I must have transmitted my thoughts through cyberspace, because just as I'm about to click the 'Submit' button for my profile, Jules phones.

'Don't forget to send in a photo for your profile.'

'I'm not going to include a photo.'

'Why not?'

'Because I want to meet men who are sensitive, brave, adventurous and patient, and who are more interested in getting to know me as a person than what I look like.'

'Bullshit — you know as well as I do that such men don't exist. What's the real reason?'

'I don't have a photo of myself that doesn't make me look like I'm stoned on a bad hair day.'

'What about those photos you had done for your wedding anniversary? You look great in them. I could even fall for you myself.'

I've forgotten about the glamour photos I gave to Jeremy as an anniversary present. The sort where the photographer takes three hours to do your hair and make-up, dresses you in a black strapless number and a feather boa, and makes you pose and pout and look so unlike yourself that your friends say, 'Is that really you? You look fabulous!'

'But those photos were taken over ten years ago. No one will believe I look like that now.'

Jules sighs with mock exasperation. 'Remember what I said about putting yourself on a level playing field. Make a choice. Ruthless honesty and eternal loneliness, or a bit of harmless subterfuge and hordes of panting men?'

That's one of the things I love about Jules. He makes the most complex moral dilemma sound so simple. He doesn't wait for my answer. 'Give me the photo you want to use and I'll scan it and email it to you.'

I dig out my glamour album and leaf through it. Is that sultry woman with the fashionably tousled just-got-out-of-bed blonde hair and the seductive come-back-to-bed eyes, really me? I insisted on taking the album with me when I left Jeremy even though technically it belonged to him.

'When I'm old and wrinkled,' I told him, 'I'm going to surround myself with these photos to remind myself that once upon a time, even if for only a few hours, I could turn a man into a quivering jelly.'

I decide on the photo in which I'm gazing into the camera as if I'm about to make love to it. It's a head and shoulders shot; and because I'm wearing a strapless dress, it gives the effect of my being topless except for the diamond pendant — which the photographer assured me was genuine — glistening on my chest.

Now all that remains is to decide on my eMatch pseudonym. What the hell, let's go with the prevailing theme of deception and delusion. I type in the name 'Sexyandsultry'.

Then I click on 'Submit'. 'Your profile will be approved within 2 days. You will be notified by email.'

Now all I have to do is sit back and wait for the deluge of replies Jules is so confident I'll get.

Chapter 3

'The thing is, I know exactly what sort of man I want.' I snap the menu shut. 'I want a man like Darius.'

'Really?' Jules looks up from his intense study of the Surf Club lunch specials. He's taking forever to make up his mind, and whatever he chooses, he'll decide that my meal looks nicer. 'But he dumped you.'

'I mean, like Darius when I first met him. And he didn't dump me. It was a mutual parting of the ways.'

Jules raises a sceptical eyebrow. 'If you say so. I wish you'd introduced me. You made him sound like Adonis and Hercules rolled into one.'

'He was more like George Clooney with muscles and an accent. And I'll thank you to confine your envy to my meals. I don't want you ogling my men as well.'

'I do *not* ogle. I simply appreciate the aesthetics of the human body. Anyway, I'm guessing you didn't get out of bed long enough to do anything social.'

'He did make getting out of bed an unattractive prospect,' I admit. 'And for me, it was like having a juicy, tender rump steak after years of mince.'

'Speaking of steak, I'll go and order.' He grins. 'Are you having the rump?'

I shove a twenty-dollar note at him. 'My budget's not up to rump at the moment. I'll have the Thai Beef Salad.'

When I say I want a man like Darius, I'm not referring to his intellect, his charisma or his scintillating wit. It's debatable whether he possessed any of those qualities. Being a Polish immigrant, his English was basic but that was immaterial. It was his non-verbal skills I was interested in. He carried a phrasebook with him, which I'm sure was subtitled in Polish 'How To Pick Up Women', because he had learnt all the important phrases such as 'You are bootiful', 'Can I buy you a cocktail?' and 'Do you live around here?'

And I'm sure the Polish phrasebook also recommended the gym as an ideal place to pick up women because that's where I met him. I'd just joined my local gym after six months of self-imposed exile as a result of my marriage break-up. Six months in which I locked myself inside the townhouse I'd moved into with the children, working my way through a mountain of chocolate, a masochistic marathon of romantic comedy DVDs and a pile of self-help books. I emerged from my therapeutic cocoon with a flourishing crop of pimples, a spreading backside threatening an imperialist take-over of my body, an aversion to Hugh Grant due to overexposure and an inability to start the day without saying 'You are a worthy person and I love you' to myself in the mirror.

As I stood in the doorway of the weights room, wondering which of the intimidating machines I would try to master first, I spied a gorgeous creature leaning against the Pec Dec, talking to a skimpily dressed young blonde. His brief shorts and cut-off t-shirt showed off his perfectly proportioned body with bulges in all the right places. I wrenched my eyes away from his bulges to his face, with its olive skin, shock of dark hair and eyes that looked almost black from where I was standing, full of mystery.

There was nobody using the Pec Dec. I willed my trembling legs to move in that direction. As my Adonis saw me coming, his casual gaze started at my feet and worked its way up to my face. A corresponding wave of tingles worked its way up from my toes to my scalp, not missing any of the bits in between. Never had I been so grateful for the oversize t-shirt that hid the worst of my bulges. He stared directly into my eyes — closer up, his were the colour of dark chocolate — and raised an eyebrow.

I felt the heat suffuse my face. When was the last time I'd felt the thrill of an instantaneous attraction? When the high school heart-throb had sauntered over to my desk and sat down next to me; and I'd just about wet myself with excitement until I discovered it was only to ask me to pass a note on to Wanda Higginbottom. Is this what men experience every time they see an attractive woman? How on earth do they ever get anything done when their body is in a constant state of sexual arousal?

I managed to seat myself on the Pec Dec without falling off and decided to put it on one-kilo weight. There was no way I was going to sweat and groan and go red in the face with this man watching me. At that moment I could have done all three without laying a finger on the machine.

'You new?' he asked, smiling. His voice, deep and a little raspy, matched the rest of him.

'Yes,' I croaked.

'Me too. We go for coffee after?'

My head, acting independently of advice from my brain, nodded. Here was a man who didn't bother with the social niceties of getting to know you, to determine whether you were available or not. And I had the feeling that if I'd refused he'd have shrugged his shoulders and wandered off to find another vulnerable creature to ensnare in his web of seduction.

I am not going to sleep with this man today, I told myself sternly in the shower after my workout, as I swiped at my legs and underarms with a razor.

'So you think he's going to examine your legs and peer into your armpits while you're having coffee?' The Voice asked. I poured shampoo on my head and scrubbed vigorously to drown it out.

I arrived at the cafe on the Mooloolaba Esplanade where we'd arranged to meet and spied Darius sitting at a corner table. His smile, as he saw me approaching, quickly turned to a look of horror as he stared at my legs.

I looked down to see rivulets of blood streaming down both my legs. It looked like a madman had attacked me with a razor, which wasn't far from the truth. I'd cut myself while shaving my legs but had been in such a rush I hadn't noticed.

Darius hurriedly pulled out a chair for me as if he thought I might collapse. 'Your legs! What happens?'

I smiled weakly. 'I was shaving them.'

Darius looked blankly at me, so I attempted to demonstrate by running an imaginary razor over my legs. 'Using razor, to get hair off.'

Darius looked perplexed. 'Why?'

Why? Because I'm socially conditioned to believe that bare legs are sexier, and much as I would love to take a philosophical stance and cultivate my body hair wherever it wants to grow, I'm too chicken. But not being able to express that sentiment in Basic English for Polish Visitors, I didn't say anything.

'Woman in Poland, they keep hair on legs,' Darius said. 'Men like hair.'

Great. I'd just slashed myself to pieces trying to make myself attractive, to no avail. I took a wad of tissues from my handbag and was about to mop up the blood when Darius said, 'Here, Soozie, let me do it.'

He took the tissues, crouched down beside me and gently dabbed at my legs until they stopped bleeding, much to the interest and amusement of the other patrons. After two large Scotches, (for medicinal purposes only), a two- course lunch and the coffee I went there for originally, I found myself in his beachside unit.

The term 'afternoon delight' hardly did it justice — it was more afternoon-complete-and-utter-ecstasy. Like all great lovers, Darius had the ability to make me feel as if I was the most beautiful woman in the world. With achingly erotic slowness, he removed every item of my clothing one by one and looked at me as I stood there, naked and with a sudden desire to duck behind the curtains.

'You are bootiful, Soozie,' he said. 'I make love to every part of your body.'

He was as good as his word. Soft kisses, becoming more masterful as our lips found their rhythm, fingertips stroking every inch of my body so lightly yet so expertly, finding parts of my body that I had never thought of as being sensual — behind my ears, under my arms, in between my toes.

I surrendered myself totally to my senses and lost all awareness of where I was or what time of day it was. I suddenly became aware of Darius talking, but he sounded miles away.

'Not yet,' he was saying, 'you don't come yet.'

Then he started with his tongue, every inch of my body from head to toe, sometimes soft moist kisses, sometimes more insistent with his gentle probing tongue. He had some sort of inbuilt radar that knew exactly what I wanted him to do — he even kissed the cuts on my legs. I wanted it to last forever and I tried to prolong it by making myself think about the basket of washing waiting for me at home. But even Zac's smelly socks couldn't stem the tide of pleasure and then it happened, taking me by surprise – that breathless moment just before orgasm when the world stands still in one soundless freeze-frame then wave upon wave of pleasure, racking my whole body. It seemed to go on for an eternity, and I could hear someone moaning and realised it was me.

Then Darius entered me and we moved together in a rhythmic dance — slow and deliberate at first then becoming faster and more frantic until Darius shuddered and collapsed on top of me. I lay completely still for a few moments in the numbness of total satiation, drinking in the musky dampness of his body. I opened my eyes and saw him studying my face.

He smiled and stroked the strands of sweaty hair off my face. 'That was good?'

'Good is probably not quite the word I would use,' I said, finding a voice from somewhere.

'Making love is hard work — I bring you snack.'

He rolled off me and got out of bed. I watched his magnificent butt disappear into the kitchen. He returned five minutes later, still naked, carrying a tray. On it were two bowls of strawberries and ice-cream, and two glasses of iced chocolate. It doesn't get much better than this, I thought, being served afternoon tea in bed by a naked George Clooney clone with whom you've just had the most mind-blowing sex. When I'm old and senile, this will be one experience I can relive over and over. 'Oh, no!' the grandchildren will cry, 'Grandma's doing speed laps in her rocking chair again!'

Think of something else, for God's sake. I gaze out the window at the beach scene below me. The sky is a gentle but unrelenting blue and the sun bounces off the waves. It's the first week of the spring school holidays and the vast expanse of smooth hard sand is dotted with beach umbrellas and families enjoying the first warm week after winter. Seagulls cluster near the water's edge, pottering hopefully around for tidbits.

Two lifeguards stand with their backs to me, in their red and yellow sweatshirts and red shorts that don't quite disguise the rounded curves of their firm buttocks. As if by signal, they both whip off their hats and shirts and step out of their shorts. As they stroll down to the surf, their Speedos cling to their butts like a lover's hand, and I can almost see every muscle in their butt cheeks flexing and releasing in perfect rhythm...

Jules nudges me and I jump. 'I'm back.'

'I was just admiring the view.'

'I bet.' He hands me a glass of champagne. May as well sublimate my desires.

'It would never have lasted,' Jules says.

'What wouldn't?' Although I know what he means.

'You and Darius. You can't do casual sex.'

'It's not that I can't do casual sex, I don't want to. It makes me feel empty and unsatisfied. Emotionally, I mean.'

'Why complicate things by bringing emotions into it? Sometimes you just need to get your rocks off.'

'That's a laugh, coming from someone who falls in love at least once a week.'

The fact that I'm not a one-night stand person — or even one-afternoon stand — meant that my post-coital elation after my first sexual encounter with Darius was marred by niggling feelings of guilt. And there's something very weird about fronting your children when you've just had a torrid session of sex with someone you picked up in the gym that morning. As I walked in the front door, I hoped I'd managed to cover all traces of what I'd been doing. I'd had a shower and done my hair and make-up, but people often exude a certain glow after sex, and I wondered if I was still bathed in a post-coital aura.

'Where have you been?' Cara demanded. 'I was supposed to be at netball training twenty minutes ago.'

'What's for dinner, Mum?' Zac asked.

Okay, no post-coital aura. Or they hadn't noticed it. Sometimes I wonder if they'd notice if I walked in naked. At that moment, though, their self-obsession was a relief.

Darius turned out not to be a one-afternoon stand after all. We continued to see one another once or twice a week for coffee or drinks and invariably finished up at his place having earth-shaking sex. Until six months later, as we lay in bed sharing a Turkish delight, he said, 'Soozie, I have job in Brisbane. I leave next weekend.'

I'd tried to imagine that I was in love with Darius, because it made it easier for me to justify our relationship. But I knew I was kidding myself. At thirty-eight, he was seven years younger than me and we had nothing in common except sex and food. But I knew I'd miss him. Okay, I'd miss the sex just as much. All right, maybe more.

'Brisbane's not far,' I said. 'You might want to come up for the occasional weekend.'

But even as I said it, I knew he wouldn't. And I was right about missing the sex. Having experienced the ultimate in sexual pleasure, I crave it now that it's gone.

'At least I still have Fred,' I say.

'Who's Fred?'

'My vibrator.'

'See? What did I tell you?' Jules's eyes gleam with triumph. 'It's not that you don't want to do casual sex — you can't! You've even become emotionally attached to your vibrator. You've given it a name, for God's sake!'

'Don't be ridiculous, of course I'm not emotionally attached to him. I mean, it. It just seems more friendly to give it a name. After all, it's going places where no man has been for the last 12 months.'

Jules studies my face. 'Hmm, looking a bit peaky, dark circles under the eyes. You've been giving Fred a bit of a workout.'

Admittedly, my bedroom has resembled an amusement parlour over the last couple of nights, as Fred and I experiment with different speeds and rotations, accompanied by flashing lights and a chorus of humming and vibrating. The climax of the night is always an orgasm that racks my whole body and goes on forever until I summon the energy to turn the switch off. I know one thing for sure, I'll never do this by hand again. Another case of manual labour being superseded by technology.

'The reason I'm looking so tired is I have to wait for Cara to go to sleep before I can use it, because her bedroom is next to mine. Then when I'm sure she's asleep I have to add on another hour to give her time to get into her REM sleep. There'd be nothing more embarrassing than your teenage daughter complaining that your vibrator woke her up.'

'You could always tell her it was your back massager,' Jules suggests.

'She's not as gullible as your mother. They probably study vibrators at school in human relations. Anyway, once the school holidays are over I can use it during the day when the kids are at school.'

'That'll certainly make me think twice about calling in unannounced,' Jules says.

'Don't worry. I'll put a 'Do Not Disturb' sign on the front door. I can understand why some women prefer their vibrators to sex — the conversation and foreplay are lousy but you're always guaranteed an orgasm, and you don't have to listen to it snoring afterwards or make it breakfast in the morning.'

'Speaking of orgasms, have you had any replies from eMatch yet?'

'My profile approval only came through a couple of days ago.'

'And you mean to tell me you haven't checked every fifteen minutes to see how many kisses you've scored?'

'Okay, I did at first,' I admit. 'But only for the first few hours. Nothing came through, and I was already over deadline for the magazine article for *Family Circle*, so it's been head down and bum up.'

'One of my favourite positions. What was the article about?'

'Low cost ways to give your home a makeover. And before you laugh, it's not from personal experience, I got a couple of comments from experts and made the rest up.'

'Situation normal, then. After all, you are a creative writer. Speaking of which, I bet when you check your emails there'll be a queue of panting admirers falling over themselves to share your spa.'

'You think so?'

'I know so. I'll bet you,' Jules picks up the cocktail list and studies it, 'a Tropical Lust that you'll have at least fifty kisses.'

'You're on.'

Chapter 4

I deliberately keep myself in suspense by not logging on until after dinner. After all, it's the anticipation that's at least half the fun.

Dinner is the usual mix of appreciation of good cuisine and stimulating conversation.

'Do I have to eat this broccoli?' Zac asks, pushing it round his plate with his fork and piling a mountain of mashed potato on top of it in a vain attempt to hide it. He then spoons rivulets of gravy over the top of the mound for a geographic effect.

'You're disgusting,' Cara says.

'No I'm not. If you want disgusting, listen to this.' He races off upstairs and comes back with his bible, the *Guinness Book of Records*. He finds the section called 'Unusual Skills' and recites, 'The greatest distance that a marshmallow has been shot from one person's nostril and caught in another's mouth is 4.96 metres.'

'That's not disgusting; that's gross,' Cara says.

'My only comment is, why?' I ask. 'If someone asks you to pass the marshmallows, wouldn't it be more polite to just hand them the plate?'

'A bit of snot on the marshmallow might add to the flavour,' Zac suggests.

'You're way past gross,' Cara says. 'I can't stand to sit at the same table as you.'

She gets up, takes her plates into the kitchen and stalks off.

'How can you stand and sit at the same time?' Zac enquires.

'That's enough. Eat your vegetables or you won't get dessert.'

'What's for dessert?'

'Marshmallows.' I disappear upstairs before he can think of a reply.

I shut the door of the study, a sign to the children that I'm not to be disturbed, and log into my eMatch email address.

I click on 'Inbox'.

I swear if I wasn't already sitting down, I'd have fallen into my chair with a painful thump. There are eighty-two new emails in my inbox, notifications from eMatch that someone has sent me a kiss. I scroll disbelievingly down the list. The fact that it's Monday and the weekend is the most popular time for online cruising may have a lot to do with it, but still – that's eighty-two men who liked my profile enough to want to meet me.

Of course it's not really me they want to meet, it's the glamorous, passionate, belly-dancing, skinny-dipping, gourmet-cooking Sexyandsultry, but who cares? I'm revelling in my new femme fatale status. I go back through the list again.

Sexyman 51 sends you a kiss

Contact for free from FullofFun

Yourplaymate sends you a kiss

Bikerboy sends you a kiss

Contact for free from Lovemetender

And seventy-seven more. Looks like I'm up for the cost of a couple of Tropical Lusts.

I log into the home page of eMatch and click on 'How it Works'. My screen is immediately filled with little red-lipsticked mouths, all pouting and making kissing noises. Then the blurb appears.

'When someone sends you a kiss, it means they have read your profile and would like to contact you and vice versa, if you send someone a kiss. The recipient of the kiss can choose from a number of standard replies, ranging from "flattered you are interested but do not wish to correspond" to "interested and looking forward to receiving your email."

'It is free to send and reply to a kiss, but for further contact one party must pay for a contact stamp. He or she can then contact the other person by email, directed via the eMatch site so that neither person's email address is revealed. Once that contact is established, it is up to each person to decide how much personal detail, such as email addresses or phone numbers, to reveal. If someone sends you a "contact-for-free" stamp with their kiss, it means that they have already paid for you to contact them.'

I peruse my list of emails again. Of the eighty-two kisses I've received, ten have been sent with a contact-for-free stamp. So ten of my ardent suitors are so keen to meet me that they have already paid for me to contact them. Perhaps they've done so out of a sense of chivalry. On the other hand (and I'm trying not to be cynical here), perhaps they are so desperate, ugly or socially inept that they figure it's the only way they'll get a reply.

I decide to test my theory by checking out a couple of contact-for-frees. I find FullofFun's profile. His photo reveals a round, chubby face with glasses — looks like he's full of calories as well. He's forty-five, separated, a postal worker. Likes country music, horror movies and jogging on the beach (obviously about as often as I go the gym). He says, 'I am a homebody at heart and have been told I have a great sense of humour.' Why does his great sense of humour have to be vindicated by other people's opinions? It probably means he has no sense of humour at all. Am I being too analytical? Hell, I've got eighty-one other men to choose from. I give him a mental cross.

I check out Lovemetender's profile. No photo — obviously hoping for his inner beauty to be discovered. Forty-eight, divorced, two kids, computer technician. Likes rock'n'roll, especially Elvis (what a surprise), only reads newspapers and magazines, loves all Clint Eastwood movies and car rallies. A country and western Elvis petrolhead — I have a mental picture of a tall, thin guy in jeans, checked shirt and slicked back hair, Elvis style, standing beside his souped-up Commodore. Another mental cross.

It looks as if there might be some validity in my theory. I put the contact-for-frees on hold for the time being. Yourplaymate sounds intriguing so I log into his profile. There's a photo of an attractive guy with dark hair and brown eyes, reminiscent of Darius. He's fifty-one, separated, one child, and is in the medical profession. Even more intriguing although if he was a doctor I'm sure he'd say so, so chances are he washes the bedpans. He likes all types of music, reads crime novels, his favourite movies are science fiction and romantic comedies — especially Meg Ryan movies (a man who likes romantic comedy, you owe me for that one, Jules) — and enjoys pushbike riding and bushwalking.

In the blurb, he says: 'I am a romantic at heart and looking for that special lady whom I can woo and lavish my affection on.' I'm a sucker for being wooed and lavished affection on, so I forgive the awkward preposition at the end of the sentence and give him a mental tick.

I skim briefly through the profiles of my other admirers. They include five from Sydney, three from Melbourne, two from Adelaide, and even two from Perth, four thousand kilometres away. Obviously distance is no obstacle to the male sexual instinct. I'm not interested in the out-of-towners, as long distance relationships are too difficult and time consuming to maintain. I enter the 'reply to sender' menu and send each of them a reply that reads 'Sexyandsultry is flattered you are interested but does not wish to correspond any further'.

That leaves me with seventy-one men to peruse at my leisure. For the first time in my life I might have a little black book. But it's been twenty years since I've been in the dating scene and I could probably benefit from some advice. I call Myf and Annie and inform them of my dilemma. There are a couple of greyish clouds in the distance that could mean rain, so we'll skip the walk and have coffee at my place.

***

Myf and Annie turn up with a couple of bottles of chardonnay, having decided that the selection process will be more efficiently assisted by the ingestion of alcohol rather than caffeine.

'Got them from the bargain bin,' Annie says. 'The liquor store guy described them as unpretentious.'

Jules is having a couple of after-work drinks, but says he'll pop by afterwards and do I mind if he brings Max? Not at all, I reply, a gay viewpoint might be very valuable, though how, I'm not sure.

I've printed out the profiles and they lie there in a pile on the dining room table, like a pile of school essays waiting to be marked.

'God, look at them all,' Myf says. 'I didn't think there were so many desperate men on the Coast.'

'Thanks a lot.'

'Did you offer some sort of incentive — like free sex for the first fifty replies?' Annie asks.

'I'm so hurt that you can't believe that it's my gorgeous looks and irresistible charm that have attracted all these replies,' I sigh. 'Okay, I'll show you why.'

I show them the Sexyandsultry profile, which I've also printed out. As I expected, there's an uproar that registers at force nine-and-a-half on the Richter amusement scale, and I spend the next half hour fielding comments and suggestions about sexy books, spas, indoor sports, nude surfing etc., ranging from plain lewd to anatomically impossible. When it comes to discussing sex, men have nothing on women, particularly women under the influence of chardonnay.

'I love the photo,' Annie says. 'But what happens when they meet you and discover that you've changed a little since then?'

'You bowl them over with your wit, charm and chutzpah,' Myf says. 'Not every man wants a woman who's drop-dead gorgeous.'

Her pronouncement is uttered with the sublime self-assurance of someone who knows she is drop-dead gorgeous. At forty-two, Myf looks thirty and is tall and willowy, with long blonde hair that she usually wears up, giving her a regal aura. She walks as if she's wading through golden syrup and exudes sensuality in a cloud, like perfume. Her parents, who were holidaying in Wales when she was conceived, named her after the Welsh legend about a woman called Myfanwy, who was so beautiful that no man could compose the words to describe her beauty. Her name has indeed proved to be prophetic. I've yet to meet a man who hasn't fallen under Myf's spell.

'And not every woman wants a man with a big penis,' I reply.

'Talking of penises, listen to this,' Annie says. ' "You sound like just the sort of woman I've been looking for and I know we would have lots of fun together. I also love to swim in the nude. Maybe we could meet at the beach one day." His name is — wait for it —Romantic Guy.'

'You can't get much more romantic than that,' Myf says. 'Your first date at a nude beach. At least you wouldn't have to worry about what to wear.'

'Yes I would,' I say. 'I'd worry about which shade of tanning lotion to put on and whether I had enough stretch mark concealer. What about this one? Sexy Swinger: "I am currently in a long term relationship but boredom has set in as it does after you've been together for a while and my partner and I are looking for someone who would like a bit of fun with both of us. No strings attached and discretion assured."'

'That would make an interesting slant for your book,' Myf says. 'Swinging for the over-forties — do's and don'ts.'

'Swinging with no strings attached. Too dangerous for me. He should find himself a trapeze artist.'

The chardonnay proves itself to be unpretentious as predicted, and the more we drink the more unpretentious we become. The profile analyses involve a detailed discussion of the motivations, expectations and imagined sexual expertise of each contender. Whatever gaps are left in the information we fill with our own highly imaginative speculations. Our mission is to weed out the obvious misfits and deviates and make up a short list of acceptable suitors, although Myf is against the idea of a short list.

'It's too small a number to get a proper statistical random sampling. If you're serious about the research aspect, you should date them all,' she insists. She's studying statistics as part of her university course.

'She's serious all right,' Annie says. 'I've never seen anyone so serious about getting laid in my whole life.'

It's at this moment that Cara chooses to surface from her bedroom and come downstairs. She stops in her tracks, her gaze alighting on the wine bottles and glasses.

'Fuck,' she says loudly, turns on her heel and walks back upstairs. A momentary hush descends as we digest this comment.

Then with unerring instinct, Zac, who up until now has been watching TV in the next room, oblivious to his surroundings, pokes his head in the doorway.

'No dinner, I s'pose?' he says. 'Guess I'll be calling child welfare.' And quickly disappears.

That's it. He's banned from watching 'The Simpsons'.

'Oh fuck,' Annie says. We all look at her.

'Speaking of child welfare, I told Richard I'd be home at six o'clock. The kids will be screaming for their dinner.'

'Hasn't he ever heard of takeaway?' Myf says. 'Ring him and tell him you're in a business meeting.'

Annie thinks for a minute. 'Why not? I haven't been out on my own for ages.'

She grabs her mobile phone out of her handbag. 'I won't ring him though because he'll be pissed off. I'll just send him a text message.'

What a great modern invention is text messaging — instantaneous communication with anyone, anywhere, when you don't want to talk to them.

'Urgent business meeting with Myf and Susie. Get takeaway for dinner. Home later.' She presses the send button. 'And I'll put it on silent so I can't hear it if he rings me — that way I won't feel guilty.'

'What's there to feel guilty about?' Myf says. 'I bet he comes up with that excuse all the time.'

'It's not an excuse,' Annie says defensively. 'He does have business meetings. But to be honest, lately I'm glad when he doesn't come home till late.'

She promptly bursts into tears. The fates of my seventy-one ardent admirers are left hanging as I put my arm around her and pat her shoulder. Myf refills her glass.

'I'm sorry,' she gulps, in between sobs. 'I've been so depressed lately. Richard's working long hours to get his consulting business off the ground, the kids are being ratty and I hate my job — it's all I can do sometimes not to stab these cranky old biddies in the head with a curling pin while I'm doing their perms.'

'I know how you feel,' I say. You're caught up on the merry-go-round of daily routine — doing the same chores, seeing the same friends, talking about the same things. In-laws over once a week, sex twice a week (in a bad week, it's the other way round). It's as if when you bought your calendar for the new year, every activity for the next 12 months was already written in it, for your convenience. Then one day you realise you hate your life, but there seems to be no way out. When I came to that point in my life, while I was still married to Jeremy, I left my job as a newspaper journalist and began freelance writing.

Annie dissolves into a fresh flood of tears. 'And then there's our sex life!' she wails. 'It's about as exciting as looking for cracks in the ceiling, which is what I do when we're having sex!'

Cara chooses this particular moment to brave another appearance from her bedroom. She rolls her eyes and I can see the thought bubble floating above her head — 'Is sex all adults ever think about?'

'I'm going to Jay's place,' she announces. 'At least I'll get some dinner there.'

'You stay right here,' I command. 'I'm about to order some pizzas.' She scowls and stalks off. Zac makes an appearance again (What is this, a vaudeville act?) but with a typical male abhorrence of tears, backs away when he sees Annie crying. He stands in the doorway rubbing his stomach and making faces, mouthing the words 'I'm starving' before falling to the floor in a simulated death from hunger.

Myf comforts Annie while I phone Jules on his mobile. 'Are you coming over soon?'

'I'm on my way.' I can hear Whitney Houston belting out 'I Will Always Love You' in the background, accompanied by a whining high-pitched sound.

'Can you bring over three large pizzas, a couple of bottles of chardonnay and a couple of family blocks of Dairy Milk chocolate? And what's that horrible noise?'

'That's not a horrible noise; that's Max singing. Sounds like we're just in time for the party.'

'More like therapy at the moment. But if you hurry up with the supplies, we'll work up to the party.'

There's no more wine until Jules arrives so I burrow into the depths of my pantry and retrieve half a bottle of Stone's green ginger wine, which I'd forgotten I had.

'What's this shit?' Myf says.

'It's a very exclusive wine. Made from the grapes that got stuck in between the peasant's toes when they were treading the grapes.'

I pour us all a glass of wine. Myf sticks her nose into her glass.

'You're right; a bouquet just like peasant toe-jam.'

We all brave a few sips, accompanied by much coughing, spluttering and semblance of retching.

'It smells so much better than it tastes,' Myf pronounces. Annie agrees in between sniffles that 'it's a unique imbibing experience'.

By calling on our inner reserves of fortitude, we manage to finish off the bottle and during the process we come to the following conclusions;

1. Not all men are bastards; but those who are bastards don't know they are bastards, and those men who aren't bastards are always taking the blame for them.

2. It's impossible to tell a bastard from a non-bastard because some men can seem like a non-bastard for ages and lull you into a false sense of security, then whammo! He does something really bad and you discover he's a bastard after all, but by then he's reeled you in and got you hooked.

3. Myf and I decide that Annie should develop a 'fuck the world' attitude and embrace a policy of hedonism — drink more wine, eat more chocolate, go to the movies more often, work on her tan, then if she doesn't discover the meaning of life at least she's had a fantastic time not discovering it.

'I'm not a "fuck the world" type of person,' Annie sniffles.

'Of course you are,' Myf says. 'You just have to learn how to do it.'

'It's easy to for you to say; you don't have a husband and kids.'

'If you're feeling happy and fulfilled, your husband and kids will be happy too,' Myf says.

By now Annie's tears have dried up. Her lips tighten. 'I fail to see how being a fat, drunk movie addict with a tan is going to make my husband and kids happy when the house is a pigsty with no food in the cupboard, because I've eaten and drunk the grocery money.'

'You don't have to go to those extremes; you just have to get your priorities right.'

Annie is looking daggers at Myf. At that moment, with impeccable timing, Jules bursts through the door hugging three large cardboard boxes.

'We're here! Let the party begin!'

A figure steps out from behind Jules holding a plastic bag containing two bottles. He looks as if he's just stepped off the set of 'The Bold And The Beautiful', still in his actor's pose as he leans lightly against Jules's shoulder. He's tall and compactly built with not an ounce of flab. His shoulders and biceps bulge out from his cut-off shirt and his black jeans look as if they've been poured onto his body as liquid and left to set. Surely he couldn't be wearing any underwear. His face is perfectly proportioned — square-shaped with a firm jaw and deep-set blue eyes, fine nose and full, sensual mouth. His fair hair is cut in a fashionable almost crew cut.

I dart a glance at the others. Myf has managed to retain her usual outward composure, but I can tell by the look in her eyes and the slight parting of her lips that she's impressed. Annie's anger has been transformed into a look of amazement, with her jaw in danger of scraping the ground.

'Everyone, this is Max. Max, this is everyone,' says Jules.

'Hi, everyone,' says Max, and in those two words, the illusion of the perfect man evaporates into the atmosphere of stunned silence. Max makes Boy George sound macho.

He and Jules bring the pizzas and wine over to the table. He doesn't exactly mince; it's more like a slow sashay. I raise my eyebrows at Myf and Annie, and I know they know exactly what I'm thinking — what a waste of a magnificent specimen of manhood.

As we all tuck into pizza and more wine, during which time Zac has resurfaced and walked off happily with half a pizza, Jules asks how the short-listing has been going.

'And by the way, Sexyandsultry, don't forget those cocktails you owe me. I'm looking forward to my Tropical Lust.'

'Ooh, so am I,' purrs Max.

'The short-listing got sidetracked because of Annie's depression,' I say, 'which we've already solved with our Stone's Green Ginger Therapy — it tastes so horrible you immediately forget all your problems.'

'I'll have to remember that,' Max says. 'I've been depressed all my life. Maybe that's my problem; not enough green ginger wine.'

'Why?' asks Annie.

'I was born depressed. It comes from being gay. Being gay is hell, absolute hell!'

A tear rolls out of his eye and down his baby-smooth cheek. What's happening here? First Annie, now Max. Is it a full moon tonight? Or is it that Venus is under the influence of Saturn, causing Jupiter to be out of alignment with Mars and everybody's lives to be in a mess?

'He had an argument with his father on the phone tonight before we went out,' Jules explains. 'His father has a Harley Davidson and tattoos, and breeds Rottweilers.'

'It's not like everyone thinks, all leather and chains and picking up men in public toilets,' Max sniffles. 'Most of us just want to find Mr Right and settle down and live happily ever after.'

We ply Max with wine and chocolate, and lots of helpful comments. 'It's hard enough for us heterosexuals to find Mr Right, what makes you think it should be any easier for gay people?'

Then Jules chimes in with 'How hard do you think it is for bisexual people? We don't know whether we want to meet Mr Right or Miss Right.'

I know that Jules's anguish over his sexuality is real to him. We've spent many hours discussing it at length, usually after a relationship has folded, but to me it's an affectation.

'But sooner or later you have to make a choice if you want to settle down,' I say. 'Just because you're attracted to both sexes doesn't mean you're destined for a lifetime of trying to decide between the two. It's like being a kid in a lolly shop wanting to buy everything but you can't because you'll make yourself sick, so you have to make a choice between the caramel chews and the strawberry creams.'

'I'd go for the all day suckers myself,' Myf says. Then follows a discussion on the various merits of double entendre confectionary, with aniseed balls and gobstoppers vying for a close second to all day suckers.

'I didn't even get a chance to try all the lollies in the shop,' Annie says. 'I married the first man I slept with. And he's turned out to be a bit of a jelly baby. Especially when he's had a few drinks.'

Then follows a discussion on the effects of alcohol on (a) sexual performance in general, (b) ability to fall asleep during foreplay and (c) ability to fall asleep during sex. It's agreed that men are more susceptible to (b) and women to (c).

Cara comes down from her room again just in time to hear Myf declare, 'That might be true of older men, but younger guys can drink and keep it up all night.'

'Absolutely!' Max agrees. Cara glances briefly at the human debris — Jules and Max lolling on the couch, and Annie, Myf and I slumped around the dining table surrounded by empty pizza boxes, chocolate wrappers and wine bottles. She rolls her eyes and marches back up to her room.

I swear if that kid rolls her eyes one more time, her eyeballs will be permanently lodged in the back of her head. It's amazing how a sixteen-year- old with attitude can put a damper on things. We all exchange guilty glances then Annie realises it's midnight.

'Fuck, Richard will be furious.' She grabs her mobile phone. 'No missed calls.' She sounds disappointed.

'Forget about Richard,' I say. 'I'm sure he hasn't died of starvation. He and the kids will have had Kentucky Fried Chicken, the kids will have gone to bed in their clothes without a bath and Richard will now be blissfully snoring in front of the telly. And everybody's happy except you because you're too busy feeling guilty about going out, getting drunk and talking about sex all night.'

'Well, since you put it like that, pass the chardie please,' Annie says.

By two am we've come up with some variations on the Not All Men are Bastards theory, with some input from Jules and Max.

Amended Theory

1. Not all men are bastards, but gay men are less likely to be bastards because they have more feminine qualities.

2. OK, gay men are more bitchy, but bitchy is not the same as bastard.

3. Unless you know Ross, the barman from Secrets.

4. Scientists will one day discover that bastards emanate a certain kind of body odour not identifiable to the naked nose and will invent a bastard detector, a portable instrument that a woman (or a man) can keep in his or her handbag, which will alert them when they are in the vicinity of a bastard.

5. This will undoubtedly be the most important invention of the century by enabling women (and men) to avoid bastards. Only a small percentage of masochistic women who actually like bastards will breed with them, resulting over time in the elimination of the bastard from the human species

6. This will then free scientists to concentrate on more important things like finding a cure for cellulite (a proper cure, not just drinking lots of water and massaging your thighs with the cosmetic equivalent of an enraged porcupine).

7. As John Lennon said 'You may say that I'm a dreamer'. A world without bastards and cellulite is something to which we can all aspire.

At midnight I call a cab and bundle them all into it. My pile of profiles has been forgotten, but at least Annie and Max have cheered up. 'Don't forget to drink a litre of water before bed!' I yell as they leave, then after checking that the children are asleep, I flop into bed.

Chapter 5

I'm on a stage, lying in a barrel with my head and feet sticking out either end. There are thousands of faces in the audience below staring at me. There's a man standing beside me. I can't see his face but he's holding a saw above his head as if he's about to plunge it into me.

'Ladies and gentlemen,' he cries, 'I am about to saw this woman in half before your very eyes.'

I cringe as he brings the saw down, but instead of sawing my body he is sawing my head. Back and forth, back and forth. Oh, the pain!

I open my eyes. I'm staring at my bedroom wall but the man is still sawing my head, in perfect excruciating rhythm. My mouth is so dry I can't feel my tongue. I wish I'd taken my own advice about drinking a litre of water before bed.

I look at the clock. Nine o'clock. Jeremy will be here any moment to pick up the kids — he sticks religiously to the every second weekend and half the school holidays routine.

I throw on a sarong, avoid the mirror and stumble downstairs.

A cacophony of vaguely musical sounds is blaring out from the TV, and Cara and Jay are nestled up together on the couch again.

'Turn that rubbish down!' I bellow. Oops, did I just say that? I sound exactly like my mother. That thought's enough to sober me up.

Zac is sitting at the dining room table eating a bowl of ice-cream and chocolate topping, surrounded by the detritus of the night before.

'Have you got a hangover?' he enquires.

'No,' I say. I'm lying, he knows I'm lying, and I know he knows I'm lying. What's the point? Maybe I can turn it into a learning experience for him.

'Actually I have. I've got a whopper of a hangover. And it's not an experience you'd put yourself through if you had any sense. So let that be a lesson to you — don't ever stay up till two am drinking wine and solving the problems of the world. Because when you wake up the next day, the world is still exactly as you left it; and you have an extra problem of a hangover to deal with.'

Lessons from a Mother to Her Son. I can just see it as one of those whimsical little books you pick up from the front counters of bookstores for $8.95. On the front is a photo of a doting mother smiling down at her chubby baby boy. Inside, on each page, is a pithy little saying accompanied by an impossibly angelic photo of the boy at each stage of his life.

Lesson Number One. '*Do not drink alcohol to excess, as it is vexatious to the spirit and makes you feel like shit in the morning.*'

'Thanks for the advice,' Zac says.

He points to the profiles scattered all over the table and decorated with wine stains and greasy pizza patches.

'Who are all these men? Are they your boyfriends?'

There's a duet of sniggers from the couch.

'Of course not, it's just some research I'm doing for a book.'

Lesson Number Two. 'Do not ask your mother embarrassing questions about her sex life, and she will return the favour by not asking you about yours when you're old enough to have one.'

There's a knock at the door and Zac flies over to open it.

'G'day, mate.' Jeremy's smile is forced and his normally rotund face is drawn, with deep lines etched under his eyes. His denim shorts hang loosely on him. A tidal wave of remorse sweeps over me. Why am I feeling like this? He's the one who had the affair.

Who knows how much longer it would have gone on if I hadn't found out? I was checking his coat pockets before taking it to the dry cleaners and found a receipt from a restaurant that he and I hadn't been to. He'd tried to tell me it was a business lunch; but surprisingly for a lawyer, he's a rotten liar. He'd been having it off for the last 12 months with Alison, the office junior trainee 20 years younger than him. She had personal problems due to her unhappy childhood (cue violins) and she had confided in Jeremy. Over time, his friendly, fatherly advice had obviously become less fatherly and more friendly.

Of course, everyone knew except me. When the gut-punch of shock had diminished, I could almost laugh. It was all so cliched, I felt as if I were playing a part in a bad soap opera. Then came the anger. How dare he have an affair when I was the one who was sexually unsatisfied? I should have been the one to run off and find myself a toy boy! Though in reality I don't think my conscience would have allowed me to do it, I was incensed that he'd got in first. When I told Jeremy I was leaving him, he was ashen-faced.

'Please, Sue, can't we discuss this? I didn't mean for this to happen. We'd grown apart and I hadn't even realised it, and I don't think you had either.'

But I was so choked up with emotion I couldn't discuss it then. Now that my hurt and anger have dissipated, our relationship has settled into a space somewhere in the middle between awkward and amiable.

Jeremy sees me. 'Hi, Sue, how are you?'

Maybe the reason he's looking so tired is that his relationship with Alison is starting to reveal some cracks. I dismiss the thought that it might be due to their shagging each other senseless. They've been living together for two years now and besides, there's a difference between tired/sated and tired/stressed. Jeremy definitely looks the latter.

I detect an amused glint in his eyes. I glance in the hall mirror and am confronted by a woman with hair sticking out at every geometric angle and bloodshot eyes ringed with smudged eye make-up. It's the rumpled raccoon look — a great look for ex-husbands to eradicate any remaining doubts they may have about the end of the marriage.

Luckily I don't have to answer the question because Zac pipes up with, 'Mum's got a hangover.'

Lesson Number Three. 'Treasure those moments of intimate honesty your mother shares with you and do not betray the confidences divulged — even if you think you're stating the obvious.'

'I hope it was worth it,' Jeremy says. I swear I can hear a note of envy in his voice.

Cara disentangles herself from Jay, goes over and throws her arms around her father's neck.

'Is it all right if Jay hangs out with us today, Dad?'

'I suppose so.'

Jeremy doesn't sound too thrilled at the prospect of having another son for the day. I know from what the children have told me that Alison tries hard to do the happy families bit when they stay there.

'Thanks heaps, Jerry,' Jay says, ambling over to the door. He's tall and gangly, like a stick insect, with the same predatory air. And Jerry! Trust Jay to come out with that — there are Jeremys and there are Jerrys, and my ex-husband is unmistakably a Jeremy.

When the door closes behind them, I take two Panadol, clear away the mess from last night and stack the dishwasher. Then I grab my swimmers and towel, and head for the only thing that in my experience is a surefire cure for a hangover — a swim in the ocean.

***

It's almost midday and the sun has quite a bite to it. The beach is packed with the weekend crowds. It's always nerve-wracking going to the beach at the beginning of the new season when I'm not used to my body being on public display. I find a spare square metre of sand on which to drop my towel and keys, and make my way to the water, my feet sinking in the soft, warm sand.

I try to convince myself that no one is looking at me in last year's faded, stretched swimmers with my pale, and contrary to my eMatch profile, less than fit and toned body. I want to break into a run to hasten the journey but I know that will only draw more attention to me. I imagine the entire beach being enveloped in a deathly silence as all eyes turn to me and a voice booms from the lifeguard's tower, 'Would the woman in the blue swimmers kindly not frighten the other beachgoers by wobbling into the water like an oversize jellyfish?'

At the water's edge I hover, gasping as the icy waves lap at my ankles like insistent Arctic terriers. Rather than prolong the agony I wade out waist deep and plunge headfirst into the waves. I surface, breathless — the coldness is unbelievable. The ocean wraps itself around me and clings to me like an icy, silken sheet. It rolls and moves with my body and won't let me go, and gradually I succumb and become warm in its embrace. I want to stay there forever, locked in its rhythm.

Swimming nude, I decide, would be a very sensual experience if I could pluck up the courage to visit a nude beach. I'm sure that I really would enjoy the water lapping over my naked body and then at least one part of my profile would be true. But the thought of appearing naked in front of complete strangers who will pretend not to be looking but who will be sizing me up thoroughly is rather daunting.

I catch a wave to shore, wade out of the surf and walk as quickly as I dare, up to my spot on the sand, pretending not to care that my wet swimsuit is clinging to every lump and bump on my body; and I feel like a bowl of tapioca.

I put what I hope is an abstracted expression on my face as if I have more important matters to be concerned about — like third world poverty or beach erosion — than whether my nipples are visible through my swimmers and if so, is that good or bad considering there's a rather dishy lifesaver over there. But then, he's not going to be looking at me anyway with all the beach babes around, except maybe nostalgically because I remind him of his mother. I finally arrive at my towel and wrap myself in its warm, sandy folds.

By the time I've walked home again, I'm feeling distinctly more alive. The headache has gone and I'm ravenous. I fix myself a triple-decker sandwich and a cup of strong tea, gather up my pile of wine and pizza stained profiles and settle myself on the patio. The tentative short list of lucky applicants we made last night before we became sidetracked got lost in the melee, so I'll have to start again.

What control can be exerted, what power can be wielded over my own fate and that of others, just by the stroke of a pen! I compose three piles — the definitely nots, the maybes and the definites. The definitely nots include lovers of country and western music, those with more than four spelling mistakes in their profile (It might sound like literary snobbishness, but what sort of relationship can I have with a man if I'm constantly correcting his spelling?) and anyone over fifty-five.

By the end of the afternoon, I've come up with twenty-six definitely nots, twenty-five maybes and twenty definites. This is no longer a fantasy, a joke, a 'what if' scenario. This is reality, these are real flesh and blood men. I'm getting ready to date twenty men, with another twenty-five in reserve, all of whom will expect me to be a gorgeous, slim, athletic, belly-dancing, skinny-dipping sex goddess, who will read erotic novels to them in the spa and whip up a gourmet meal before doing amazing gymnastics in the bedroom. Am I completely deranged and delusional? Or just crazy?

Robin Storey

PART TWO

Perfect Sex

Chapter 6

MY DATING DIARY

SATURDAY, 12 OCTOBER

I've decided to keep a diary of all my eMatch dates — likes and dislikes, impressions and experiences — as it will be impossible to remember them all by the end. And I'll need to have all this information at my fingertips when writing my book (names and incriminating details changed to protect the guilty, of course).

I've just had a date with my first eMatch candidate — lunch with Mr Big, alias Patrick, a solicitor from Noosa. As none of the ten who sent me a contact-for-free stamp merited a selection in the definites, I bought contact stamps for my twenty definites. I sent each an email in which I thanked him for his interest and supplied a few more tidbits of information about myself — just enough to arouse further interest without specifically mentioning any of my wide variety of erotic pastimes. I haven't rated my definites in order of preference — Mr Big happened to be the first to reply.

Initially, I wasn't sure if he fancied himself as king of the local mafia or endowed with more than his fair share of sexual equipment. After one date with him, I'm still none the wiser, nor do I want to be.

The photo in his profile displayed a younger, slimmer version, a Mr Not-Quite-So-Big. At forty-eight, his body is showing signs of the ravages of a well-lived middle age, he's almost bald and has the ruddy complexion of the seasoned drinker. His less than impressive rating on the hunk scale didn't prevent him from believing that he was the most fascinating person in the world — his achievements both in and out of the workplace were the only topic of conversation throughout the entire lunch. When I managed to get a few words in about myself, he made a token effort to listen then steered the conversation back to himself. I pictured him in a scene of attempted seduction — 'You've just had a hysterectomy? That's great — how about coming back to my place for a nightcap and some wild sex?'

His profile stated that he was divorced with two adult children, that he was well-travelled and financially secure, with interests including all water sports, bushwalking and the ubiquitous 'picnics in the country and moonlit walks along the beach'. If the profiles I have read so far are to be believed, the countryside of the entire nation must be jam-packed with men lounging on picnic rugs, gazing adoringly into their companion's eyes over smoked salmon and devilled eggs; and the beaches at night must be scenes of mayhem and potential collisions, with all those couples out for their romantic walks.

It transpired that Patrick's idea of water sports was pottering along the Noosa River in his thirty-foot cruiser, imbibing copious amounts of champagne. Bushwalking referred to mooring the boat near Noosa Woods and passing by one or two bushes on his way to the bottle shop to replenish his supplies. As for picnics in the country and walks along the beach, I decided the only attraction they would hold for Patrick would be as opportunities to lure you into a secluded spot in the bushes or to tackle you behind the sand dunes.

I know I'm hardly in a position to criticise Patrick's liberties with the truth, and before our date I had managed to whip myself into a nervous frenzy. I was convinced that he'd take one look at me and either refuse to believe that I was 'Sexyandsultry' or refuse to go ahead with our date on the basis of misrepresentation.

'Don't be ridiculous,' Annie and Myf said as they were helping me get ready. Annie had cut and styled my hair into a soft bob with blonde highlights. 'It takes years off you,' she said, which was supposed to be reassuring, but only made me wonder how old and frumpy I'd looked before.

Myf gave me the benefit of her fashion advice. 'I don't care what Jules says — you can't wear a long black skirt to lunch, even in Noosa.' She found a flowing pink wraparound skirt in her wardrobe — a one size fits all — and a pink and white rosebud print blouse designed to show just a hint of cleavage, which it would have, if I'd had any to show.

So Myf rushed back home again and fetched her Wonderbra, which did a wonderful job of creating mountains out of molehills, and I paraded around in front of the mirror in various poses — side-on then leaning forward, admiring the sensual curve of my breasts spilling out over the top of my bra.

'Do you think it's too much cleavage for a first date?' I asked.

' You're Sexyandsultry, remember?' Myf said. 'Just don't lean forward too much. You want to tantalise him, not invite him to jump in. If you drop something on the floor, leave it there.'

Then I decided I didn't like the way Myf's skirt clung to my bum and thighs, so Annie rushed home and came back with a pair of her Wonderpants. They resembled a pair of long stretchy shorts, like a modern-day version of the girdle my mother wears.

'You wear them over your knickers — they have bottom and thigh control panels,' she explained.

'Good idea,' Myf said. 'The last thing Susie needs on a first date is her bottom and thighs running rampant.'

I stepped into the Wonderpants; and as I pulled them up to my waist, I felt all my insides squishing together. Annie was right about the control panels — it was a totalitarian regime there, inside my Wonderpants. They performed miracles, creating a smooth, bump-free line under the skirt.

'These are fabulous,' I said, putting on my high heels and swirling around in front of the mirror. From a distance and with my eyes half closed, I could almost imagine myself to be Cameron Diaz.

'They're not in the least bit sexy,' Annie said, 'but they do the job. And they're multi-functional too — you can't eat much with them on and they also act as a sort of chastity belt. It would take a very determined man to get his hand inside them.'

'In a busy Noosa restaurant at lunchtime, that's a remote possibility,' I said. 'But in any case, with my Wonderbra and Wonderpants he'd get a shock no matter where he put his hand.'

I had to admit I looked pretty damn good when my personal attendants were finished with me. I modelled my new look up and down the catwalk of my bedroom, and they wolf-whistled in stereo.

'You've got nothing to be nervous about,' Annie said. 'You look exactly like your profile — slim, fit, and attractive with a great bod. He'll be bowled over.'

'You look great,' Myf agreed. 'You can't even tell that the great bod has been artificially created.'

Cara and Zac came in to see what all the commotion was about.

'Wow, you look pretty hot, Mum,' Cara said. 'I hope you're going to be back at a reasonable hour. And don't let him drive you home if he's been drinking.'

Zac had a strange look on his face that I've seen once or twice before. It's the realisation of a boy who suddenly sees his mother as a sexual being and not just a food dispenser who nags, and to whom the revelation is unwelcome and uncomfortable.

'I hope you're not going to bring him back here,' he said. 'I want to watch "Vulcans of the Universe". There's lots of killing and blood and guts — not suitable for adults.'

You're safe there. There's no way I'd bring him back here unless I wanted to get rid of him. It's a comforting fallback though — if any of my suitors become too eager and don't get the hint, I'll invite him home and set the children on to him.

Patrick and I had arranged to meet in a beachfront restaurant at Noosa called 'Café Ciao'. He'd offered to pick me up from home but I declined. I've decided on two cardinal rules for internet dating.

1. Always arrange to meet them somewhere for the first date so I can check them out in person before I let them know my address.

2. Make sure I drive myself to the venue for the first date. If I know I have to drive home, I'll limit my alcohol intake. When I've had a few drinks, I tend to rave and disclose all sorts of things I'd be too embarrassed to mention when I'm sober.

Patrick was sitting at the bar when I arrived. As I expected him to look like his photo, I almost didn't recognise him. He certainly didn't seem to be disappointed with my appearance in the flesh, jumping off his stool to give me a hearty handshake. My initial feeling was one of relief, followed by a gradual glow of smugness as the lunch progressed — here was someone who actually surpassed me at being an impostor.

After two courses and a bottle of wine, most of which Patrick consumed himself, he took my hand in his. It was warm and sweaty and I jumped. I'd been on the lookout for sudden moves, but my guard was down. He dropped my hand.

'Sorry, didn't mean to startle you. Tell me,' and he leaned forward, ostensibly to rearrange the salt and pepper but really to get a better view of my cleavage, 'how is the belly dancing going?'

Silly me, here I was thinking he wasn't interested in me at all.

'Er ... fine, thanks.'

'Perhaps you could give me a demonstration one day.'

He gazed into my eyes while at the same time trying to keep one eye focused on my cleavage, resulting in a weird, cross-eyed effect.

'The class is in recess at the moment. I've probably forgotten everything I've learnt.'

'Oh, I'm sure you could improvise. After all, the moves are very reminiscent of the sex act. It's an interesting enigma, don't you think — those Middle Eastern women who have to be so submissive in every other aspect of their lives, performing a dance that's so suggestive and sensual.'

Any minute now he's going to demand I give a performance right here on the table. I leaned back casually in my chair (Sorry, old boy, the peep show is over) and feigned horror as I looked at my watch.

'Oh, look at the time, I really have to go.'

Patrick overcame his obvious disappointment by insisting on paying for lunch, perhaps thinking it would stand him in good stead for future assignations. He insisted on walking me to my car, enveloped me in his arms and pressed me tightly against him. He reeked of wine, garlic and aftershave, and the hard lump of his erection pressed against me.

'It's a pity you have to go,' he breathed into my ear. 'I was just starting to get to know you.'

My stomach was cramping as my insides protested at their prolonged restriction by the Wonderpants, and I started to feel faint.

For God's sake, don't pass out now and give him the perfect opportunity to apply mouth-to-mouth resuscitation.

Just then my handbag started ringing. Whew! Saved by the bell. I disentangled myself from Patrick's grip, dug around inside my bag and pulled out my mobile phone. The Caller ID said 'Home'.

'When are you coming home?' Zac demanded.

'I'm about to leave. What's the matter?'

'I've got a really bad headache.'

'Take some Panadol.'

'There's none left.'

'Ask Cara to walk down to the shop and get some.'

'She's locked her bedroom door. I think she's asleep.'

I felt a rush of blood to my head. I gave Cara specific instructions to keep an eye on Zac. I could only hope she was in her bedroom by herself.

'I'm leaving now — I'll be home in half an hour. I'll get some Panadol on the way.'

'Can you hurry up — I'm feeling really sick. And there's no ice-cream left.'

'You shouldn't be eating ice-cream if you're sick,' I snapped.

I pressed the end button and gave a weak smile. 'Boys! Horrible creatures, then they become men.'

'We're not all bad,' said Patrick, lurching towards me. I ducked gracefully under his arm, unlocked my car door and scrambled inside.

'Thank you for a lovely lunch, Patrick. It was nice to meet you,' I said out the car window as I started the engine.

'You haven't given me your phone number,' he called as I drove off.

'Send me an email!' I yelled back.

As I drove home along the motorway, The Voice, who'd been silent for ages due to my dull, blameless lifestyle, reasserted itself with gleeful smugness. *You're such a coward, Susan Hamilton. You should have told him right then you didn't want to see him again.*

But he'd been drinking; he might have turned nasty.

'*Bullshit. Telling him by email that you don't want to see him again is a cop-out.*'

OK, so I'm gutless, dishonest and a prick teaser. I never claimed to be perfect.

END OF DIARY

Chapter 7

Opinion is divided during our post-walk coffee as to how and when I should have told Patrick I didn't want to continue our association.

Myf is all for the immediate, upfront approach.

'You should have said "It's been nice talking to you, but I don't think we're compatible." It saves him from getting his hopes up — and anything else — and then having them dashed, and it saves you from feeling guilty for doing it.'

'It sounds perfectly simple when you say it,' I reply, 'but very hard to put into practice when he's got you in a clinch, breathing garlic in your ear and trying to touch your spine with his penis.'

'I agree,' Annie says, 'and anyway, why spoil a nice afternoon? For him, anyway, considering he paid for it. You can at least leave him with one nice memory of you.'

'Timing is of the essence,' Myf says. 'If you're going to be mercenary about it, tell him after he's paid the bill but before he has a chance to get you in a goodbye grope. By the way, did Mr Big live up to his name?'

I shrug. 'Bit hard to tell through his clothes. And anyway, I was trying to pretend it wasn't there — his erection, I mean.

It's exciting when it's someone you're attracted to but it's horrible when it's not.'

***

I canvass Jules's opinion at lunch at the Surf Club. We're too late to claim a window table, but score one underneath a model of a lifesaver suspended from the ceiling in a diving position with a relay stick in his hand, as if he's about to dive head first into someone's lunch. With his rippling muscles and wearing only his Speedo swimmers (or DTs — dick togs, as they're commonly known), it's easy to see that the model is anatomically correct, which probably accounts for the plastic smile on his sculpted, suntanned face.

'I wonder if the artist made a proper penis under those swimmers,' I muse. 'Or maybe he just did a good imitation because he knew no one would ever know the difference.'

Jules looks up and considers the bulge. 'It certainly looks realistic from where I'm sitting. Maybe he had a real-life model.'

'You mean suspended from the ceiling, swinging about on a wire like a fairy in a pantomime, yelling "can I come down yet?"'

'No, you idiot, perhaps he had a real lifesaver pose for him in DTs just to get the exact size and shape of the penis. I can't believe we're having a discussion about the sexual properties of a dummy.'

I agree that things are pretty desperate when you start ogling dummies, but to make matters worse, I have to sit and listen to Jules rave on about Max.

'He's everything I've ever wanted in a man — he's kind, considerate, generous and he's going to help me give my unit a complete makeover. And we've got so much in common — he likes music, ballet and art as well, and he's sensational in bed. What more could you want?'

'That's great, but is he everything you've ever wanted in a woman?'

'What do you mean?'

'Does this mean you've renounced women forever?'

'Of course! And anyway, Max is everything I've wanted in a woman as well. He's very emotional — he'll cry at the drop of a hat, as you saw the other night. The other day we were watching some re-runs of 'The Brady Bunch' — you know the one where Alice decides the family doesn't need her any more and leaves — and I heard this noise, and there was Max blubbering like a baby. I like that in a man.'

I admit there's something appealing about a man who's not afraid to show his emotions, but with Max I'd be afraid that if he saw anything really moving, like the scene in 'The Waltons' where John Boy wakes up from his coma during a bedside Thanksgiving, he'd have a complete breakdown.

'Talking of men,' I say, 'even if we're using the term somewhat loosely, I need a male viewpoint.' I recount the Patrick scenario.

'Now just imagine, we've had a nice long lunch, you think I'm hot stuff and you want to see me again. Would you prefer I told you then and there that I don't feel the same way, or would you rather I save your ego and not spoil a nice afternoon and email you in a couple of days?'

Jules grins. 'I know you want me to say option b, but I won't. I'd much rather know straight away, so I can start working on my next conquest. And don't give me that bullshit about saving his ego — that's just your excuse for not wanting to be honest. The poor guy has probably been fantasising all week about watching you do the dance of the seven veils on your next date.'

'Not any more. I emailed him yesterday and told him I'd enjoyed our lunch but I didn't think we had enough in common to continue our friendship.'

'He likes sex and you like sex — for a lot of men, that's as much in common as you need. So that's one down, how many more to go?'

'Forty-four altogether if you include the maybes.'

**

I'm in bed by 10 pm — most unusual for me. I'm trying to get some beauty sleep before my breakfast date tomorrow with candidate number two, Flying High. But my mind is spinning with all the issues that have arisen since I began this project that I haven't foreseen.

For example, when am I going to find the time to date all these men? If I count the maybes in with the definites and date two men a week, it's going to take me twenty-two weeks or over five months to date them all. And that's not allowing for the fact that there may be at least a few who will be presentable enough to date more than once. Even two men a week is stretching it a bit, bearing in mind I have a family to look after and writing deadlines to meet.

And issue number two. When, if ever, do I tell them they're part of a literary exercise? On the first date? Before our first kiss? After they ask me to marry them?

And issue number three. What if I find someone I'm really attracted to and want to have sex with? While that would be great – after all, if I'm truthful, that's as much the aim of the exercise as writing a book – that would mean the end of my research. Once sex comes into it, it's a whole new ballgame for me, and I wouldn't feel comfortable dating other men.

Instead of being forced to make a choice, perhaps I could negotiate. 'Darling, I'd love to go to bed with you but I have another twenty-five men to date yet, so let's make a date for June next year!'

There's no way round it. I'll have to create another rule. Cardinal rule number three: no sex with any of the candidates.

Cue derisive laughter from The Voice. *'Come on, you know damn well that if you find your Mr Right, the book won't mean a thing to you.'*

I bury my head in my pillow to drown it out and decide to deal with these issues in my usual manner — by complete avoidance.

Chapter 8

MY DATING DIARY

SUNDAY, 20 OCTOBER

Fuck, fuck, fuck. Cardinal rule number three is in danger of being swallowed up in a vapour of steamy sex, disintegrating in a volcanic explosion of passion and drowning in a surging ocean of desire.

But I digress. This morning I dragged myself out of bed at six o'clock, figuring I'd need at least an hour and a half to wake up and get ready for my eight o'clock breakfast at Billy's Cafe with Flying High, alias Sexy Phil.

I'd named him Sexy Phil purely on the basis of the one phone conversation we had to arrange our date. His voice had a deep, hypnotic resonance that made my insides go soft and marshmallowy. He hadn't included a photo with his profile, saying he was happy to email a photo after contact; but I'd forgotten to ask him for one, and when he phoned me I was so mesmerised by his voice that I forgot to ask him again. In his profile, he described himself as having a solid build with dark hair and blue eyes. Could this be a euphemism for fat with grey hair — okay, dark grey hair — and blue contact lenses?

He also said he was forty-seven, divorced with three adult children and a commercial pilot employed as a crop duster. As well as flying, he likes surfing, fishing and loves to experiment in the kitchen. Did this mean cooking or trying new positions on the kitchen table?

His blurb read, 'I would like to meet a woman who laughs at the same jokes as I do, with whom I can have long conversations about anything and nothing, someone who is my best friend as well as my lover, and be my soulmate who will cherish and love me as much as I cherish and love her.'

It was a bit over the top and greeting card-ish, but I was attracted to the spirit of romantic idealism. As I stumbled into the shower, I tried not to think of all the past occasions in my life when a man with a sexy phone voice had turned out to be the complete opposite in the flesh.

I made up my face to hide the bags under my eyes and put on my faithful, all-occasions denim skirt with a white blouse buttoned up to the neck. I've learnt my lesson about cleavage on the first date.

Cara was still asleep, and Zac was watching the Sunday morning cartoons.

'Where are you going?' he asked suspiciously.

'I told you last night — I've got a breakfast date.'

'You told me you'd make pancakes for breakfast,' he whined.

'I don't remember that.'

'You did — you promised!' His note of petulance rose higher.

'I don't remember making that promise, but okay if you want pancakes, I'll make them.'

By now, it was seven-thirty. I banged around in the kitchen, threw the ingredients into a bowl and poured the mixture into my non-stick frying pan. Unfortunately, my frying pan has seen better days and the non-stick stuff has worn off. The pancake batter stuck to the bottom of the pan, and the pancakes disintegrated into a gluggy mess when I tried to turn them over.

I deposited the pancakes in the bin and slammed the dirty dishes into the sink. 'Don't panic,' I said to Zac, 'you'll get your pancakes.'

I drove down to the local McDonald's, waited in the interminable drive-through queue and ordered a serve of hotcakes. When the attendant asked me if I wanted drinks, I snarled at her, 'If I'd wanted drinks I'd have asked for them, and I don't want any fries either'. I waited in the parking bay for ten minutes while they cooked them, took them home and plonked them on the table.

'There's your pancakes, I'm going.' I gave Zac a peck on the cheek and left.

Lesson Number Four from Mother to Son. Nothing worthwhile is ever achieved in a hurry. Your goals need to be nurtured and tended lovingly and carefully if they are to be attained — they will not be achieved through haste, anger or guilt. And it's the same for pancakes.

It was already eight o'clock. I'd been planning to walk to Billy's Cafe on the Mooloolaba Esplanade, but now I had to drive. By the time I found a car park three blocks away and arrived at Billy's Cafe, it was eight-twenty. The sun was already high in the sky, the ocean was shimmering postcard-blue and the Esplanade was abuzz with the Sunday breakfast crowd.

I scanned the crowd. Phil had said he'd be wearing a red shirt and denim jeans. There was a gorgeous guy sitting by himself in the corner with two cups of coffee. What a pity that's not him, I thought, but he's wearing a blue shirt, which really suits him because it brings out the blue in his eyes and his olive complexion...

The gorgeous guy got up and came towards me. He was over six feet tall and well-built. 'Are you Susan?' he said.

Once he opened his mouth, I couldn't mistake him. His mellifluous tones reverberated in my ears, shot straight through my stomach and bounced down to my knees, which were in danger of giving way.

My mouth emitted a strangled noise, like a lost kitten. 'Ye...ee...ss.'

'Hi! I'm Phil.' He held out his hand.

I stared into the blue brilliance of his eyes. 'But you said you'd be wearing a red shirt!'

I regretted it the instant the words were out of my mouth. My tone was accusing, as if I were the sort of person for whom last minute changes of wardrobe were too upsetting to the order of the universe. But I was still in shock — I'd prepared myself for the worst (thongs, a bushy beard and a beer gut) and I was certainly not expecting someone whose animal magnetism almost knocked me off my feet.

'Sorry,' he said, smiling, 'My red shirt was in the wash.'

He went to drop his hand when I didn't shake it, so I hurriedly grabbed it and pumped it up and down. 'Lovely to meet you,' I squawked as sparks of electricity shot through my body.

Did he feel them? He held my hand for a few seconds before saying, 'Come and sit down. I took the liberty of ordering you a cappuccino. I hope it's not cold.'

He rushed to pull my chair out for me and I wobbled thankfully onto it. I sipped my cappuccino. It was only just lukewarm, my penance for being late.

'It's just right,' I said. I apologised for my lateness and recounted the pancake story.

Phil gave a warm, easy laugh. 'My youngest left school last year. He was a real handful at that age. It must be tough doing it on your own.'

The waitress came to take our order and as Phil scanned the menu, I studied him. He didn't look forty-seven; his olive skin was smooth with just a few laugh lines, his hair was dark with only a hint of grey, and his body, although solid, displayed not an inch of flab. I could see the definition of muscle underneath his shirt and jeans.

I was visualising him lying naked on my bed — I'll have to get a new doona, my present one is a bit threadbare — when he looked up at me and said, 'What'll you have, Susan?'

I blushed and looked down at the menu. 'I'll have the pancakes with maple syrup and grilled banana. May as well have the real thing, the way they're supposed to be cooked. I won't tell Zac though — he'll be so jealous.'

One plate of pancakes, one Eggs Benedict (his breakfast) and six cappuccinos later (three each), we were still sitting there. The breakfast crowd had gone and the lunchtime crowd was starting to filter in. Phil was one of those rare men, a good listener as well as a good conversationalist, and by the end of the morning, he knew the story of my life; or at least the *Reader's Digest* version, condensed and edited.

For my part I learnt that he'd been married twice and divorced for five years. He was a radio announcer (and I bet he had an ardent female following) before he became hooked on flying and became a pilot. His current contract as a crop duster takes him all over Australia, from the east coast to the remote regions of Western Australia.

'Isn't that rather dangerous?' I asked, recalling having read somewhere a list of the most dangerous occupations, with crop dusting right near the top, just below mercenary soldier.

'It is,' Phil agreed. 'Even when you're experienced, there's always a risk, a factor of unpredictability. But that's what I love about it. There's nothing to compare with that rush of adrenalin you get when you're taking off — you really know you're alive. And then being up in the sky, so far away from civilisation, just you and the plane, as if you're suspended in a vacuum of time and space. Often I think I'd rather be in a plane then on the ground.'

His eyes had taken on a dreamy glaze. 'You look like you're up there now,' I said. 'Is it better than sex?'

His eyes refocused on me and he raised an eyebrow. I nearly melted into my seat. What is it about me and eyebrows?

'As good as,' he said.

He leaned forward and looked into my eyes. From the corner of my eye I could see a few dark chest hairs peeking out of the top of his shirt and his aftershave enveloped me in its fragrant aroma. My heart started beating like a chorus of tribal drums.

'You know,' he said, 'you're nothing like I expected.'

Oops. The tribal rhythm missed a few beats. 'What were you expecting?'

'Someone very ... you know ... out there, vivacious, flirtatious...'

'Sex on legs?'

'Something like that. Not to say you're not attractive, you are, but all that stuff about being a passionate woman who wants a passionate man, getting your gear off in the water, wanting to try indoor sports — it doesn't really sound like you.'

I was insulted. How dare this man, who had only met me three hours ago, try to tell me that I wasn't a wanton sex kitten?

'I am passionate,' I said hotly, 'when the mood and the man suits me. Admittedly I haven't swum in the nude for a while, but the weather's been lousy the last few years. And as for indoor sports, I'm the age champion for Twister and I'm pretty good at Trivial Pursuit, as long as you don't ask me any science questions.'

Phil laughed. 'I like your sense of humour anyway, and I'm glad you've got a few brains. You don't come across in your profile as the intellectual type.'

'So you contacted me because you thought I was a bimbo? Is that what you want for your soulmate?'

Phil's eyes twinkled. 'Touché. I contacted you because you sounded fun. And you are, only not quite in the way I visualised.'

He'd probably visualised me under the table by now, demonstrating my passionate nature by giving him a blow job while he was sipping his cappuccino.

'Well, you're not what I expected either,' I said. 'I pictured you as the original sensitive new age guy, valiantly searching the world for his soulmate, someone he can pick flowers with on a summer's day or read poetry to in front of the fireplace on a cold winter's night.'

'I can do sensitive and poetic, if you like.' He took my hand and stroked the back of it with his thumb, deliciously feather-light strokes that sent a tingle up my spine. 'But I can't show you just yet because I have to go away to Western Australia tomorrow for four weeks.'

'Oh.' There didn't seem much else to say. He turned my hand over and started stroking my palm with his fingers in light circular motions. If I wasn't so turned on, I would have laughed. It reminded me of a game my mother used to play with me, which I passed down to my own children. 'Round and round the garden like a teddy bear', you say while drawing a circle on their palm, then 'one step, two step', as you walk your fingers up their arm, followed by 'tickle you under there', as you tickle them in the armpit, guaranteed to bring on paroxysms of giggles every time.

I wondered if Phil was suffering from arrested development, if any minute he would suddenly come out with 'One step, two step', up my arm and then 'tickle you under there', while making a lunge for my breasts.

He must have read my mind because he moved my arm closer to his hand and started stroking the inside of my arm, long gentle strokes from my wrist up to my shoulder and back again, only a hair's breadth away from brushing my breasts on the way through. Underneath the table, our legs were just touching — I don't remember how that came about as when we first sat down, we were at opposite ends of the table. Even through his jeans I could sense his powerful thigh muscles. Goosebumps were breaking out all over my body, and I was glad I'd worn a respectable blouse because I could feel my nipples getting hard.

'Unless,' he continued, 'you want to come to my place tonight. I'll give you a break from cooking up a storm, and I'll cook for you instead.'

He reverted to tracing circles around my palm. So much for round and round the garden, this was the R-rated version and it wasn't my underarm I want him to tickle.

'I'm tempted,' I said. We both knew I wasn't referring to the dinner.

'If you're wondering about my culinary abilities,' Phil said, 'I'm a pretty passable chef. I do a great Thai chicken curry — quite spicy so you have to drink lots of wine.'

His fingers moved up my arm again. My erotic trance was shattered by a muffled ringing from somewhere in the distance. It went on and on, and stopped. Then it started again. I suddenly realised it was coming from my handbag, which was under the table.

I picked it up and unearthed my phone. As I suspected, the caller ID said 'home'.

'When are you coming home?' Zac demanded. 'Josh wants me to go over to his place; but his Mum can't pick me up, so I need you to take me over there.'

If I were home, I would have told him to walk or ride his bike, but now wasn't the time to become involved in an argument with a sulky adolescent.

'I'll be home soon,' I said, mustering all my self-control to sound normal.

'Can you hurry up, please?'

The spell was broken. The look on Zac's face as I'd flung his pancakes at him before leaving flashed into my mind, giving me an uncomfortable jolt in the stomach. Cardinal rule number three blazed before me in neon lights.

Don't do it. Remember your book. No involvement.

This isn't involvement; this is just sex.

Yeah, right.

'Are you still with me?' Phil asked. He'd stopped stroking my arm and was holding my hand in between both his hands. They were warm and reassuring.

'I'd love to come to dinner, but I promised to help Zac with his English assignment tonight.'

It was a lie and he probably knew it, but I was saving face. I couldn't very well say, 'I can't come to dinner at your place because I know you'll seduce me, and my conscience is telling me this won't be good for me.'

'That's okay,' Phil said. 'I should get an early night anyway. I've got to get up at the crack of dawn tomorrow.'

He walked me to my car, and I shivered in anticipation of a goodbye kiss. But he only brushed my cheek with his lips, then put his mouth to my ear and murmured, 'I'll call you when I get back.'

END OF DIARY

***

We analyse my date with Phil in every goose pimply detail over coffee.

'With all that chemistry happening, it's a wonder you didn't both self-combust,' Myf says. 'I don't know why you didn't take him up on his offer of dinner.'

'Because I knew I was on the menu as dessert.'

'The problem being?'

'If I start a relationship now then that's the end of my research and my book.'

'Who said anything about a relationship? This is sex, baby, animal attraction, lust, whatever you want to call it. And why will it mean the end of your research?'

'I don't think I can do sex with one man and still date others.'

Myf gives an exasperated sigh. 'But think of your book! Having a sexual involvement will make it more interesting — no one will want to read it unless there's sex in it. Think of it as art; all writers have to make sacrifices for their art.'

'Some sacrifice,' Annie observes, 'giving up not having sex.'

'I'm not sure I want to include my sex life in the book anyway,' I say. 'It's a bit up close and personal.'

'I'm all for being up close and personal,' Annie says. 'Then those of us who don't have a sex life at all can at least get some vicarious pleasure from it.'

There's an undertone of bitterness in her voice. Her face is drawn and her eyes ringed with dark shadows. She and I have had some long, teary phone conversations well into the night when Richard has been at work.

'What's happened?' I ask.

Her eyes well up with tears. 'I went to the doctor because I haven't been sleeping or eating and he hardly said a word to me, just gave me a prescription for anti-depressants and told me to come back in two months. Then I went to another doctor to get a second opinion and he gave me a referral to see a psychiatrist. I thought, this is crazy, I don't need either of these, so I tore up the script and the referral, and went to the TAFE college and enrolled in a fashion design course for next year.'

'That's great! You've talked about that for ages.'

'But it will mean giving up my job because it's a full time course, and Richard is really angry with me because he says we need the money and he'll have to work 100 hours a week instead of 80. So now he's not talking to me at all and he's moved into the spare bedroom.'

'Oh shit.'

'I don't care about the sex,' Annie says. 'Our sex life was pretty hopeless anyway, just the occasional fumble under the sheets in the morning before the kids got up. I'd be still half asleep and afterwards I'd hear Richard humming away in the shower and I'd think, 'Did we just have sex or did I dream it?'

'I love morning glories,' Myf says. 'Jason never used to be a morning person, but I've converted him. He's always got an erection in the morning, so I play with myself a bit to make myself all hot and horny, and while he's still asleep I just hop on top and away we go. He says I'm the best alarm clock he's ever had!'

'He really knows how to flatter a girl.' I turn to Annie. 'This doesn't sound good. What are you going to do?'

'I don't know,' she sniffles. 'All I know is I can't go on living like this. The kids are upset and always asking me why Daddy's so grumpy and why won't he talk to me and even the dog is acting strangely. When Richard comes home, he goes and hides under the bed and I swear I'm going to join him!'

'Well, there's only one immediate solution that I can see,' Myf says.

'I hope you're not going to suggest anything pertaining to the word sex,' I say.

Myf looks affronted. 'Of course not! Do you think I'm completely insensitive? There's only one other thing, besides sex, that will bring those endorphins rushing back.'

She gets up and goes to the counter. After a few minutes, she reappears bearing a plate on which is perched a mountainous slice of Chocolate Obsession — a triple layer mud cake with a middle layer of chocolate mousse, topped with icing sugar and a nest of plump strawberries. Rivulets of fresh strawberry sauce trickle down the sides of the cake, forming a gleaming pool at the bottom, which flows into two scoops of ice-cream and a huge dollop of whipped cream.

All eyes are on Myf as she conveys the sacred object of gluttony to our table and places it ceremoniously in front of Annie. I swear I can hear a synchrony of salivation — the men over Myf and the women over the cake.

Annie looks aghast. 'I'll never be able to eat all of that!'

Myf produces three forks with a flourish. 'Susie and I will be only too pleased to help you out. After all, what are friends for?'

Annie has only a couple of token forkfuls of cake; so Myf and I polish it off, groaning with delight at every mouthful. There's a duel of forks to get the last bit on the plate and we lean back in our chairs, sated.

'I don't know about you, Annie, but my endorphins are racing around in my brain as if they're in a pinball machine,' I say.

'I get enough pleasure just knowing that it's you two who'll be suffering the pimples and the cellulite,' she replies. 'Anyway, let's talk about something else. When are you seeing Phil again?'

'He's going to ring me when he gets back in four weeks.'

'Four weeks!' Myf grins at me. 'When you see him again, you're going to crack, I can guarantee. Just remember the two R's — research and recreation — and don't fall in love with him.'

'You know me, love 'em and leave 'em — that's my motto.'

Chapter 9

I'm scrolling through the fifty new kisses I've received since I did my short list and at the same time trying to decide which lucky definite will be my next date. Juggling all these men is hard work and rapidly turning into a full-time occupation. I have also bought contact stamps for the twenty-five maybes and sent each an email. 'I'm looking forward to getting to know you, but I'm about to go on holidays and will contact you upon my return.'

Suitably vague, but hopefully at least some of them will be interested enough to hang in there until I return from my mythical holiday, giving me a pool of reserves to draw on in the unlikely event that I run out of men.

A knock on the study door makes me jump. Without waiting for an answer, Cara bursts in and flings herself on my bed, sobbing loudly.

'What on earth has happened?' Even as I ask the question, I know it's something to do with Jay.

'Jay cheated on me,' she gulps, which starts a fresh flood of tears. I sit on the bed and wrap her in my arms. It's like holding a bird that's fallen out of a tree, a fragile bundle of sharp bones and delicate softness, heaving and shuddering. She snuggles her head into the crook of my shoulder, like she used to do as a child. Since she's become a teenager, she's shied away from physical demonstrations of affection — except for Jay.

Her pain sears through my body and I feel a desperate urge to burst into tears myself. But I have to be strong for her, to give her solace.

Eventually the sobs subside into a series of sniffles and nose-blowings. I stroke her hair. 'Want to tell me what happened?'

'Jay went to a party last night. I didn't know he was going. He didn't even invite me, and he met another girl there and he kissed her, and now he doesn't know whether he wants to go out with her or me.'

All I can think of to say is an eloquent 'Oh, shit'.

'So I said, "I'm not hanging around waiting for you to make up your mind — you and I are over".'

Good on you, kid, don't take any crap. A good lesson to learn early in life.

'But I've changed my mind now. I don't want to break up — I want him back!'

'Are you sure about that? Even if he says yes, how do you know he won't do the same thing again? In fact, you can almost guarantee he will.'

'You don't know that.'

Damn right I do. But she doesn't want advice from someone as ancient and uncool as I am. Someone who can't even remember what it's like to be in love. I hold her till her tears dry up, make her some hot chocolate and tuck her into bed.

***

A spooky quietness has enveloped the house. One minute the walls are reverberating with the usual Saturday morning cacophony of screeching guitar grind from the Dead Arctic Seals and the inane blaring of the TV, and the next minute, complete silence. The children have just left with Jeremy for the weekend and it's as if all traces of their existence have been obliterated.

After all this time, I'm still not used to having every second weekend to myself. I look forward to it with a passion then when it arrives, I wander aimlessly around the house. It's not as if I don't have plenty to do, it just takes me a while to become accustomed to the freedom of choice.

A metaphor for life perhaps, I reflect on my way to Jules's place for dinner with him and Max. Perhaps if I ever find my perfect match, I'll discover that he's not what I wanted after all. Maybe there is no man who can fulfill all my sexual, intellectual and emotional needs. Perhaps I'll have to settle for two out of three (but which two?).

Max insists on trying out his new cocktail recipe on me, so that forestalls any further deep thinking. He's called it Oblivion. It's fruity and potent — like its creator, Jules proclaims, downing his second — but I have to refuse any more on the high probability of it living up to its name. Max then whips up a fragrant Thai fish curry with melt-in-your-mouth coconut rice. Is there no end to this man's talents? He's moved in and redecorated Jules's entire apartment, replacing the stark chrome and metal look with delicate Chinese antique furniture, colourful rugs, fringed lamps and other exotic accessories in an Asian theme, giving the place a warm, cosy ambience.

After dinner we sip our coffee on the balcony, listening to the crash of the surf in the distance. Max has filled it with so many pot plants and hanging baskets of greenery that it's like sitting in the middle of a jungle.

'Any minute now I expect Tarzan to come swinging through the trees and leap onto the balcony,' I say.

'I've got a lap-lap somewhere, I think,' Max says.

'Ooh, cute,' Jules coos. He gives Max's thigh a squeeze. They exchange the sort of meaningful look between lovers that makes the onlooker feel intrusive.

A lump rises in my throat. I haven't seen Jules this happy for a long time. At the same time I felt a deep stab of envy. I'm still suffering from a serious case of skin hunger. Fred and I have spent many happy hours together, but he is sadly lacking in the kissing, touching and cuddling department.

'I read an article recently,' I say, breaking the silence, 'about an experiment that scientists did by wiring up some men and women and measuring how often they thought of sex. Don't ask me how, maybe they emit some kind of electrical signal when they think about it, and they discovered that men thought about sex thousands of times per day, far more than women.'

'That's hardly a startling revelation,' Jules observes.

'I know, but the startling revelation is that I think I'm abnormal. I think about sex all the time — even when I'm trying not to think about it, it just pops into my head. By the end of the day, I'm exhausted after indulging in all my fantasies.'

'Perhaps you should find a hobby,' Max suggests. 'Or get a pet.'

'It's only because you're not getting any,' Jules says. 'Deprivation is the mother of obsession. Anyway, it's your own fault — you've been inundated with men all wanting to race you off.'

'That's the scary part. Never mind them racing me off — last Sunday, within five minutes of meeting Phil, I had us lying naked on my new doona, and I was the one doing all the seducing!'

'You should have consulted me before you bought a new doona,' Max scolds, 'I could have done the whole bedroom for you.'

'I haven't bought it yet; it was while I was having this fantasy that I realised I needed a new one.'

Jules and Max then continue the discussion on feather versus synthetic doonas and what colour scheme would best suit my bedroom.

'I can't believe this is happening. We start off talking about sex and you two have turned it into a CWA meeting. Any minute now you'll whip out the scones and jam.'

'This *is* about sex,' Max argues. 'The decor is very important in setting the mood. You couldn't possibly seduce anyone in a bedroom where the quilt cover clashed with the walls — it would be an absolute disaster!'

'I'd be a bit careful of Phil,' Jules says. 'He sounds like a Mr Smooth. I don't want to see you get hurt, Susie.'

'We're going out on a date, not getting married. But don't worry, I'll be wearing my full emotional armour.'

Usually the shoe is on the other foot when it comes to being hurt. I've lost count of all the late night conversations and boozy sessions I've shared with Jules after each of his relationships has folded. I hope it's different this time with Max — next to my own desires, my dearest wish is for Jules to find someone with whom he can settle into a long-term relationship. It would certainly save me a lot of sleepless nights and hangovers.

'Anyway, Phil's away for the next few weeks and I've got plenty of other men to amuse myself with.'

Chapter 10

MY DATING DIARY

SUNDAY, 17 NOVEMBER

If today is Sunday, it must be Peter, no hang on, Ken. Or was it Mike? I've dated six men in the last three weeks, which accounts for my confusion. I've decided if I don't speed things up, this book is never going to be written. Although I haven't set an end date for my research yet, I presume there will be one — either I will meet the man of my dreams and live happily ever after (unlikely) or I will collapse with exhaustion, muttering a litany of male names as they cart me away to the madhouse (likely).

I soon realised I needed a systematic collation of information as well as my dating diary. I've bought a stack of manilla folders and have allocated a folder to each man I date. In it I put a copy of his profile, any emails he has sent me and notes about each time we meet — first impressions, positive and negative attributes, my thoughts and feelings and any other relevant information. So far I have eight folders — Patrick, with COMPLETED written across the front; Phil, with TO BE CONTINUED; and the six others I've dated (summary below).

The initial deluge of kisses has slowed down, but they're still flowing in at the rate of between ten and twenty a week, at least half of whom live out of town, sometimes interstate. 'A man will travel the world for a beautiful woman,' Myf proclaims, 'but he'll go to the ends of the earth for a good fuck.'

I'm pretty efficient now at weeding out the definitely not's and dividing the rest into definites and maybes. After reading dozens of profiles, you get a feel for the personalities behind them, even allowing for the necessary hype. Photos make it even easier because I maintain that good looks aside, you can tell a lot about a person's character from his face.

Then I have the problem of organising my definites into a dating schedule and keeping them interested. Sometimes I give the excuse that I would like to get to know them a bit more by email first before we meet, but that doesn't always work. One of my definites, Hotmale, alias Russell, wrote plaintively, 'You said you'd gone to a work conference for a week, three weeks ago, and you're still there. I would love your job — where can I apply?'

Another, Youngatheart, wrote, 'I don't know what you've got against meeting me in person — I'm really quite respectable, as you can see from my photo. I'm neither a mass murderer nor a rapist, and I'm quite prepared to believe that you're not a psychopath. So, what's stopping us?'

With that attitude, I think Youngatheart, alias Dave, deserves to be demoted to a definitely not and emailed with my 'Ms Hamilton regrets' platitude — 'I regret to tell you that I have met someone else and fallen madly in love. I wish you the best in finding a partner'.

It's no loss. I still have another thirty definites on my list, including the recent arrivals.

SUMMARY OF DATES SO FAR

Wayne (alias Newlife)

Age: 45

Lives: Noosa

Marital Status: separated, 2 kids, 11 and 9

Occupation: civil engineer

Interests: abseiling, canoeing, adventurous type.

First date: Saturday, October 26, dinner at Noosa (Italian) then coffee

Personality: outgoing, thrives on being the centre of attention, the sort of person who includes the waitress in the conversation and tells tasteless jokes to the drinks waiter

Looks. Positives: tall, nice teeth, dresses well

Negatives: has the beginnings of a gut, very hairy arms and hands, suspect he has a hairy back as well, which is a real turn-off for me, despite the fact that Sean Connery has one.

Is he sexy? He emanates a certain raw sexiness and hints that he is very accomplished in that area, which immediately arouses my suspicions.

Can I imagine myself going to bed with him? maybe, as long as I'm on top (because of the hairy back)

Summary of date: I had quite an enjoyable time, except for a few awkward moments when he asked, 'And what erotic novel are you reading at the moment?'

My mind went blank. 'The Story of O,' I blurted out. It just popped into my head, because I'd heard of it somewhere.

'Oh yes, I've seen the movie, it's rather erotic, especially the bit where he puts her in a dog collar.'

I hurriedly changed the subject. I didn't want him to think for a moment that being in a dog collar would turn me on.

I declined his suggestion of a walk on the beach after dinner as (a) after our previous conversation I thought it might entail a collar and lead and (b) I had a feeling I might end up with sand in more places than just between my toes. But he wouldn't let me get away without a goodnight kiss and after clamping his lips on mine and employing enough suction to swallow me whole, he murmured, 'If you want a passionate guy, baby, then I'm your man'.

Rating out of 10: 7. Needs tuition in slow, tender kissing

Will I see him again? Undecided

Peter (alias Happyguy 50)

Age: 50

Lives: Caloundra

Marital Status: separated, no kids

Occupation: software developer

Interests: computer magazines, scientific journals and garage sales

First date: Wednesday, October 30, lunch at a beachfront cafe at Caloundra

Personality: intense, needy. I felt as if I were being drawn into his web of deep-seated and complex problems. Happyguy would have to be the misnomer of the century.

Looks. Positives: appears to have all necessary limbs and functioning bodily parts

Negatives: gangly build, greasy hair, long dirty fingernails, none of which were evident in his photo. And he had the temerity to mention that I looked nothing like my photo.

Is he sexy? the answer is obvious.

Can I imagine going to bed with him: Ditto

Summary of date: Exhausting! He is the sort of person who should stay in bed all day (alone) because he attracts disaster wherever he goes. For my benefit, he relived his traumatic childhood with an abusive father, his narrow escape from two house fires, the death of his dog, a near death experience in a car accident, the death of his first wife from cancer, his mother's admission to a psychiatric hospital and his latest disaster, his second wife leaving him six months ago — I daresay she wanted to get out while she was still alive and healthy.

All this was recounted in a low monotone with unnervingly intense eye contact, as if daring me to express disbelief at his chronicle of tragedies. I'm sure that if I'd come up with any personal misfortunes of my own, he'd have been quick to upstage me.

The strange thing was that he'd managed to make himself sound interesting and amusing in his profile, so he either has a creative streak, which is yet to become evident, or someone else wrote his profile for him. I'm tending towards the latter option.

At the end of our meal I quipped, 'So I guess your nickname is Lucky.' He looked at me blankly. Then I realised I'd witnessed the greatest tragedy of all — no sense of humour.

Rating out of 10: 2

Will I see him again? No. He doesn't need a partner; he needs a grief counsellor.

Harry, alias Goodfella

Age: 48

Lives: Maroochydore

Marital Status: separated, 2 adult kids

Occupation: owns a printing business

Interests: golf, tennis, nothing out of the ordinary (so I thought)

First date: Friday, November 1, Drinks at the Maroochydore Surf Club.

Personality: Pleasant, easy to talk to, good sense of humour

Looks. Positives: nice muscle definition, good biceps, firm butt, strong thighs — and a nice face too

Negatives: no negatives that I could see

Is he sexy? yes

Can I imagine going to bed with him? yes, I already have (imagined it, I mean)

Summary of date: Harry seemed like a nice, run-of-the-mill sort of guy until he mentioned that he is a naturist, and my alleged fondness for skinny dipping prompted him to contact me. However, Harry doesn't just swim in the nude, he does everything in the nude where possible — from relaxing at home to going away for weekends and holidays with other naturists. I got the impression he thinks nudism is the answer to war, injustice and inhumanity.

'I decided not to say anything about it until I met you,' he said. 'Some people think we're kooks or perverts.' I hastily assured him I wasn't one of those people. If anything, I probably qualify as a kook or pervert myself. Is it kooky or perverted to be turned on by picturing a man vacuuming or cleaning the bath in the nude? Or playing tennis or volleyball at a nudist camp? I've often wondered why they don't play more sedate sports at nudist camps, like croquet or lawn bowls, where it's less likely that unrestrained parts of the body will get in the way or be damaged. I'll pluck up the courage to ask Harry if I see him again.

We only had time for a couple of drinks as Harry had to attend a family function. Unfortunately, he was the perfect gentleman and just gave me a kiss on the cheek.

'I'd like to see you again, and you're welcome to keep your clothes on — unless you want to take them off,' he added, with a cheeky grin.

Rating out of 10: 8.

Will I see him again? maybe, but how much of him, I'm not sure.

Ken, alias Yourplaymate (one of the first profiles I logged into — my Darius lookalike in the medical profession who is looking for a lady he can lavish his affection on).

Age: 45

Lives: acreage, Eudlo

Marital status: separated, one child, 16

Occupation: nurse

Interests: pushbike riding, bushwalking, animals (keeps a menagerie on his property) gardening (grows organic fruit and vegetables)

First date: Monday, November 4, lunch, Organic Delights Cafe at Maroochydore

Personality: serious, likes to engage in deep and meaningful conversations, quite a sensitive new age guy.

Looks. Positives: nice brown eyes, warm smile, doesn't look his age, despite his profession and all the outdoor work he does, nice hands with slim elegant fingers. A man's hands is one of the first things I notice about him — Jules says it's because I'm always thinking six steps ahead and anticipating what those hands might be doing to certain parts of my anatomy.

Negatives: Dress sense could do with an improvement. If I'm going to the trouble of rearranging my internal organs by squeezing myself into a pair of Wonderpants, wearing a Wonderbra to create an illusion of bosom and spending half an hour putting on my face, he can at least wear a pair of jeans that aren't ripped and frayed, and an ironed shirt.

Is he sexy? He has a certain kind of rumpled, boyish appeal.

Can I imagine going to bed with him? Maybe, if I didn't have to share the bed with any animals.

Summary of date: Very organic. He chose the venue for lunch, as he only eats organic food. If that's the secret of his youthful appearance, I'll have to try it myself. Admittedly the food was delicious — I had a huge slab of spinach and feta pie with salad, and a monstrous mango and banana smoothie. Even though I was stuffed to the eyeballs, I could feel myself glowing with virtuous good health.

Ken is an animal fanatic. He wanted to do vet science but his grades weren't high enough, so he did nursing instead. But he's compensated for that by letting his pets have the run of his house — from cats and dogs to hens, and even a donkey and a pig. It reminds me of a book I used to read to the children about a farmer who kept all his animals inside the house and woke up every morning sharing his bed with an assortment of creatures. Strangely enough, there was no wife mentioned in the book.

Ken was also eager to share spiritual experiences and philosophies. 'I have a friend who does belly dancing, and she finds it a very spiritual experience. With all that release of sensual energy, it gives her a sense of oneness with the universe. Do you feel that too?'

'Er … no, I haven't experienced that,' I said. Which was not at all surprising, considering the closest I've ever come to a public performance baring my stomach was when I went to the Year Seven fancy dress ball as a genie, and Ronnie Barton chased me around the school hall trying to rip the plastic ruby out of my navel.

'Tell me,' he said a few minutes later, after slurping up the last of his spinach and cucumber juice, 'have you ever practised tantric sex?'

I was beginning to feel naive and one-dimensional. 'I'll have to admit to being a tantric sex virgin.'

Ken proceeded to enlighten me, but from the way he described it, it seems to consist of two people lying together getting extremely turned on but not actually doing anything about it, because they're concentrating on being spiritual. While it appeals to my innate sense of laziness, I think my desire for divine fulfillment would soon be overcome by more earthly needs.

Rating out of 10: 5

Will I see him again? Doubtful. A bit too alternative for me. The organic food thing would become rather tiresome after a while (do they make organic Tim Tams?) and I suspect it's a case of love me, love my animals. Thinking back to his profile and his desire for that special lady whom he can lavish his affection on, I'm wondering how many legs she's required to have.

Mike, alias Outdoorguy.

Age: 51

Lives: Coolum

Marital Status: divorced, 4 kids from 17 to 25

Occupation: high school teacher

Interests: as his pseudonym suggests, outdoorsy, high adrenalin stuff — windsurfing, mountain climbing etc., although with four kids he must have spent some time indoors.

First date: Friday, November 8, drinks and dinner at Coolum Surf Club

Personality: casual, laid back, self-assured nature, can imagine him getting on well with teenage kids

Looks. Positives: open, tanned face, though weather-beaten.

Negatives: unruly sun-bleached hair, looks as if he's just walked out of the surf and neglected to brush it. A bit short for my liking, he's only just my height, which means I would tower over him in heels — not that it's going to be an issue, as it turns out.

Is he sexy? Not really, might be after a couple of drinks (me, not him)

Can I imagine going to bed with him? Maybe, again if I'd had a couple of drinks and closed my eyes (but then I'd probably go to sleep).

Summary of date: Embarrassing. Discovered in the first few minutes that not only does he teach at Cara's school but he's her maths teacher. I've heard her mention Mr Beecham a few times, and Mike told me his surname in his first email but not being good at maths, I didn't put two and two together.

'Unfortunately, Cara has taken after me in the maths arena,' I told him.

'She does her best,' he said kindly. 'I can't ask any more than that.'

'There's no way I'm going to tell her that I've been out on a date with you,' I said. 'That would be the most uncool thing I could ever do to her.'

Mike grinned. 'If I'd known that 'Sexyandsultry' was Cara's mother, I would have arranged a private parent-teacher interview long ago.'

If only Cara knew that not only did I date her maths teacher but he propositioned me as well! I flirted briefly with the idea of sleeping with him in exchange for passing Cara in maths, but after noticing his rough and calloused hands, decided it was too big a sacrifice for a mother to make for her daughter.

Rating out of 10: 5

Will I see him again? No. Mike agreed that for ethical reasons, further social contact was out of the question; but he was disappointed, as he'd been looking forward to taking me abseiling. As heights terrify me, and my adventurous spirit is confined to dating dozens of strange men, that's another good reason not to see him again.

Derek (alias Yachtie54)

Age: 48

Lives: on yacht moored at Noosa Sound

Marital Status: single, no kids

Occupation: semi-retired, part-time boat builder

Interests: sailing, snorkelling, playing the guitar

First date: Saturday, 16 November, a day sailing on his yacht

Personality: Blunt, down to earth, has a sort of rough and ready charm, calls a spade a fucking shovel

Looks. Positives: great body, good muscular development, very fit and tanned, has a large nose, which could be a positive attribute if the supposed correlation between nose size and penis size is correct, or perhaps this is just a myth generated by the ancient masculine species *Proboscis gigantor.*

Negatives: looks like the wild man of Borneo. In his profile photo he's clean-shaven with short hair, but since then he's let it all hang down. He has a bushy beard, one of my pet hates, and his blonde-grey hair is shoulder length and tied back in a ponytail. Perhaps I could persuade him to tie his beard up in a ponytail as well, or even plait it.

Is he sexy? in a primitive, Neanderthal way.

Can I imagine going to bed with him? If he keeps his hair under control, this would be one occasion when I wouldn't mind rocking the boat.

Summary of date: very enjoyable. I took quite a risk going sailing with him on our first meeting, even though we only sailed around Noosa Sound and along the river. He'd made it sound so enticing I had to agree. Remembering the movie *Dead Calm,* in which Nicole Kidman is trapped on a yacht for days with a psychotic killer, I kept my mobile phone within reach all day. Who I was going to call and how they were going to help me if he suddenly lunged at me with a knife, I hadn't decided.

We had a lovely day lazing around on the deck, drinking champagne and eating a delicious lunch of honey roasted chicken and wild rice that he whipped up himself. He went up a huge notch in my estimation after that — I maintain there's only one thing sexier than a man wielding pots and pans in the kitchen, and that's a man on his hands and knees scrubbing out the shower.

When the wind came up a little, he cut the motor, and I was able to lie back and admire his rippling muscles as he trimmed the sails and all those other nautical things sailors do.

As he wore only a pair of board shorts, I had plenty of opportunity to admire his body and to imagine making love on the tiny bunk in his low-ceilinged cabin, an act that would require great ingenuity and economy of movement — an ideal opportunity to try Tantric sex.

We pulled into a secluded little bay along the Noosa River and it wasn't until he stripped down to his DTs that I realised that in all my excitement getting ready for my seafaring adventure, I'd forgotten my swimmers.

'I don't mind at all if you swim in the raw,' Derek said. 'I know it's one of your favourite pastimes.'

I put on a demure look. 'Maybe when I know you a bit better.'

'I can tell you everything about myself in ten minutes.'

'You've either had a very boring life or you're an exceptionally fast talker,' I said. 'And I'll opt for the second.'

He conceded defeat gracefully and dived into the water. I watched him glide through the water, executing porpoise dives and back flips — all for my benefit, like a dolphin in a show at Seaworld.

After a few minutes, he hauled himself out of the water and stood about two feet away from me as he dried himself. There's something about a man in DTs. You can't not look at his crotch. Your eyes are drawn there as if by some magnetic pull, in much the same way men are compelled to stare at the breasts of a well-endowed woman. I tilted my head back and looked directly into his eyes.

'How was the swim?' I asked, pretending not to notice out of the corner of my eye that everything was jiggling and swinging as he towelled himself dry in what seemed an unnecessarily vigorous manner.

'Fan-fucking-tastic.' He flung his towel over a chair, picked up a tropical print sarong and draped it around his waist. Most men I've seen wearing a sarong look as if they're playing dress-ups from their wife's wardrobe, but Derek managed to not only look completely at ease in a sarong but positively sexy.

'Seeing as I can't talk you into swimming naked with me, can I make you a mango daiquiri?'

I could hardly refuse, as he'd somehow divined that mango daiquiris are my favourite cocktail. By the end of the day, he'd also asked me if I wanted to stay for dinner, had I ever made love on a boat and would I like to? I answered no, no and maybe, but not tonight.

Rating: 7.5 and 10 out of 10 for persistence. (the .5 was for the mango daiquiri which was sensational, but I could only drink half of it as I had to drive home). When he dropped me off to shore in the dinghy, he gave me a hug and a lingering kiss — more than a peck but not quite a full-bodied knee trembler. His beard was soft and tickly against my chin and I was surprised at what an enjoyable sensation it was.

Will I see him again? Maybe.

END OF DIARY

***

Progress reports are tabled and each man pulled apart like an insect under a microscope. I feel sorry for the poor guys, oblivious as they are of their fate.

Myf thinks Derek is the most promising prospect so far. 'He doesn't have a wife or kids, and it sounds as if he's quite well-off. He might be the next best thing to your rich old man with a nasty cough.'

'But why has he never been married?' Annie asks. 'I'm always suspicious of men who haven't been snaffled by a woman at least once — it makes me wonder what's wrong with them. Maybe he has some weird sexual fetishes. Did you say he has a big nose?'

'On the largish side. I may be sorry I asked, but why?'

'I saw this movie recently about a guy who had an enormous nose. It was one of those weird foreign films and he did the most incredible things with it, in fact he preferred using his nose over almost anything else...'

Her voice trails off, her face glowing pink.

Myf snorts into her cappuccino. 'It gives a whole new meaning to the term nose job,' I suggest.

'Anyway,' Annie says hurriedly, 'I think Harry sounds more interesting. I've always wondered what they do in those nudist camps. You should go as an undercover reporter and write an article about it.'

'Where would I put my notebook and pen?'

'It's obvious you're not attracted to any of them as much as you are to Phil,' Myf observes. 'There's nothing like a bit of sexual tension multiplied by absence and anticipation to add some spice to your first date.'

Swarms of butterflies have been doing gymnastics in my stomach since I received a phone call from Phil yesterday. He's back from his travels and we've arranged to go out for dinner on Friday night. Of course I'm not going to sleep with him, Cardinal rule number three will be uppermost in my mind. But just the thought of a slow, tender kiss is enough to make me tingle all over.

***

I'm no sooner in the front door than Cara bowls in, eyes sparkling. 'Guess what? Jay and I are back together again.'

'Oh. Is that a good thing?'

'Of course! He was drunk when he kissed Ebony. He's begged me to forgive him and we've talked things over, and I've agreed to give him another chance.'

'Being drunk is never an excuse for bad behaviour,' I tell her. 'He shouldn't have been drinking anyway — he's underage.'

Cara gives me a look that says 'what prehistoric rock have you just crawled out from?'

'I know, Mum, but he made a mistake and I've decided to forgive him. Haven't you ever made a mistake?'

Plenty. And I wish you could learn from my mistakes, but you have to make your own. I'll stand helplessly on the sidelines and watch; and then help you pick up the pieces.

I smile. 'I hope it works out,' I say with a lot more conviction than I feel.

Chapter 11

I swear I'll never be able to look at chocolate again. I must have demolished close to an entire 200-gram block, but I'm not looking at what's left because I don't want to know.

According to my research, chocolate boosts your levels of serotonin and endorphins, the chemicals in the brain responsible for your feelings of calmness and wellbeing. If that's correct, I should be so calm as to be practically comatose. I wish I was — instead, I feel like throwing up. Cara and Zac, relishing the opportunity for role reversal, have been scolding me for being such a pig and pointing out that if I'd shared the chocolate with them, I wouldn't be feeling so ill.

Lesson Number Five from Mother to Son: Don't ever hope to understand the special mystical bond that exists between women and chocolate. What you will need to understand is that on occasion, you will have no hope of competing with a block of Cadbury's Fruit and Nut Chocolate.

Unfortunately I can't tell the kids the real reason for my pig-out so they'd at least have some sympathy — my disastrous date with Phil on Friday night.

It started off well. We had an intimate dinner at a cosy Thai restaurant in Coolum with ocean views. Phil had offered to pick me up but I told him I'd meet him there, thinking that if things got hot and heavy, I could leave whenever I wanted.

I knew he lived at Coolum, not far from the restaurant. From the time I got into the car until I arrived at the restaurant, I was chanting a mantra to myself — 'Don't go back to his place'. I saw the words clearly in lights, like the huge neon signboards erected by the Department of Transport on the side of the road with admonishments such as 'Every K over is a killer'. Only this one said in large, orange, moving letters — 'DON'T GO BACK TO HIS PLACE'.

My other insurance to protect me from giving in to my carnal desires was my Wonderpants, which I wore under my long black skirt. I'd bought my own pair so I could give Annie back the pair she had lent me. There was no way I'd want Phil to see me in those passion killers and even worse, witness my body wobble all over the place like a blancmange when I took them off. I should have known that a mantra in ten-foot high neon letters and my vanity would be no match for my raging hormones and Phil's persuasive persistence.

During dinner, he was the perfect date — charming, attentive, laughing at all my jokes and regaling me with amusing anecdotes about some of the outback characters he'd met on his crop dusting adventures. He was even more attractive than I remembered him — his skin had tanned a shade darker, and in his cream silk shirt and perfectly pressed trousers, he looked as delicious as the plate of stuffed chicken fillet in front of me. He told me that his wife had left him for his best friend, just as unoriginal as having an affair with the office junior, and we agreed that my ex-husband and his ex-wife would make a perfect couple.

'I've had a few relationships since then,' he said, 'but there's been no one that I felt I could connect with on a long-term basis.'

He took my hand in his and stroked it gently. A shiver of delight zoomed up my spine. 'I have a feeling you could be the woman I've been looking for,' he said softly, turning my hand over and starting the 'round and round the garden like a teddy bear' thing on my palm.

Just then the waiter appeared and asked if we'd like to see the dessert menu. 'I couldn't fit another thing in,' I said. The Wonderpants were starting to cut into my waist.

I looked at my watch. It was 11 o'clock. We'd been eating and talking for three hours and I realised with a sudden sense of surrounding stillness that we were the only people left in the restaurant.

Phil leaned forward and put his mouth to my ear. 'Would you like to go for a walk on the beach?' His lips brushed my ear lobe as he spoke and his breath was warm and heavy in my ear.

You'd be better off going home now; you're only making things hard for yourself.

I hope so.

Don't be flippant. You know you hate getting sand in your clothes.

'Okay,' I said.

It was a crisp, clear night, with just enough breeze to ruffle the stillness. The beach was deserted — the multitudes of romantic men from eMatch who love moonlit strolls on the beach obviously don't frequent Coolum beach. We took off our shoes and walked hand in hand along the firm sand. After a few minutes, Phil stopped and turned to me, taking both my hands in his. The lights and noises of civilisation were just across the road but they seemed miles away. On the beach, with just the gentle lapping of the waves in the background, it was eerily quiet, as if we had stumbled onto another planet.

'I missed you while I was away, Sue,' Phil said.

My heart did a leapfrog into my throat.

'Did you?' It came out as a croak. I missed you too, so much that I had to date six other guys while you were away.

'I really did. I missed your conversation, your sense of humour and ... your sensuality.' He traced a line around my face with his finger. 'You're a very exciting woman.'

He cupped his hands around my face and kissed me — tentative, gentle, exploring. Then, as our lips blended into a fierce rhythm, Phil drew me closer to him and his erection was almost bursting out of his pants.

We kissed for what seemed like hours. I had one of those strange experiences in which I'm standing outside my body watching myself and I was thinking, 'Please make the world stop right now, I want to do this forever.'

It was a while since we'd come up for air and I was feeling a bit lightheaded. 'Oh, God,' I moaned, which is hard to do when you've got your tongue inside someone else's mouth.

Taking my moans to be those of passion, Phil crushed me against his chest and kissed me even harder.

'I mean, oh, God!' I moaned again, reluctantly pulling away from him. A combination of nervousness, a large meal and the constriction of my Wonderpants had resulted in a massive stomach ache.

Phi looked at me. I felt feverish and I was perspiring. 'You really are a passionate woman,' he murmured. 'I can see I'll have to take you back to my place and cool you down.'

If I go back to his place I can go to the toilet, take off my Wonderpants, which will give me instant relief, stuff them into my handbag, have a quick cup of coffee to be sociable then go home.

What about the mantra and the Department of Transport sign? And Cardinal rule number three?

It's just a cup of coffee.

This is self-delusion to the point of insanity!

You think I haven't got the willpower to resist his advances?

Absolutely. If you take one step into his house, you will be powerless.

Phil put his arm around me, undid the top two buttons of my blouse and ran his fingers lightly over my chest, letting them rest momentarily in my cleavage, courtesy of my Wonderbra (also new). He put his mouth to my ear again and asked huskily, 'Would you like to come back to my place and have a coffee?'

See? Just what I said. A cup of coffee.

Is that before, after or during?

When you're in an agony of indecision there comes a point when you make up your mind, and nothing that happens afterwards can sway you from your chosen path.

'Okay, just a quick one,' I said.

I followed him in my car to his house. As soon as we got in the door, I made a beeline for the toilet while Phil prepared the coffee. I unpeeled my Wonderpants and collapsed on the toilet in a spasm of relief. It was all I could do not to moan out loud in appreciation. I'd only brought a small evening bag with me and after I'd stuffed the Wonderpants in it, it bulged at the seams and the clip wouldn't do up properly.

I walked back out to the living room holding my stomach and bottom in as best I could. Phil was sitting on the couch, with two steaming mugs on the coffee table beside him.

'Now, where were we,' he murmured, as I sat down beside him. Before I had a chance to taste my coffee, we were in the bedroom feverishly tearing each other's clothes off.

After a few minutes of foreplay, Phil was ready for the main event. He pulled me on top of him and tried to insert his penis into me, but I rolled away, whispering 'not just yet'. I continued teasing him with my tongue. It felt so wonderful to be experiencing sexual intimacy after so long that I could scarcely believe it was happening. Phil rolled on top of me and whispered, 'I'm so horny, I want to get inside you.'

'I want to be really aroused, so aroused I can't stand it,' I said, and I took his hand and placed it between my legs. He stroked me and sucked my nipples for a little while and then pushed my legs apart, saying 'I just want to feel you. Only a minute, I promise.'

Another one to add to the list of Greatest Sexual Cons, along with 'I promise I'll pull out before I come' and 'Of course I'll respect you in the morning'.

'All right,' I said, 'but I'll hold you to that. Only a minute.'

He entered me and started thrusting in a slow, powerful rhythm. 'Oh God, that feels so good,' he moaned. He started to move faster.

'Hang on, a minute's up,' I said.

'Okay,' he panted. 'I'm stopping right now.'

I felt his penis contract inside me and he collapsed on top of me. He lay there for a couple of minutes panting then murmured, 'I'm sorry, babe, I didn't mean that to happen, I got carried away.'

He lifted himself onto his elbows and smiled down at me. 'It's all your fault, you shouldn't be so incredibly sexy. When you started moving your hips like that I just couldn't help myself.'

'I'm sorry,' I said. 'Next time I'll just lie still like a lump of wood so you won't get prematurely excited.'

I tried to keep my tone light, and if he took offence at my mention of premature excitement, he didn't show it.

'I'm sorry you didn't come,' he said. 'What would you like me to do?'

I looked up into the deep blue of his eyes. There was something about his tone of voice — like that of the waiter in the restaurant when he'd asked if we wanted dessert, knowing it was his obligation to ask, but obviously hoping we'd refuse so he could finish up and go home.

'Don't worry about it,' I said. 'I don't think it's going to happen for me tonight — I'm really tired. What I would love is that cup of coffee I didn't have a chance to drink.'

'Your wish is my command,' he said. Was that a note of relief in his voice? 'You stay there and relax — I'll bring it in to you.'

He got out of bed, threw on a pair of boxer shorts that were hanging on the end of the bed and went out into the kitchen.

Relax from what? Any sexual excitement I felt had quickly drained away, leaving me feeling as flat as if I'd been run over by a steamroller.

What did I tell you?

Shut up, next time will be better. I'll just have to be a bit more assertive.

A ring tone jerked me back to the present. Phil's mobile phone was on the bedside table. After a few rings it stopped.

Then it started again — the caller obviously wasn't going to give up. I got out of bed, wrapping the sheet around me in a tangled mess (how do female movie stars in bedroom scenes manage to look so damn cute wearing a sheet?) and picked up the phone. The caller ID said Julia. I carried it into the kitchen and held it out to Phil who was filling the coffee plunger with boiling water.

'Phone call for you.'

He hesitated before taking the phone. 'Hullo,' he said, turning his face away from me.

'How are you?' His tone was guarded.

'Nothing much, what about you?' He busied himself getting the coffee mugs down from the cupboard as he talked.

'Yeah, that should be fine. About 5 pm.'

He listened for a while then said, 'Let's talk about it tomorrow. See you then.'

He pressed the end button and smiled at me. 'Just a friend. Some people have no concept of time.'

'She must be a pretty good friend to be ringing you at midnight,' I said.

'How did you know it was a she?'

'I saw the caller ID.'

Phil shrugged. 'She thinks because she's a friend she's got a right to know what's going on in my personal life. You know what women are like.'

At first I thought it was meant as a joke, a sly dig, but then I realised that underneath the casual tone was an implied threat — mind your own business.

Suddenly I felt humiliated and foolish. I didn't want to be there a minute longer. 'Don't worry about the coffee,' I said. 'I'm going.'

I marched back to the bedroom with as much dignity as I could muster, wearing a sheet that trailed behind me like a bridal train. I dressed, grabbed my evening bag and walked through to the kitchen. Phil had decided to forgo the coffee as well and was sitting at the breakfast bar with what looked like a Scotch.

'Why the sudden change of heart?' he said.

'I don't think I'm the one destined to be your soulmate. I'm sure you have plenty of other willing applicants for the position.'

'Is it because of the phone call?'

'Not only the phone call. I've come to the realisation that this is not what I want. Thanks for dinner.'

As I walked out the front door he called after me, 'You shouldn't have picked up the phone anyway; it was none of your business.'

Maybe he was right but it didn't matter. I'll be eternally grateful to Julia, I thought as I backed out of Phil's driveway. She's saved me from more hurt and humiliation later on when discovering that there's at least one other woman in his life and probably more. I put my foot down and sped along the street that joined up with the motorway going south.

You never learn, do you?

'Just shut up,' I said out loud. The tears started to flow as I raced along the deserted motorway. At one point I noticed I'd clocked up 130 kilometres per hour, so I eased up a little. A hot, salty torrent of tears filled my eyes so rapidly it almost blinded me.

As I stopped at the traffic lights at the top of the Mooloolaba exit, I reached over to my evening bag to grab a tissue. Then I remembered I didn't have any — my evening bag was stuffed full of my Wonderpants. In the absence of anything better, I pulled them out and blew my nose heartily on them.

When I arrived home, Cara was still up, entwined on the couch with Jay, watching a DVD. 'Are you all right, Mum?' she asked. She and Jay stared at me, and I realised I was still clutching my Wonderpants.

I stuffed them back into my evening bag. Jay got up. 'I'd better be going.'

It was then that I noticed Zac asleep on the floor beside the couch, still in his shorts and t-shirt, with his head on a cushion and a rug thrown over his legs. He was clutching his pillow to his chest as if it was a lifebuoy. His hair had fallen over his face into his eyes, and his mouth was slightly open as he snored softly.

'He said he wasn't going to sleep until you came home,' Cara said. 'He rang you a couple of times, but you didn't answer.' She added pointedly, 'You must have been otherwise occupied.'

She got up and followed Jay to the front door to say goodbye. Struggling to stifle the guilt rising up inside me, I knelt down beside Zac and shook him gently to wake him so I could put him to bed — the days of being able to pick him up and carry him up to bed are long gone. But he remained steadfastly asleep, and I gazed at his pudgy face framed by the mop of dark hair. For once, his interruption might have been a good thing. It might have saved me from making a total fool of myself.

This vulnerable half-child, half-other being made me ache all over inside. I went into the kitchen and made myself a cup of coffee, and instead of milk, I poured in a large splash of Tia Maria.

So, dear diary, that's why I'm depressed. I'm a woman of forty-five — mature age, supposedly — but I feel as if I'm nineteen again. I've allowed myself to be taken in by soft words and silken fingers, like fairy floss — sweet and enticing but dissolves into nothing the minute you taste it.

Cardinal rule number three — no sex while researching — is back on the agenda. My mission statement is 'to apply myself to the highest principles of scientific research without the distractions of physical and emotional involvement'.

From now on, it's just me and Fred.

END OF DIARY

Chapter 12

I'm looking forward to basking in a major outpouring of sympathy from Myf and Annie during our walk and coffee. But Myf doesn't turn up at the appointed time and isn't answering her mobile phone, so Annie and I do the walk without her. Afterwards at coffee we indulge in the only proven way to get a man out of your system — a slice of Chocolate Obsession, with extra cream. This time Annie has a whole slice to herself in a show of female solidarity.

'Sex with Phil doesn't even rate a mention compared with this,' I sigh.

'A classic case of needing a bastard detector,' Annie agrees. 'All that Prince Charming stuff was just to lure you in, then wham, bam thank you ma'am and a chat to the other girlfriend on the phone afterwards.'

'Jules said he thought Phil sounded like a Mr Smooth. He won't be able to resist saying "I told you so".'

'It's the good looking ones who are the worst,' Annie says. 'They're so used to women falling all over them they think they don't have to make an effort. Ugly men are better in bed because they have to make up for their lack in the looks department with other attributes. So I've been told,' she adds.

Just then Myf arrives in a whirlwind, draws up a chair and flings her handbag on the table.

'I can't believe it,' she says through clenched teeth, 'what an absolute bitch!'

Her lips are pursed into a tight line and her face is white with fury. Other than that she looks her usual glamorous self, and I can feel the interest of the grey-haired gent at the next table cranking up a couple of notches.

'Who?' we chorus.

'The girl who's been screwing Jason. What an absolute fucking bitch.'

There's silence as we digest the news.

'When did you find out?' I ask.

'This morning. I called around to Jason's place to give him a surprise present. He was acting very strangely and didn't want to let me in; so I just barged in, and then I saw a woman's handbag and shoes on the couch and the bedroom door was closed. So then it was all perfectly clear.'

'Did he admit it?'

'Only after I threatened to go in there and see for myself. Her name's Rachael, she's in one of our psychology classes; and they were just good friends and he didn't mean for it to go any further, blah, blah, blah, usual bullshit, and they want to get married and settle down. And the worst part is, she's got legs like tree trunks and looks like Marge Simpson on a bad hair day!' So I said "don't bother inviting me to the wedding, have a nice life" and walked out.'

'Perhaps he loves her,' Annie suggests.

'He did actually mention the word love,' Myf spits out. 'If that's love, he can have it. She'll turn into one of those fat, frumpy women, he'll have a mortgage, a couple of snotty nosed kids and no sex life. If that's what he wants, good luck to him.'

I suspect Myf's pride is hurting her as much as the break-up of the relationship. In all the years I have known her, she has always been the dumper, rather than the dumpee, as soon as the excitement wears off the relationship or her partner shows signs of wanting commitment.

'As the saying goes, there's plenty more fish in the sea,' Annie says.

'If you like gropers and sharks,' I reply. 'Why don't you try abstinence for a while? It's very good for the soul. Read some philosophy, go for long walks, explore your inner self, free yourself of the addiction to sex.'

'I'm not addicted to sex,' Myf says frostily. 'And why are you, of all people, extolling the virtues of abstinence?'

'Because most of the time it's been forced on me when I haven't wanted it. But I had six months of voluntary abstinence after I left Jeremy and it was the best thing I ever did. I learnt how to talk to myself in the mirror, caught up on all my DVD viewing and put on five kilos.'

'I may be missing something but there doesn't seem to be a lot to recommend it.'

'What's the longest period of time you've gone without sex?' Annie asks.

Myf thinks for a while. 'A month. That was after Neil died.'

Myf's husband Neil, who was some years older than her, died a few years ago, leaving her a wad of money. They had no children so wise investment on her part has enabled her to be a professional student for the last few years. Since Neil's death, Myf had become a serial toy boy dater. There's something psychological there though I'm not sure what, and

I don't think Myf knows either. Maybe that's why she's studying psychology.

'A month is not a long period of mourning,' I observe.

'Who said I was only mourning for a month? Having a relationship with Daryl helped me to get over my grief.'

'I bet you couldn't go without sex for six months,' Annie says.

'Of course I could. But why would I want to?'

'For the challenge,' I reply, 'and sense of achievement. You said the other day that you've been feeling at a bit of a loss since uni finished for the year. Imagine how much you could do with your life without men and sex to distract you.'

'What are the stakes?'

'Chocolate Obsession,' Annie says. 'You win the bet, Susie and I will buy you a slice. You lose, you buy us one each.'

Myf looks incredulous. 'You want me to give up sex for six months for a piece of cake?'

She watches me as I shovel the last few crumbs of Chocolate Obsession into my mouth and let out a sigh of sated contentment.

'Okay, it's a deal.'

Annie and I stare at her.

'You're not serious?' I ask.

'But if I'm going to put myself through such torture, I want more than just a piece of cake. It's the whole cake or nothing.'

Myf can be a hard woman when the occasion demands. Annie and I agree to up the stakes to a whole Chocolate

Obsession cake, borrow a pen from the waitress and draw up a list of rules on a paper napkin.

1. From today, November 27 until May 27 next year Myf is not to indulge in any form of sexual contact with a man. This includes any form of heavy petting (as they call it in sex manuals) clothed or unclothed, and contrary to Clintonesque theory, oral sex.

'What about kissing?' Myf demands. 'Kissing isn't sex.'

'Theoretically, no,' I reply, 'but why would you put yourself in the way of temptation by getting into a passionate clinch?'

Myf reluctantly concedes the point.

2. As we will obviously not be stalking Myf, peering in her bedroom windows or setting up a spy camera in her wardrobe, this bet relies on her honesty to be successful. She is to own up straight away if she gives in to temptation.

3. Vibrators are not only permitted but compulsory.

4. Myf should keep a journal of her thoughts and feelings during this time, so she can chart her journey of personal growth and development.

'Stuff the personal growth and development,' Myf says. 'I'm only doing this for the Chocolate Obsession. It's all going to be a bit of a yawn, actually. I'll have to find myself a hobby.'

'What about crocheting or patchwork quilting?' I suggest. 'Something where you're not going to meet any men. Maybe you could join the CWA.'

Myf gives me a look that makes words superfluous. As we get up to leave, the neighbouring gent, who's been casting surreptitious admiring glances at Myf, looks quickly away. But I've already caught him out.

'By the way,' I say, 'what was your surprise present for Jason?'

'I had a Brazilian wax. Now it's going to be totally wasted.'

We walk out to a spasm of coughing and spluttering from the next table.

Chapter 13

MY DATING DIARY

SUNDAY, 28 DECEMBER

Between my disastrous date with Phil and Christmas, I've managed to date a further ten men. No wonder I collapsed in a near coma on Christmas Eve.

First was Ray the architect. He had sad eyes, drooled a lot and reminded me of a cocker spaniel. Women with big breasts were especially saliva-inducing, which fortunately counted me out. Simon the personal trainer had muscles where I didn't think it was possible to have muscles and almost crippled me when he hugged me. Lennie the stockbroker demonstrated over dinner how the stock market works by the creative positioning of the cutlery and condiments, although I didn't have the heart to tell him he'd lost me way back at the salt and pepper.

I exchanged tuna recipes and playgroup anecdotes with David, a full-time sole parent. Nick the security officer had been learning taxidermy and wanted to show me his mounted boar's head and Steve the sculptor wanted me to do a nude sitting for him, for purely artistic motives, of course. Mick the retired (i.e. redundant) bank manager recounted the bizarre story of how his second wife ran off with his first wife.

'You tell me why both my wives turned out to be lesbians,' he demanded, belching loudly and finishing off my wine.

Rob the wine salesman was such an enthusiastic connoisseur of his own products that he was drunk before I even met him, and that was a lunch date. Keith the dental hygienist said I had beautiful teeth and gave me a free carton of dental floss and Andy the musician offered to teach me how to play the lute, no strings attached.

I've become an expert on fielding questions, comments and suggestions about skinny-dipping, belly dancing, erotic novels, spa baths, gourmet cooking and being a passionate woman. I've also discovered for myself the truth of Jules's observation about internet dating — that exaggeration of your qualities is not only acceptable, it's mandatory.

'Athletic build' means there are muscles somewhere underneath the epidermis of spreading flab, 'my friends tell me I'm good looking' means his friends are delusional, 'good sense of humour' is demonstrated by an endless supply of jokes about blondes, nuns and oral sex; and 'sensitive' refers to his moist eyes when describing his footie team's win at the grand final.

I guess that when these men — or some of them at least — met me for the first time, I fell far short of their expectations of a 'Sexyandsultry' woman, but apart from a couple of snide 'I didn't recognise you from your photo' remarks, they were polite enough not to say so. In fact, many of them have been eager to continue seeing me after our first meeting, but contrary to Jules and Myf's advice, I've taken the coward's way out. I emailed them with my standard 'Dear John' reply – 'I have met someone else and fallen madly in love. I am sorry to have to write this letter. You're a lovely guy (this bit occasionally required me to grit my teeth) and I wish you luck in finding a partner.'

Besides Phil, the only other man I have met through eMatch to whom I have felt any strong attraction is Lennie the stockbroker. While Phil was handsome in a classical, movie star way, you could only describe Lennie as classically ugly. He's Jewish, though non-practising, with the typical large nose, thinning dark hair, eyes too close together, large, thick-rimmed glasses that make him resemble Buddy Holly and an over generous mouth. He's of average height and slight in build, and has a raspy voice that makes him sound like a younger version of comedian George Burns. Like the late George Burns, his raspy voice is due to a passion for cigars, he drinks like a fish, hates the beach and spends all his time indoors hunched over his computer analysing the stock market or reading obscure academic texts.

His profile photo was taken a few years ago, airbrushed and minus the glasses, and he somehow neglected to mention the smoking, drinking and indoor lifestyle. On the face of it, he's someone I'd normally run a mile from, but he's also clever, quick-witted and entertaining company; and occasionally the façade of cynical detachment reveals a crack of vulnerability. His wife died of cancer two years ago and he admits he's still grieving for her.

I'm strangely fascinated by Lennie's ugliness and during our first meeting at dinner, I was hypnotised by him as he recounted various amusing anecdotes from his past. I found that the more I stared at him, the better looking he became. My mind became desensitised with increasing exposure and alcohol, and by the end of the night he was beginning to take on an alluring aura. He didn't attempt to kiss me, just shook my hand and said, 'That was fun, let's do it again soon.'

Since then, just before Christmas, Lennie has emailed me every day, wanting to arrange another date. I've been stalling, using Christmas and New Year as an excuse. The truth is, I'm a bit afraid of my attraction to Lennie — there's something unstable and on the edge about him, and I'm unsure about further involvement. But I keep thinking of Annie's theory about ugly men being the best in bed.

Don't start, I warn The Voice, before it has a chance to retaliate. I'm just speculating.

END OF DIARY

Chapter 14

I flop down onto the armchair, damp with sweat. Why do I feel the need to clean the house from top to bottom before a party? It's not as if anyone will notice or even care, and I'll have to do it all again tomorrow to get rid of the aftermath.

I run through my mental inventory. Alcohol, a full fridge and esky, tick. Food, enough party pies, and salami and cheese to soak up the New Year's Eve excesses, tick. Paper napkins and plastic plates, tick. No way am I going to wash up after forty people. Clean loo and extra loo paper, tick. Children soon to go to Jeremy's, big thankful tick.

The phone rings. I can't muster up the energy to get up. It stops and after a few minutes, Zac comes in and hands me the cordless phone. 'It's Grandma.'

I take the phone. 'Happy New Year, Mum.'

'Susan, what is going on there?'

'What do you mean?'

'I've just been talking to Zac. He tells me you're never home because you're always out on dates, with a different man each night.' Her voice is shrill. 'And he said something about you doing research into sex.'

'I'm not researching sex, Zac's got hold of the wrong end of the stick.' And boy, would I love to give him the right end. 'I'm doing research for a book on internet dating.'

'Internet dating? Isn't that rather dangerous?'

'Not if you're careful. It's no more dangerous than meeting someone at a party.'

'It doesn't sound as if you're setting a very good example to your children, Susan. How many men have you dated?'

Lie to her. Say three. 'About eighteen.'

'Eighteen?'

Her voice is on the upper register now, like an opera singer warming up. Then silence. Has she passed out from shock? I feel a prickle of guilt for not lying to her; to someone who married her first boyfriend, hearing the news that I've dated eighteen men in a short space of time must be akin to my admitting to prostitution.

'I don't like the sound of this at all. You've been out with eighteen complete strangers?'

'Everyone's a complete stranger until you get to know them, Mum. Even Dad was when you met him.'

'That's different. I wasn't going out with seventeen other men at the time. *And* I married him.'

'I'm sorry, Mum, but if you expect me to marry all these men, it's out of the question. I couldn't stand all those mothers-in-law.'

'It's not funny, Susan. I'm worried about you — and the children.'

'Honestly, Mum, there's nothing to worry about. All the men are thoroughly screened before I even meet them, and I'm not having sex with any of them.' Well, hardly any.

'I should certainly hope not.' Her tone of voice implies that she has no desire to even entertain that possibility. 'I don't think your father's going to be very impressed either.'

I can't believe it — I'm forty-five and she's still using the hoary old 'wait till your father hears about this' chestnut.

'I already know, I've been listening in on the other phone.' My father's voice booms in my ear. 'Try not to worry, Pat. If Susan says she's being careful and everything's all right, then we have to trust that it is.'

My mother lets out a martyred sigh. 'All right. But promise me, Susan, the minute anything happens, you call me and I'll be on the first plane.'

'Okay, I promise.' I have no idea what she means by 'anything'. After I hang up, I look for Zac to give him a tongue lashing but he's mysteriously disappeared.

Lesson Number Five from Mother to Son. It is imperative to learn what your grandparents need and don't need to know. They do need to know all your cricket team's scores, your favourite ice-cream flavour and what you want for Christmas. They do not need to know how many men your mother is dating and whether she is having sex with any or all of them.

***

By 9 pm my apartment is crammed with bodies and buzzing with chatter, the walls reverberating with the raunchy strains of the Rolling Stones. When I invited everyone to bring a friend or two, they took me at my word. The crowd overflows from the courtyard into the living room and kitchen.

Max has brought his own coterie of admirers who keep everyone amused with their outrageous anecdotes, recounted with the flair for drama at which certain gay men excel. It always amuses me to watch Jules when he's in their company — by a process of unconscious osmosis, his voice goes up an octave, his hands start fluttering in the air like delicate little birds and I swear I've seen him mincing, which he categorically denies. 'I'll admit to a bit of falsetto and the occasional giggle,' he declares, 'but no way do I mince!'

Annie arrives on her own with the Cold War showing no signs of abating. Richard's gone to another party on his own so Annie has left the kids with Richard's parents. 'They think it's normal for a married couple not to talk to each other,' she tells me. 'Richard's father hasn't said anything of more than one syllable to his mother for years.' Her careworn face sparks up when Peter, one of Jules's advertising colleagues, comes over and introduces himself. He's the sort of person who engages you in a deep and meaningful conversation within two minutes of meeting you, which puts a lot of women off, but in this instance he couldn't have picked a better target. He and Annie are soon deep in animated discussion.

Myf, looking sensational in a slinky black dress with high heels and her hair up, plays court to a steady stream of admirers all night with the air of a Nordic queen dispensing favours to her courtiers. 'Hope you're browsing and not buying,' I mutter in her ear as I pass by. She glares at me and later corners me in the kitchen as I'm opening a bottle of wine.

'That was really cruel, asking me here,' she hisses. 'I've had to turn down three dates already. I could be at home watching "The Science Show".'

'So sorry for putting you in temptation's way. I didn't know myself there'd be so many gorgeous young guys here tonight. How many days is it now?'

'How should I know? I'm not ticking them off. All I know is I've got one hundred and forty-five days, twenty hours and fifteen minutes left. And if you're any sort of a friend, you won't even mention the word sex between now and then.'

'This is going to be so good for you.' I can't help the air of smugness. 'Now you know what the rest of us mere mortals have to go through every now and then. This will really develop your empathic side.'

Myf gives a very unempathetic reply as she stalks off, cutting a swath through the crowd like the parting of the waters.

Max and Co put on an impromptu drag queen act without the drag, singing and dancing to 'Big Spender', 'Goldfinger' and other classics from Jules's Best of Bassey CD, using bananas as microphones. This goes over extremely well although the performances render the bananas inedible. Two sets of neighbours arrive to complain about the noise but relent when I offer complimentary drinks and a front seat view of the show. Jules joins the act for the finale, swinging his hips and casting smouldering looks at the audience. So much for not mincing

By three o'clock in the morning, everyone's gone home, except for a couple of bodies on the living room floor, and Jules and Max. Max is poking around in my kitchen in a drunkenly futile attempt to make coffee. Jules, who up until now has not uttered one word of 'I told you so' about Phil, proceeds to make up for lost time.

'Didn't I tell you he'd break your heart?' he demands, stabbing in the direction of my chest. 'If that sleazebag ever comes within ten feet of me I'll break his legs! Then we'll see how smooth Mr Smooth really is!"

If Phil was within ten feet of Jules right now, it's doubtful he'd be too concerned about the threat coming from a guy with glazed eyes and sticking-up hair, wearing a T-shirt saying 'Kiss my arse — it's better looking than my face' and fluorescent pink sandshoes.

'And you can stop laughing. If it wasn't for Max, I'd marry you just to keep you safe from deadshits like him.'

'Please don't let me stop you, darling,' Max cuts in. 'I'd hate to think I was in the way. Susie, you've run out of milk.'

'That's a sign it's time to go home. I'm calling you both a cab.'

I'm so tired I could drop on the spot and already a hangover is hovering. When the cab arrives, I practically push Jules and Max out the door, their cries of 'Happy New Year!' echoing in the still night air. Annie left earlier in the night with Peter, both sneaking out the front door when they thought no one was looking. I caught Annie's eye and she waved, and looked sheepish before disappearing. I can't help speculating on the fact that while not exactly ugly, Peter resembles a short, dumpy version of Gerard Depardieu, right down to the large nose.

Chapter 15

MY DATING DIARY

SATURDAY, 15 FEBRUARY

I f a hypothesis can be proved by one test case, I can support the theory that ugly men make the best lovers.

Last night, Lennie and I finally did the deed that I've been trying desperately not to think about for the last few weeks. In my fantasies I tried to replace Lennie's head with Brad Pitt's head, but it didn't work and his real head kept popping back onto his body. In the end it didn't matter — in the dim light of the flickering candle by his bed, with his glasses off and about to go down on me for the third time, Lennie was Brad Pitt, George Clooney and Johnny Depp all rolled into one.

I don't consider myself particularly impressionable when it comes to men, with the exception of expensive restaurants, lavish gifts and fast cars —Lennie provided all three. From our first date, he has picked me up in a stretch limousine, wined and dined me at the most exclusive restaurants and lavished upon me an endless succession of gifts — huge bunches of flowers so that my house resembles a florist's shop, boxes of chocolates (much to the kids' delight) and bottles of French perfume. The pièce de résistance is a small fur-lined box, in which nestles a diamond necklace and a pair of diamond earrings. The more I protested that I couldn't accept them, the more Lennie insisted I take them. I haven't worn them and because I don't know what to do with them, I've hidden them from potential burglars amongst a pile of towels in the linen cupboard. It makes me nervous having something so valuable in the house.

When I remarked that I wasn't aware that stockbrokers made such a good living, Lennie just winked. 'After my wife died, I realised the value of living in the moment. My money's no good to me when I'm lying in a coffin.' Which was a strange thing to say, considering he spends most of his time immersed in the world of money.

On our second date, he reached across the table for my hand. 'I know I'm no Brad Pitt,' – I jumped guiltily, could he read my mind? – 'but I sense an attraction and I would love to go to bed with you, but if and when is completely up to you.'

So last night as I was getting ready to go out, I was tingling all over, because I knew it was going to be The Night. The reason I knew that, apart from it being Valentine's Day, was that I decided not to wear my Wonderpants.

You know you're being bought, don't you?

I don't come cheaply — at least someone recognises my true worth.

You realise that the 'if and when we go to bed is up to you' stuff is just a con, don't you? To make you feel as if you're in control. Of course you're going to sleep with him when he's taking you to expensive restaurants and buying you gifts and saying all the usual romantic bullshit.

Your cynicism is getting out of control, I told The Voice. The money thing is just his insecurity coming to the fore —

he's a sweet guy and we have a lot of fun together. And he's really ugly.

So is this an act of charity? Be Kind to Ugly Men Week?

I was saved from further ridicule by the arrival of the limo, filled with fresh flowers and champagne and Lennie peering out through a forest of roses. On the way back from dinner at a stylish Noosa restaurant we kissed and fondled in the back seat, and I felt as if I were in high school again. When we arrived at Lennie's riverfront apartment at Maroochydore, surprisingly modest for someone with such an extravagant lifestyle, he lit a candle, put on a CD called 'Greatest Love Songs of the Century' and led me into the bedroom. We spent the next few hours alternating between tender and fiercely passionate sex until daylight crept through the curtains.

I've never been particularly ambitious when it comes to orgasms — one per lovemaking session of the normal garden variety is fine by me. I know that according to modern sexual ideology I'm not reaching my full potential. On my orgasm report card I'd only merit a B — could try harder. If I really worked at it, I could be having multiple orgasms every time — G spot orgasms, tantric orgasms, psychic orgasms, feng shui orgasms, out-of-body orgasms — the sky's the limit. And Lennie was my self-appointed tutor.

He managed to make me come three times, which is a personal best for me. He also managed to have three orgasms himself, but I wasn't game to ask whether that was his PB. With an amazing capacity for delaying orgasm and a rapid recovery rate afterwards, I estimated he spent three quarters of the night with an erection.

By the early hours of the morning, I was so tired and sated that I almost fell asleep before Lennie achieved his third orgasm. He was moving slowly and rhythmically on top of me when he let forth an anguished 'Helen!' and collapsed on my breast, sobbing his heart out.

I lay there, unmoving. What should I do? Nowhere in the etiquette manuals do they tell you the correct procedure when your lover yells out his dead wife's name at the moment of climax and then bursts into tears. I didn't know whether to be flattered or insulted, whether to pat him and murmur 'there, there' or get out of bed and make him a cup of tea.

Lennie's sobs gradually faded. He lifted himself off me, grabbed a hanky from the bedside drawer and blew his nose. 'Sorry,' he rasped, 'got carried away by the emotion of the moment. I'll get us a drink of water.'

While he was clattering around in the kitchen, it occurred to me that he might have had some artificial stimulation. I checked his bedside drawer for telltale packets of little blue pills but there were none. If he were taking Viagra, he might keep them elsewhere.

Who cares? I'm going to enjoy this relationship immensely.

END OF DIARY

***

Whoops! Did I say relationship?

See? What did I tell you? You've had sex with the guy once and now you're in a relationship. So much for research.

The research has finished, so shut up and stop harassing me.

I hadn't realised until just now that I'd made that decision. But I think the time has come to start writing. I've got more than enough raw material to work with and in any case, most of my 'reserves' have lost interest and ceased contact. There's only so long a guy can hang around before some other gorgeous belly-dancing, skinny-dipping woman of passion catches his eye. I'm still receiving a steady flow of kisses from new admirers and I'll keep my profile active. It's good for the ego and there's still a chance, however slight, that my Mr Right is floating around in cyberspace.

***

The correlation between ugly men and great sex is explored objectively and with a scientific eye for detail by Annie, Myf and me — as befits the requirements of research.

'I've never slept with an ugly man in my whole life,' Myf says, 'and I've had some pretty spectacular sex. Although,' she adds, 'an ugly man is looking a hell of a lot more attractive to me now than two and a half months ago.'

'When your six months is up, you should try one for a bit of variety,' Annie suggests, as if we're discussing a new breakfast cereal.

'On the basis of my experience,' I proclaim, 'I'm prepared to wholeheartedly endorse the ugly man equals great sex theory. And in the interests of science, I'm prepared to undergo further sexual encounters with my subject to verify my initial findings.'

'Your dedication to your research is admirable,' Myf says. 'But a random sample of one subject is hardly a sound statistical basis on which to prove a hypothesis. Anyway, there's an added variable here in that your man is rich as well and we all know that if a man is rich, he's not ugly.'

'Good point,' Annie says. 'Who was it who said, "I never met a rich man I didn't like?" '

'You did,' I say. 'But I agree, it should have been someone famous, like Zsa Zsa Gabor.'

'Anyway, I'll back your theory,' Annie says. 'Peter wouldn't win any beauty contests, but he's dynamite in bed.

I'd forgotten it was possible to have sex any other way apart from the missionary position with the lights out.'

Annie and Peter did the deed on New Year's Eve, as I suspected, although by then it was early New Year's Day. Wracked with guilt, she told Richard and he moved out the next day. I suspect this relationship won't be long-term — Peter has only been separated from his wife for six months and has two small children, and Annie is balancing on a seesaw of emotion. But at the moment she exudes that air of sensuality of a woman who knows she is wanted and desired.

'Why do our conversations always end up being about sex?' Myf asks.

'Why not?' I reply. 'What other experience is so commonplace and universal to the human race, yet unique to each person and capable of arousing just about every emotion from misery to ecstasy?'

Silence. Not bad for an off-the-cuff remark.

'I never thought of it like that,' Annie says with awe.

'It puts a whole new slant on it,' Myf says, 'now that you've just confirmed I'm the only person in the world who's not having sex. When you're getting your quota of bonks you don't care about other people's sex lives. But now I see it everywhere! The other day this couple were practically having it off in the coffee shop – he was feeding her pieces of cake and she was licking the icing off his fingers and then he started kissing the cappuccino froth off her mouth. They were like monkeys in the zoo — I didn't wait to see what they did with the donuts.'

Annie and I exchange surreptitious grins. It's one of the delicious ironies of life that she and I are both having great sex (in my case, one session and anticipating more) and Myf is missing out entirely. She insists she hasn't succumbed to temptation, although we've only got her word for that — and her expression of martyrdom, like a dieter in a pastry shop.

'Continuing with today's theme, I presume you'll be seeing Lennie again?' Annie asks.

'He's at a conference at the moment, but he's going to ring me when he gets back.'

'By the sound of it, if you see him too often you won't have any energy left to write your book.'

'Don't worry, all under control. I'll ration him out into manageable portions.'

Myf snorts.

'And you won't do anything silly like fall in love with him, will you?' Annie says.

'Absolutely not. Apart from the sex, he's totally not my type.'

***

MY DATING DIARY

FRIDAY, 11 APRIL

ABSOLUTELY AND IRREVOCABLY

THE FINAL ENTRY

I didn't anticipate any more entries — after all, my research is done and I'm almost halfway through writing my book. But I didn't anticipate the turn of events either, and only now, a week later, can I write about it. Anger. Humiliation. Embarrassment. All grist to the writer's mill.

A week after Lennie's return from his conference, I hadn't heard from him, so I swallowed my pride and emailed him. 'How was the conference? Looking forward to catching up when you're free.'

There was no response, not to follow-up emails or phone calls, which went straight to MessageBank. Surely he wasn't deliberately avoiding me? Not when his last words to me were, 'That's the best night I've had for a long time — let's have lots more.' Maybe he drank and/or smoked himself into a heart attack at the conference and was in hospital, or worse, dead. I considered calling round unannounced to his home but talked myself out of it. It wasn't something you did to someone you'd only been out on a few dates with, notwithstanding the all-night sex. Besides, I was afraid of what I might find — his week-old dead body, a secret stash of women's clothing or some other dark secret I'd rather not know about. I was right about the dark secret.

On Friday night last week, I was cooking dinner to the background of the TV news in the living room when I heard, 'A stockbroker appeared in Maroochydore Magistrates Court today charged with fifty-three counts of fraud. Leonard Rothstein, 50, a self-employed stockbroker of Maroochydore, was alleged to have used money from his clients' trust funds for his own financial gain.'

I rushed over to the TV in time to see Lennie's slim, three-piece suited figure being ushered down the steps of the courthouse by a large bald man, obviously his solicitor. He didn't look at the TV camera and appeared to be in deep conversation with the bald man as they strode towards the carpark.

'Police are still investigating Mr Rothstein's affairs and expect to lay further charges in the near future. Mr Rothstein entered no plea today and was remanded to appear again on 9th of May.'

I sank onto the couch and stared accusingly at the TV, the purveyor of the bad news, while the lamb chops burnt to a cinder. That certainly put everything in perspective — the flowers, limousines, and expensive restaurants I'd been enjoying at the expense of his unfortunate clients, who were oblivious to the fact that a complete stranger was enjoying the good life with their money.

And shit! The necklace and earrings! Still in my linen cupboard wrapped up in the hand towels. Could I be charged with receiving stolen goods? Not exactly stolen, but more than likely bought with embezzled funds. Or am I an accessory after the fact?

I've spent the last week alternating between a state of panic, expecting the police to turn up on my doorstep any minute, and cursing Lennie. 'Fuck you, why couldn't you wait another few months before getting caught, so at least we could get in some more bonking?'

That's not rational thinking, of course — the longer I'd known him, the more it would have hurt, and now, after a few days of wallowing in self-pity, I'm grateful that our relationship was only short.

When I woke up this morning, I knew what to do with the necklace and earrings. I placed the box in a Postpak and sent it to Lennie's home address by certified mail, with a note inside. 'You will need these to help pay compensation to your unfortunate victims. At least I can be thankful I wasn't one of them.' To the point and satisfyingly cathartic.

When I returned from the post office, two detectives were on my front doorstep. Our interview was mercifully brief. It was obvious I couldn't shed any light on his dealings and they weren't interested in any affairs other than business. As they were leaving, one of them said, 'He said to tell you he's sorry, for what that's worth.'

'Not much,' I said.

PART THREE

Chapter 16

I lean back against the seat overlooking the beach, tilt my face up to the sun like a sunflower and close my eyes. It's hard to believe we're two weeks into winter — the sky is a translucent blue and the sun's gentle warmth feels magical on my skin. I imagine it melting the lines on my face and putting a rosy bloom on my pallid cheeks.

I've just released myself from four months of self-imposed solitary confinement, writing my manuscript. The rest of the world has gone ahead without me as I've feverishly typed, deleted, added and retyped, surfacing only to do the essentials like shop, cook meals and ferry Cara and Zac around. And while I know the process is far from finished, with rewrites and editing still to do, I'm basking in the glow of self-congratulation.

Not a bad effort, considering I spent the first couple of weeks with a bad dose of literary constipation. It was only when I decided to switch from a factual guide to online dating, to a fictional account of the trials and tribulations of a group of women using an internet dating agency that the words began to flow. I've found it a lot easier to write about sex and relationships through the eyes and voices of other people, and it also gives me leeway to invent things when reality doesn't measure up.

The rhythmic crash of the waves below me puts me in a trance and I'm soon drifting off. My leg buzzing jolts me awake. I dig into my jeans pocket and pull out my phone. One new email.

Hi Susan,

Thanks for the opportunity to read your fiction manuscript, Love Bytes. This is the most entertaining story I've read in a while. Funny and quirky on the surface but a lot of depth there as well. You made me laugh and cry at the same time, which is no mean feat for a jaded editor.

'However, there is some work to be done. Like most first novels, it's overwritten and needs some judicious pruning, including cutting out a few scenes. I've attached a quote for my editing services, and my terms and conditions. Let me know as soon as possible if you want to proceed.

Regards,

Martin Pascoe

Pascoe Editing and Consulting

Level 1 6/157 George St Sydney

www.pascoediting.com.

I read the email a few more times for the words to sink in. On the one hand, I want to spring up and punch the air with joy. He liked it! So my fears that I've been spending all this time writing a load of codswallop are unfounded. But I'm also burning with indignation. What does he mean by 'overwritten'? As for cutting some of the scenes — which ones does he mean? I've sweated blood over them, and they're all essential to the story.

I open the invoice attachment. Gulp. A bit more than I thought. A lot more, actually. But I intend to self-publish my novel as an e-book and it's essential that it be professionally edited. And he comes highly recommended by a colleague, the editor of *Home and Garden* magazine. 'Martin's been in the industry a long time. His last job was as fiction editor of Schwarz Publishing before he started his own business. You might pay a bit more but he's the best in the business.'

Looks like more dipping into the retirement fund. Who wants to retire anyway? The good thing about being a writer is you can work until you shrivel away to a skeleton, sitting at your computer.

I hit the reply button. 'Thanks so much Martin, I'm glad you liked it. I'd like to proceed with your services, so I'll deposit the payment today and we can get started.'

I'll concede that Love Bytes could probably do with a bit of trimming, but I refuse to cut out any scenes.

***

There it is. Large and bold on my computer screen. I've created it from my imagination and now it has a life of its own. Love Bytes by Susan Hamilton. Five thousand words and six scenes trimmer than two months ago. Ready to be uploaded to e-book sites and sent out into the world.

Contrary to the old adage, people do judge a book by its cover and the cover, which Martin and I designed together, is arresting. Hot pink, with 'Love Bytes' in large red letters across the top and 'by Susan Hamilton' across the bottom. In the middle is a graphic of a computer, its screen filled with an oversize pair of full red lips, parted with teeth exposed as if they're about to crunch into something — or someone. They're alluring and a little menacing at the same time. I swell with pride. I almost wish I hadn't written it so I could buy it.

The blurb that goes with it says, 'What happens when four newly single women in their forties decide to join an internet dating agency in their quest to find a man who can grunt in three syllables and who knows the difference between a Spanish omelette and a Spanish fly?

'Excitement, trepidation, anxiety, lust, passion, anger, grief and yes, even love are all part of the experience as Jill, Claire, Amanda and Kate discover the dating scene has changed dramatically since they were last single. Is it considered bad etiquette to grope under the table at dinner? What do you say to your children when they catch you making out in the car? When is a good time to break off a relationship — before or after sex?

These questions and more will be answered in this hilarious, moving, unputdownable book.'

I'm not sure about the last sentence, which was Martin's idea. It seems presumptuous to assume readers will think the book is any of those things. 'As a self-published author you have to blow your own trumpet,' Martin told me, 'so get used to it.'

So I'm getting used to it. And now that the day I thought would never come has arrived, I'm dead tired but too excited to rest. The editing process has been just as exhausting as the writing and a huge learning curve for me. I've had to swallow my pride and accept that most of the time Martin was right. I smile as I think back over some of our email exchanges.

'I don't know why you think Jill comes across as too aggressive in the sex scene with Sexyman 69,' I wrote. 'After all, she hasn't had sex for two years — that's a lot of pent-up frustration.'

'But you paint her as such a timid wallflower type,' Martin emailed back. 'And then overnight she becomes a tigress of passion — she practically drags him into the bedroom and demolishes him. Even allowing for the sexual frustration, wouldn't she be a little more subtle?'

'You obviously don't know much about women,' I replied. 'Take a normal woman, timid or not, with a healthy sex drive who hasn't had any action for ages and put her in a room with a hunky man, and nothing is beyond imagination.'

'All right, I'll concede that,' he wrote back. 'But let's compromise and make her a little more assertive in the beginning — then it's not such a leap of credibility for men like me who don't understand women's sexual appetites.'

I did, however, win the argument about chocolate body paint. 'The scene where Nigel has a severe allergic reaction to Amanda's chocolate body paint — is this medically/scientifically feasible?' Martin emailed. 'Is there actually any chocolate in chocolate body paint? If so, perhaps it would be feasible as I have heard of people being allergic to chocolate, although not to the extent that they've passed out and had to be given the kiss of life, as Nigel did.'

'Do you really think I would write such a scene without researching it first?' I wrote back. 'It happened to a friend of mine years ago. The ingredients of chocolate body paint are: sugar, vegetable fat, hazelnuts, milk powder, cocoa powder (NB), whey, soya powder, emulsifier, lecithin and vanilla flavouring. So as you can see, there is real chocolate in chocolate body paint, and it is possible to have an allergic reaction to it. If you'd read that scene properly, you'd understand that Nigel's passing out is as much to do with his finally getting Amanda into bed after pursuing her for so long as his allergic reaction. And don't ask me if it is scientifically possible for a man to pass out through sheer sexual excitement — it happened to a friend of mine (different friend) and anyway you have to remember that Nigel is a bit of a wimp, so he's prone to pass out at the drop of a strategically placed hat.'

'I'll bow to your greater knowledge of chocolate body paint,' Martin replied. 'You have some interesting friends — you must introduce me one day.'

I re-read the email he's just sent me. 'Here it is — your masterpiece. All you have to do is upload it to Amazon and Smashwords. Don't be disappointed if you don't get many sales straight off, sometimes it takes a while to build up momentum. And don't forget to keep up your marketing!'

I groan. I wish I could afford to hire my own PR person. I've marketed my arse off over the last few weeks, resurrecting my tired old blog and putting up regular posts, doing guest posts for other writers' blogs, and Facebooking and Tweeting into the early hours of the morning after I've finished my day's rewriting. And even now I'm behind the eight ball, as all the experts say you should start marketing before you even begin your novel.

I hit the reply button. 'Thanks so much, Martin. I couldn't have done it without you.' It's true; he's been not only my editor, but also my proofreader, co-cover designer, formatter, mentor and marketing advisor — at added expense, of course. Don't worry about the cost, I keep telling myself. This is your dream. You can't put a price on turning a dream into reality.

***

I have to tell someone, to give it substance and make it real. I phone Jules at work, but he's in a meeting and can't be disturbed. Annie is at college and Myf is at uni, and both their phones go straight to MessageBank. Is this a conspiracy to spoil my excitement?

There's only one option left. I dial Melbourne.

'Hullo, dear, I'm just mixing the meat loaf, but you can talk to me while I'm doing it. How are you?'

That's my mother — doing the meatloaf for dinner at lunchtime. Organised down to the very last second.

'I'm absolutely fantastic, Mum. I have the best news in the world. You know the book I've been writing for the last few months — it's finally published. I've just uploaded it and it'll be on the internet in a couple of days.'

'That's wonderful, dear. I think I need a bit more onion. What's it called?'

'Love Bytes.'

There's silence at the other end.

'Bytes is spelt B.y.t.e.s. You know, as in computers.'

'So it's about computers?'

'You could say that.'

'But what about all those men you were dating on the internet? Wasn't that for your book? Oops, nearly forgot the parsley.'

'Sort of.'

'So your book's about internet dating?'

'That's part of it.'

"So where do the bytes come into it?'

'They don't come into it much at all.'

"I'm confused, Susan. I don't know what I did with the basil. I'll just have to use the dried stuff but it's not nearly as nice. I suppose I'll have to wait until it's published and read it myself.'

'Um ... yes.' We chat for a bit longer about mundane things and all the while I can see before me the horrifying scene of my mother reading my book.

'Anyway, dear, congratulations, that's wonderful news, I've finally found the meatloaf tin, it was right at the back of the cupboard. I'll tell your father, I'm sure he'll be just as keen as I am to read it.'

Chapter 17

I'm hastily throwing together some finger food for tonight's celebration party. If you could call Annie, Myf and me a party, as I haven't been able to reach Jules or Max; they've both had their phones turned off.

Cara and Zac are perched at the breakfast bar watching me chop up cheese and salami. I'm touched at how thrilled they are for me, considering that for the last few months I've been an autopilot mother, my mind still wrapped up in my book even when we're discussing netball practice and the latest Wii game. However, the higher frequency of takeaways and my lack of time and energy to nag them about chores and TV programs has more than compensated for my lack of attention.

'Are you going to be rich and famous like JK Rowling?' Zac asks.

I laugh. 'Highly unlikely, unfortunately, and anyway my book is definitely not for children.'

'I hope you didn't put anything about Mr Beecham in it,' Cara says, giving me her best accusing look.

She's only just forgiven me for the Mr Beecham incident. I put my foot in it a couple of weeks ago when she came home from school distressed about the maths test she'd had that day. So great was my desire to comfort her that I opened my mouth without thinking.

'Never mind, Mr Beecham told me he's impressed with your efforts, that you always try hard. I can't ask any more than that.'

She looked at me disbelievingly. 'When were you talking to Mr Beecham?'

I looked so guilty, I couldn't lie my way out of it. So I told her.

'I can't believe you dated my maths teacher! That is just so gross!'

'It was months ago and it was just one date, and I wouldn't have gone at all if I'd known beforehand.'

'Did you kiss him?'

'We didn't even hold hands. And believe it or not, we didn't spend all night talking about you, either.'

'This is so embarrassing! I'll never be able to look him in the face again! You and your stupid book — why can't you be like other mothers and work in an office!'

She flounced off to her bedroom and slammed the door. She might be a C student in maths but I'd give her an A plus for drama.

She's over it now and can finally look Mr Beecham in the face again and think of logarithms and fractions rather than he and her mother having an intimate tete-a-tete.

'There's no mention of Mr Beecham anywhere,' I assure her. 'In fact, nowhere is there even any mention of teachers. As far as my book is concerned, teachers and maths don't even exist. There is however,' I add cautiously, 'a fair bit of sex.'

Zac pulls a face. 'Gross! I won't be reading it.'

'Great,' Cara says. 'So now all the teachers, including Mr Beecham, especially Mr Beecham, will be able to read the gory details of my mother's sex life.'

'It's fiction,' I say. 'It's the characters' sex lives, not mine. And they're not gory.'

Cara looks at me resignedly. 'Alicia's mother had a book published. It's about vertical gardening.'

And I'll bet it's as boring as hell. There's not much excitement in gardening, unless you're D.H. Lawrence's Lady Chatterley. Although, she was probably more into horizontal gardening.

***

I've just changed into a clean pair of jeans when there's a knock on the door. I open it and an oversize garbage bag rustles in and envelopes me in a huge embrace, so that I'm pressed up against the layers of plastic, all crackling in unison.

'Congratulations!' it cries, thrusting a bottle of champagne into my hand.

I've seen Annie in some weird outfits recently, but this one takes the cake. It's made up entirely of garbage bags, the bottom part consisting of a pair of billowing green pantaloons with elastic below the knees and a black plastic sash at the waist and a black long-sleeved top with a green sleeveless vest over the top. With her hair cut short and dyed orange and pink, she resembles a psychedelic court jester. Since starting her fashion design course, she not only designs and makes her own clothes, she's become a born-again teenager. Any minute now I expect her to start hanging out with Cara and talking about rock groups called Sick Puppies and Putrefaction.

'It's an assignment,' she explains. 'We had to design and make something out of an alternative material. And as there aren't a lot of social occasions on which I can wear it, I thought I'd wear it tonight. A sort of mutual celebration of creativity.'

'It's fantastic,' I say heartily. 'You're the original bag lady. Don't sit still for too long though — you might find yourself being hauled out to the garbage bin.'

We decide we can't wait for Myf to arrive, so we open the bottle of champagne that Annie brought.

'Typical of Myf,' I observe, 'always late, making her grand entrance. You'd think she'd be on time for once — I haven't seen her for weeks.'

'Neither have I,' Annie says. 'I haven't seen her since we celebrated the end of her celibate period.'

In the tradition of artists, though it is debatable how much art was involved, we now refer to Myf's six months of celibacy as her Celibate Period, like Picasso's Blue Period.

'In fact,' Annie continues, 'she's been acting rather strangely. You probably haven't noticed, being engrossed in your book, but every time I've suggested getting together for lunch or a movie, she's put me off with some vague excuse.'

She raises her glass. 'Anyhow, let's drink a toast. Here's to *Love Bytes* taking the literary world by storm! *Fifty Shades of Grey*, eat your heart out!'

We clink glasses. There's a forced gaiety to her tone and her make-up doesn't quite hide the shadows under her eyes. A month ago, Peter decided to give his marriage another go and moved back in with his wife, plunging Annie into another low, even though I suspect that deep down she knew the relationship would only be temporary. But she's keeping afloat, with a little help from her friends. And champagne.

Cara pops her head in the doorway. 'Myf's here.'

Myf sashays into the room. She's making a grand entrance, all right — big would be more appropriate. Although she looks her usual elegant self with her hair up and wearing a clingy black skirt and silk blouse, she is also unmistakably pregnant.

Annie and I stare at the round bulge in Myf's stomach as if we've never seen a pregnant woman before.

'If you're not pregnant, that's the worst case of wind I've ever seen,' I say finally.

Myf has the grace to look abashed. 'I'm sorry, I know I should have told you both before, but I kept putting it off. Then when Susie rang today and told me the great news, I wasn't about to steal her thunder by saying, "Well you might have published a book, but I'm pregnant!"'

'This obviously happened during your so-called Celibate Period,' Annie says.

'I only slipped up once,' Myf says defensively. 'He caught me in a moment of weakness.'

'Who?' Annie and I ask in unison.

'Rob. I was feeling a bit down in the dumps and lonely, and he asked me out for a drink and I thought, "Why not? A drink won't hurt". And then I had two drinks and he started stroking my leg, and then I had another drink and he started nuzzling my ear...'

'We get the picture,' I say. 'Once you get to the ear nuzzling, there's no turning back.'

'But how did you get pregnant?' Annie asks. 'I mean, I thought you were on the Pill.'

'I missed it that night; I was so excited about doing the deed after so long that I completely forgot about it. I can't get over it – I'm forty-two, I thought my eggs would be almost at their use-by date, I miss one fucking pill and I'm pregnant.'

'And Rob is a student, I presume?' I ask.

Silence. Myf's looking sheepish. 'Not exactly. He's my psychology lecturer.'

'I think I'm immune to any further shock,' I say. 'But I'm going to test myself anyway. How old is he?'

'Fifty-one. And he's divorced with grown-up kids. Anything else you want to know?'

'Fifty-one!' we chorus in disbelief.

'He looks very young for his age,' Myf says defiantly. 'And he's very fit too. In fact, he's pretty good for an old guy.'

We bombard Myf with questions — Do you know what sex it is? What does Rob think about you being pregnant? Are you in a relationship with him? Are you going to keep studying?

The answers are no, he's thrilled, no and don't know.

'And I suppose,' Annie says, 'he's madly in love with you and filthy rich, and wants to marry you and keep you in the manner to which you're accustomed.'

'How did you know?' Myf says incredulously.

There are some people who are born with more than their fair share of luck and Myf is one of them. Even when things go wrong for her, they end up right. As the only child of wealthy parents, she was born with a silver spoon in her mouth, and with a rich dead husband and a loaded lover, she's graduated to the whole cutlery set.

Annie and I exchange looks and I shake my head. 'You owe us a Chocolate Obsession. Make that a whole one each.'

We settle down to some serious celebrating now that we have two reasons, and Annie and I have the responsibility of drinking all the champagne as Myf's not drinking. If Myf thinks her pregnancy is a cause for celebration, she's hiding it well — even though she looks in the bloom of health, she doesn't appear overjoyed by the prospect of bringing another life into the world.

When we've almost finished the champagne, I go into the kitchen to make coffee. Any more alcohol is going to tip me over into the rotten hangover zone. When I return, Annie has produced another bottle of champagne and refilled our glasses. 'There's one toast we haven't had yet.' She raises her glass. 'To sex, please come back, wherever you are.'

'To sex,' we chorus solemnly, clinking our glasses, including Myf with her fifth glass of soda and lime.

I look around and see Cara standing in the doorway. With her impeccable timing, she's destined to be an actor. She gives us all a look of haughty disgust. 'I'm going to bed. Good night, everyone. And can you keep the noise down, please?'

'That's what you're going to be dealing with in seventeen years time,' I warn Myf.

'The toast for sex was really for you, Susie,' Annie says generously. 'I don't think I'm up to it at the moment, but I know you've been living in a state of monastic celibacy ever since,' and she lowered her voice melodramatically, 'the Lennie Incident.'

'I appreciate your thoughtfulness,' I reply. 'But to tell you the truth, since the Lennie Incident, as you call it, I've been so wrapped up in my novel that I haven't even thought about sex.'

It's not quite true. I have thought about sex, but only when writing about it in the novel. I derived so much vicarious pleasure from the sexual exploits of my four female characters that I felt no need for my own sex life. Although I did haul Fred out from the back of my cupboard occasionally; but only when I was frustrated with my writing, so it was more for stress relief than from sexual desire. Luckily, Fred's a basic, uncomplicated type and doesn't mind being used.

'Although,' I add, 'I dare say now that I'm going to be rich and famous, I'll have men beating down my door.'

'Particularly as your book is about sex,' Myf says. 'Men love women who write about sex. I read an interview with a female writer of erotica and she said that once men find out what she does for a living, they're totally fascinated, think she's some kind of literary nymphomaniac and want to know how she gets her ideas, whether she has to do research and so on.'

'Literary nymphomaniac,' I muse. 'I like the sound of that. Classy. Like reading Tolstoy for foreplay.'

The plunger of coffee I've made sits on the table, ignored by Annie and me. Myf's off coffee as well. By midnight she's yawning and offers to take Annie home.

'It's so boring being the only person making any sense. I want somebody standing by in the labour ward with a magnum of champagne and as soon as this baby pops out, they can pop the cork and serve mine up in a bucket.'

'Great idea!' Annie trills. 'I'd much rather go shopping for champagne than baby clothes.'

She gets up from her chair and promptly trips over the leg, landing on her knees and putting a huge tear in her garbage bag pantaloons. 'Oh shit, I knew I should have used the extra-tough bags.'

After they've left, I drink a large glass of water and make a fresh pot of coffee, to try and forestall a hangover. I know it's an old wives' tale about the coffee, but I do it anyway. I take my mug into the study and log into eMatch. Just out of curiosity.

Twenty-two kisses since I last checked a few days ago. Over the last few months, I've occasionally logged in to check for new admirers, purely as ego gratification. Fortunately for my creative process, not a single one appealed to me and they all received the automatic 'flattered but not interested' reply.

I scan the profiles of my new fans. No one who arouses any interest. Mangrove Jack is quite attractive, but his spelling is atrocious. Spirit in the Sky professes to have psychic abilities, and I don't need to be a psychic to foresee that after the initial excitement of being told that 'I'm going on a long journey and Mr Right will make an appearance very soon', it will be a source of irritation. Likely Lad has a full-length photo of himself with his Great Dane, no doubt hoping that the dog, which is sitting in front of him, will hide his gut, but no such luck. A dog can only do so much.

Perhaps with all my experience in internet dating I'm becoming too picky. Then I remember Phil and Lennie. No, picky is good.

Chapter 18

The shrill ring pierces my head. I'm gradually surfacing through the layers of my consciousness, like a diver coming up from the deep. I wrench my eyes open and snatch up the receiver of the bedside phone.

'Susie!' It's a man's voice, familiar but hoarse, as if he's smoked too many cigarettes. Who is it? My brain feels as gluggy as rice pudding.

'How are you?' I say, on the premise that if he keeps talking, his identity will reveal itself.

'Fucked. Susie, I need to talk to you. Can you come round this morning?'

The penny drops with a loud clang.

'Jules, what's happened?'

'I don't want to talk about it on the phone; I'll tell you when you get here.'

'I'll be there as soon as I can.'

Jules sounds as terrible as I feel. I have a gnawing feeling this has something to do with Max. What else besides love can make a man sound like he's just eaten a bowlful of gravel?

I haul myself out of bed, make my way gingerly down the stairs into the kitchen and grab the Panadol from the medicine cupboard. This is all Annie's fault — making me drink all those toasts. I hope she's feeling as rotten as I am.

Zac materialises and opens the fridge door, an automatic response whenever he enters the kitchen — even when he doesn't want anything from the fridge.

'Morning,' he says cheerfully after burying his head inside it and surfacing with two monstrous slices of leftover pizza. 'Another hangover?'

I give him a withering look. From inside my head, it feels like a withering look, but my muscles aren't in working order yet and I suspect it's more like an ineffectual grimace.

Lesson Number Six from Mother to Son. Tact is a skill anyone can learn. Stating the obvious is not an example of tact. An example of tact is, when someone is suffering from a self-inflicted condition, you express empathy and concern. Practise every day in front of the mirror until you get it right.

I look at the clock. Five past nine. The dirty dishes and glasses are still strewn over the table. I hurriedly load them into the dishwasher, have a shower and put on my face. Lucky I've got no travel plans — those bags under my eyes would incur an excess baggage fee.

'Susan, you look like shit,' I proclaim to the person in the mirror. 'Tomorrow you will be your usual gorgeous, adorable self; but today you are a total wreck.'

That felt great, unleashing all my frustrations onto myself. Now I realise where all those self-help books go wrong — too many Pollyannaisms. You have to give yourself a thorough trashing every now and then, so you can appreciate the warm and fuzzy stuff.

I'm also coming down from the euphoria of *Love Bytes* being published. Even though I've longed for it and worked towards it with feverish determination, I now feel a sense of anti-climax. What now? Back to reality with a thump.

I throw on some jeans and a shirt, and round up the kids. I drop Zac off at the skate park and Cara at the shopping centre where she is meeting Jay. I arrive at Jules's place, and he opens the door before I've had a chance to knock.

He's in jeans and a shirt that he's obviously slept in, his hair looks like a mangled straw broom, his eyes are an unflattering shade of red, and he's sporting a couple of days stubble. He doesn't say a word, just engulfs me in his arms so tightly I can hardly breathe.

When he lets me go, his eyes are brimming with tears. 'I'll make you a cup of coffee.' His voice wavers.

I take his hand and lead him into the living room and he follows, unresisting. In the middle of the couch sits a large brown teddy bear with twinkling button eyes and a red ribbon round its neck. It's a present Max bought for Jules and it usually has its jaunty pride of place on their bed.

'You sit down,' I instruct him. 'I'll make the coffee.'

In the kitchen, the sink is filled with dirty dishes and half a dozen empty wine bottles straggle along the bench. Jules is usually a fastidious housekeeper. I clean up while I'm waiting for the kettle to boil and make two cups of instant coffee from a jar of Moccona in the pantry. I assume it's Max's purchase, as Jules would rather suffer caffeine withdrawals than drink instant coffee.

I sit on the couch with Alfonso the bear between us and put the coffee on the table. 'Thanks, babe,' he says. He picks up his mug, takes a sip, grimaces and takes another sip. 'I'm drinking instant coffee and I don't even care.' He manages a lopsided grin.

'It's Max, isn't it?'

Jules nods. A single tear makes its slow journey through the shadows of his unshaven cheek and plops onto his lap.

'It's the first time in my life I've been jilted for a Porsche.'

'He left you for a Porsche?'

'Convertible, to be precise. Smooth, sleek lines, beautiful curves, sexy and stylish — how can I compete with that?' The words tumble out with a bitter force.

'Jules, you're not making any sense. You're trying to tell me Max is having an affair with a car?'

'He may as well be.' He takes a deep breath. 'He had a phone call from his father about a week ago. His mother's had a stroke and needs long-term care, so Max's father is looking after her at home. He has a courier business and wants Max to go back home to Sydney and run it for him, so he can look after Max's mother full time. He offered him a good salary and Max was really excited — we both were, because I was going to chuck in my job here and go down to Sydney with him, but then Max's father put a proviso on the deal — he wants Max to live a decent life, as he calls it, to give up his gay lifestyle and do what Daddy says and in return, he'll be rewarded with a brand new Porsche.'

'Oh.'

'So when faced with the choice between the lover and the Porsche, he chose the Porsche. To give him credit, he did think about it for a couple of days.'

I take his hand. 'Jules, that's just ... terrible.' I'm painfully aware of the inadequacy of my response. 'Has he gone already?'

'He left yesterday. I said to him, "Why don't I come with you and find a place nearby and we can still keep seeing each other? Surely your father's not going to be tracking your every move." But Max said no, he didn't like being deceptive, he's always been upfront with his father and anyway they know so many people in the area, someone would be bound to see us together and tell his father. For Christ's sake, we're grown men, aren't we?'

He picks up Alfonso and clasps him to his chest, burying his face in his soft fur.

'Poor old Al,' he says in a muffled voice. 'I've cried so much on him it's a wonder he hasn't gone all soggy.'

'I can't believe Max gave you up for a Porsche. I'm sure there's more to it than that. Family ties can be pretty strong, you know. Perhaps he felt he needed to be there, with his mum sick and maybe not going to be around for long and his dad needing help — maybe he wanted to try and patch things up.'

'But he's not being true to himself,' Jules argues. 'It's going to be a pretty lonely life for him if he's going to give up the gay lifestyle. It's not much fun having a beautiful new Porsche to drive around in if you haven't got anyone to share it with.'

He looks at me over the top of Alfonso's head. 'When Max and I were together, I'd often get this weird feeling — we'd be doing something really ordinary, like cooking dinner or watching a video, and all of a sudden I'd see him in a freeze-frame snapshot, and it'd take my breath away and I'd almost burst with happiness. All those other times I thought I was in love ... they were nothing like this.'

He buries his head in Alfonso's chest and a steady stream of tears drips onto Alfonso's leg. I put my arm around Jules and we all sit together on the couch, he and I and Alfonso, in our silent grief, with the pale fingers of the late winter sun struggling to reach us through the French doors.

***

Who was it who said if you love, you also grieve, because one cannot exist without the other? Perhaps I read it on a desk calendar or on a station noticeboard. Jules's grief has exposed a wound I thought had healed — it's been slashed open again, and as I drive home the tears are flowing.

I realise in a moment of blinding clarity that I've never allowed myself to mourn the end of my marriage. I was too busy being angry and hurt to allow any sadness. But now it's bubbled up and refuses to be ignored.

When I fell in love with Jeremy, I felt as if I'd met my twin in male form. We talked about everything and nothing, revelled in the silliness of our humour and basked in the absolute rightness of our being together. We were lovers and best friends rolled into one, a phenomenon I had never before experienced. In hindsight I can see that even our sex life was founded on friendship — comfortable and predictable more than passionate and exuberant. I didn't mind back then; so entranced was I with having found my soulmate.

But a few years into our marriage, the rapture had settled into a complacent and mundane equilibrium. As Jeremy lost interest in sex (which he put down to stress at work), our physical intimacy and with it our emotional intimacy withered away like flowers dying on a vine. Who knew how much longer our marriage would have limped along if Jeremy hadn't strayed?

It was convenient — that affair. It gave me a reason to walk out of a lifeless marriage and be the injured party, the recipient of sympathetic platitudes and invitations to chardonnay-soaked evenings of commiseration with the Sisterhood of Women Who've Been Cheated On. Convenient because I didn't have to think about what part I might have played in the disintegration of our marriage.

There's no going back, no way of knowing whether our marriage could have been resurrected if we'd both made the effort, or if we'd even been aware it was sliding out of our grasp. How could this happen? Yesterday there were long gazes into each other's eyes, helpless laughter, and companionable silences. Today we endure forced smiles, desultory conversation and awkward silences.

I'm sobbing so hard I can hardly see where I'm going. I pull over to the side of the road and fumble around in the glove box for a tissue. Of course there aren't any, not even a pair of Wonderpants to blow my nose on. I find the cloth that I use to de-fog the windscreen and give my nose a hearty blow.

Eventually my sobbing peters out from sheer exhaustion. The last time I cried that hard and long was ... I can't remember. Maybe, never. Perhaps I've just released every hurt and disappointment I've ever experienced, right back from when my best friend in first grade, Angela Stubbins, stole my Mr Squiggle pencil. Maybe now I won't need to cry for another twenty years.

I survey my face in the rear-view mirror. Red eyes, blotchy complexion, smudged eyeliner. Let's hope Mr Perfect Sex doesn't choose this moment to make his appearance.

I start the engine and pull out into the traffic. I'm only a few blocks from home, so I call into the local DVD rental store and get a copy of *Sleepless in Seattle* from the $1 weekly section and a family-size block of Cadbury's Dairy Milk chocolate. The girl who serves me, Breeanne, is a friend of Cara's.

'Hiya, Mrs Hamilton,' she says cheerily. Then she looks at me with consternation. 'Are you OK?'

I realise that I've forgotten to wear my sunglasses into the shop to hide my ravaged face. 'Yes, I'm fine.'

She processes my DVD and chocolate then looks up and smiles sympathetically. 'Men problems, right?'

I smile back at her. 'That's a tautology, isn't it?'

Breanne looks at me blankly. What do they teach kids in school these days?

'I thought so. That's the first thing I do when I've been dumped — hire out a soppy movie and pig out on chocolate.'

'Actually, in this instance, I was the dumper, not the dumpee.'

'Good idea,' Breanne nods her approval. 'Dump them before they dump you. That's my philosophy from now on.'

'Thanks for the advice.' If she notices an edge in my voice, she ignores it and gives me another disarming smile.

'No worries. There are plenty more men out there. Have you tried the internet?'

I feel chastened at having been given relationship advice by a seventeen-year-old, albeit one who probably knows as much about men as I do, but I can't help admiring her positive attitude and resilience. Tomorrow I'll be back to hope, optimism and the feminine way — tonight, Jules and I will have a girls' night in, pumping up our serotonin levels and crying for the umpteenth time when Meg Ryan and Tom Hanks finally meet over a lost teddy on the roof of the Empire State Building.

Chapter 19

It's D-day. Or rather, L-day. Launch Day. It makes *Love Bytes* sound like the next shuttle being sent into outer space.

I'm having an official book launch at a Mooloolaba restaurant at the insistence of Jules, Myf and Annie, who know nothing about promoting books and against the advice of Martin Pascoe, who knows everything there is to know about book promotion.

'You've got the cost of having the books printed and delivered, not to mention the hiring of the restaurant, food and staff and all the other incidentals,' he said when I phoned him to pose the idea. 'Even charging guests at $30 a head, you'll need to sell an awful lot of books just to break even, let alone make a profit. You're better off sticking with the online marketing.'

But the others refused to take no for an answer and even offered to chip in with the expenses. Jules used his advertising connections to make a deal with the owner of 'Oceans', an exclusive restaurant on the Mooloolaba Esplanade with ocean views, to hold the launch there. For their thirty dollars, guests will receive a glass of champagne on arrival, a two-course lunch and coffee, and background music supplied free of charge by the owner's son, an accomplished jazz pianist. This was nothing short of miraculous for a spur-of-moment-decision made only three weeks ago.

Jules also used his contacts to do some radio and newspaper advertising for the launch and achieved his second miracle — within a week of it being announced, the entire one hundred restaurant seats were sold; and there was even a waiting list for cancellations. He's thrown himself into the preparations as if his life depended on them, glad to have something to fill his spare moments since Max left.

I take my cup of coffee out into the courtyard and re-read my speech for the fiftieth time. My stomach is churning. Making a speech hadn't even crossed my mind until two days ago when Jules said casually, 'Have you written your speech yet?'

'What speech?'

'Your speech for the launch. It's your book; you have to make a speech.'

'What sort of speech?'

'About the book, of course — how you came to write it, the research you did, that sort of thing. Make it lighthearted and amusing and a little bit risqué, just enough to make people want to buy your book then and there.'

Talking in front of a hundred people was bad enough but to bare my soul and be amusing and titillating as well...

'There's no way I can do that,' I said. 'You know how I feel about public speaking. You do it for me — tell everyone I've been struck down with a mysterious throat virus and can't talk.'

'You have to do it,' Jules said firmly. 'You're the author; it's expected of you. Anyway, the subject matter sells itself — people love to hear about sex and relationships. Why don't you read out some excerpts from the book, like the bit where

Kate and her boyfriend get sprung in the change room of the lingerie store, or where Claire gets stuck in the hotel lift in her nightie with the randy rock star?'

So I've spent the last two days wishing fervently that I'd taken Martin's advice about not having a launch. I've written what I hope is an interesting and humorous speech with just the right amount of raciness — which is very difficult to judge, not knowing whether there's going to be anyone under sixteen or over sixty in the audience and considering my own daughter (who finishes school in a few weeks but still has the potential to be embarrassed by her mother) is going to be in the audience.

I study the words I've written, trying to memorise them yet again, but I know that in the sheer panic of the moment, my memory will seize up and I'll have to resort to reading them. That's if I can coax anything at all out of my mouth.

When was the last time I made a speech? On my fortieth birthday. Under the calming influence of a couple of glasses of champagne and in front of my adoring friends and family, I managed to string a few words together in their correct sequence. Hardly comparable to standing before a crowd of complete strangers and with the even more horrifying thought that if I make a complete fool of myself, they probably won't buy my book.

I check my watch. Ten o'clock. Is it too early to have just one glass of champagne for medicinal purposes? Better not. The effect will have worn off by the time of my speech, which is in between main course and dessert.

I recall the phone conversation I had with Martin last night, in which I confided my fears to him. 'And don't give me that spiel about imagining the audience in their underwear,' I said. 'I'm so stressed I'll be standing there wondering if the audience is imagining me in my underwear.'

'If it's any consolation, the men will be,' Martin replied. 'In fact, they won't bother with the formalities of underwear, they'll be imagining you standing there at the microphone stark naked.'

'Thanks, you're cheering me up no end. Anyway, it's a women's novel, I don't think there'll be too many men there.'

'Don't bet on it. It's about relationships and sex. As soon as you mention sex men are interested.'

But it's sex written from a woman's point of view, I wanted to argue. But I refrained. For two people who've never met, Martin and I have had some interesting conversations about sex.

I fling the speech on the table. Don't think about it — que sera, sera. I wander inside and pick up my copy of *Love Bytes* from the living room coffee table. I gaze at it in wonderment for the thousandth time since the 100 copies arrived last week from the Amazon print-on-demand service.

The front cover looks twice as impressive on a real book, with the huge red lips gleaming against the lurid pink background. On the back cover, underneath the story blurb, are a couple of reviews that Martin kindly arranged for me by emailing the book to a couple of colleagues and asking them to read it.

'A rollicking read with a racy plot, a cast of whacky but totally believable characters and laughs on every page.' Vanessa Harper, reviewer, National Book Review.

'This book is a must-read for women of all ages — thought-provoking but also thoroughly entertaining.' Shelley Burger, editor, Woman's Own.

'I had to resort to strongarm tactics to get such good reviews,' Martin emailed when he forwarded them to me. I hoped he was joking.

At the bottom of the back cover is a small photo of me and an author 'bio', as they're known in the trade. I decided to splash out and hire a photographer for another glamour shot that I could also use on my author's pages on the internet. I'm chuffed with the result — my hair is moussed to within an inch of its life but still looks natural, the smoky eye make-up gives me a sultry aura; and some artistic licence with the lipstick gives my lips just enough pouty fullness. I've decided that if I ever become rich, I'll hire my own make-up artist and hairdresser so I can look like this every day.

Martin was impressed too. 'Great photo,' he emailed. I couldn't pluck up the courage to tell him I look nothing like that in real life. If we ever meet, he won't recognise me.

The author's bio was not so easy. Martin's advice was to make it short, succinct and amusing. The problem was not with it being short but making my unspectacular life sound interesting. I finally decided to sum up my life in a couple of sentences, so my readers would relate to the ordinariness of my life.

'Susan Hamilton is a forty-something freelance writer, divorced with two children. She lives on the Sunshine Coast in Queensland, Australia and her ambition is to have enough money to retire to a beach cottage where she can drink wine, eat chocolate and write more books. So please buy *Love Bytes* and persuade all your friends, relatives and neighbours to do likewise, except Great Aunt Dottie, who might object to the nudity, obscene language and sexual references.'

In any case, it's presumptuous to think that readers will be interested in the life story of a debut novelist. When I have a few novels under my belt, I can write quaint pieces such as, 'Susan Hamilton lives in a renovated terrace house with her two Yorkshire terriers, a collection of vintage wines and a houseboy. In her spare time she likes to go for trips in her BMW convertible and knit beanies for orphans in war-torn countries.'

I open the book and leaf through the pages, burying my nose in them and inhaling the fragrance of new paper and fresh print. I still can't believe this object I hold in my hands is entirely my own creation. Like a mother with her firstborn, I imagine there's nothing that comes close to the thrill of the first book.

I'm jolted out of my reverie of maternal bliss by an SMS alert on my phone. 'Good luck. Wear your best underwear. Martin.'

Thanks for the encouragement. I think. Someone is rapping at the door. It's Jules, standing on the doorstep peering through a veil of red roses and pink carnations.

'Happy launching.'

The jumbled emotions of the day suddenly catch up with me and tears spring to my eyes. Jules wraps his arms around me, flowers and all, and presses me tightly to him. For a few seconds, as I relax into the warmth of his body and breathe in his aromatic aftershave, I wonder if the line between friendship and something deeper is about to be crossed. Then he lets me go and smiles at me, and his eyes are glistening as well.

'This is such a great day for you, Susie. You deserve it. I don't know what I would have done without you over the last few weeks.'

'I don't know what I would have done without you to organise this launch. Probably not had one, which I'm thinking now is not such a bad idea.'

'Bullshit, you'll have a ball. Just think of it as a party. You can come and help me decorate the restaurant — there's a ton of balloons and streamers to hang up. That'll take your mind off your nerves.'

He busies himself lugging the piles of books into his car while I shove the flowers in a vase, and throw on some clothes and make-up. I've bought a new dress for the occasion, a knee-length black chiffon dress with a pink rose print and a frill at the bottom, feminine but clingy. Definitely a Wonderbra and Wonderpants job. Sorry, guys, any of you with X-ray vision for underwear will be sorely disappointed. With several squirts of mousse and my blow dryer, I try to transform my hair into the style I had for the glamour shots; but I end up just looking like I've had a turbulent night in the sack, which I wouldn't mind if I'd had the pleasure of the experience.

When I emerge from the bedroom, Jules gives a wolf-whistle. 'Very sexy, especially the hair. I love the tousled look — very Meg Ryan.'

'Let's hope Tom Hanks makes an appearance. In fact, if anyone even slightly resembling Tom Hanks turns up today, I can't guarantee I won't behave absolutely disgracefully. That's Tom Hanks as he was in *Sleepless in Seattle*,' I add hastily.

We arrive at the restaurant and enter through the double wooden doors painted with swirling blue waves that proclaim it to be Oceans Restaurant. The entire dining area is festooned with red and pink streamers and balloons. A couple of waiters are putting finishing touches to the tables, with red and pink napkins in the wine glasses and vases of red roses and pink carnations on each table.

'Oh look!' Jules says. 'They've put the decorations up for us. Don't they look gorgeous?'

I stare in horror at the balloons and streamers. Adorning the walls are bunches of balloons tied together — huge, red, inflated penises complete with testicles bobbing behind, jostling with pneumatically enhanced pairs of pink breasts, their red nipples perched on the end like cherries on top of gigantic strawberry ice-creams. The streamers have some sort of design on them and closer inspection reveals that it's made up of a continuous line of ink sketches of naked couples in various sexual positions — a sort of Kama Sutra conga.

'Gorgeous?' I shriek. 'They're horrible! Where on earth did you get them?'

Jules smiles conspiratorially. 'I have my sources.'

'Don't you think it's a little over the top? Not everyone wants to sit down to lunch with giant penises and overinflated boobs waving in their faces.'

'I don't see why not, it adds to the ambience. Anyway, people who are coming to the launch of a book called *Love Bytes* aren't likely to be prudes.'

My nerves are making a sudden, violent return. 'I need to go to the toilet. And when I come back, I want a huge glass of champagne waiting for me.'

When I return from the Ladies, the jazz pianist has arrived. He's young and fresh-faced, snappily dressed in dark trousers, white shirt and bow tie. He looks around the room and nods his approval. 'Love the decorations.'

He sets himself up at the piano in the front corner of the restaurant and soon the strains of I'm in the Mood for Love' float through the room. I'm making inroads into my champagne when the first people start arriving. The tickets say 11.30 for 12 and everyone receives a free glass of champagne on arrival. I smile and introduce myself and thank them for coming. I don't know any of these people and I feel like a bride at a wedding who's trying to be sociable to guests that she's never met because they're on her husband's side of the family.

Then I spot Annie and Myf arriving, and I rush over and give them a hug. Annie is looking her usual bizarre self in another of her unique creations — a short green skirt in the shape of a Christmas tree, showing lots of black stockinged leg, red platform shoes and a red sequined halter-neck top. Her hair is sparkling with red and green highlights, and her earlobes are weighed down by two enormous flashing Christmas tree earrings. But it's only October.

'I couldn't wait till Christmas to wear them,' she whispers to me.

Clutching Annie's arm is an even more exotic creature — a young male of indeterminate age with black spiky gelled hair, sultry brown eyes smudged with eyeliner, long black shorts, a purple shirt with a yellow sleeveless vest and red joggers.

'Susie, this is Toby,' she says, 'one of my partners in design.'

Toby puts out his hand and gives me a limp handshake. 'Hi, Susie,' he lisps, 'I'm her handbag for the day.'

'Well, you're certainly better looking than the battered old thing she normally carries around.'

As for Myf, I can't believe she looks as sensational as ever and she just had a baby six weeks ago. I wish I could hate her for it, but I can't. And part of the reason is that Amy is the sweetest baby I've ever seen — with the exception of my own two, of course. At six weeks, she is already the spitting image of Myf, with her tiny, angelic face peeking out from her pink bonnet. Her fate is already written in the stars; she'll be a heartbreaker like her mother.

Myf is wearing a black crepe skirt and a jacket that hides the almost imperceptible bulge she still carries from the birth, and despite wearing a baby as an accessory, still turns every male head when she walks into the room. The slight shadows under her eyes are the only indication she's experienced a major lifestyle change in the last few weeks.

'I hope Amy behaves herself,' she says. 'Rob offered to look after her for me, but she's too fond of the boob to leave her. If she starts to play up I'll just have to whip it out.'

'Be my guest, you'll feel right at home here,' I say, indicating a couple of balloon breasts suspended on the wall near us.'

'I think I could give those boobs a bit of competition,' Myf says. Her blouse clings to her full, rounded breasts and her top button casually left open reveals a glimpse of an ample cleavage. When I was breastfeeding I felt like a cow — fat, bloated and full of milk. Myf's bigger breasts and the extra weight she's carrying on her hips just make her look more voluptuous. If I try, I think I could hate her a bit.

Cara materialises beside me with her friend Alicia. I've lent her my car so she can pick Zac up from school. When I asked him if he wanted to come to the launch, he considered it for a few seconds, obviously weighing up the benefit of having the day off school against the drawback of having to sit through a lunch with a lot of dreary adults and my speech.

'I've never heard you make a speech,' he said. 'Not a proper one when you weren't drunk, but I think it would be boring anyway.'

'Especially if you're going to talk about all your boyfriends,' he added.

Lesson Number Seven from Mother to Son. Sometimes it is acceptable to tell a lie — for example, telling someone whose fear of public speaking is surpassed only by the fear of being eaten alive by tarantulas that you know her speech will be a roaring success. In this case, not only acceptable but compulsory.

Cara and Alicia are wearing the usual teenage uniform of hipster skirt and midriff top exposing acres of smooth brown flesh. In the last few months, Cara has shed her gawkiness and filled out, and with her hair streaked blonde and shaped in a shoulder-length bob, she's now quite a stunner. She and Jay are no longer an item — he's had one metal-lipped dalliance too many — but she keeps him hanging around hopefully in the background as a spare in case she finds herself, horror of horrors, dateless one Saturday night.

'Alicia and I have a table in the corner near the door,' she says, 'so if anything embarrassing happens, we can make a quick getaway.'

'Cool decorations,' Alicia says.

Cara opens her mouth, but I forestall her. 'Don't say anything. They weren't my idea.'

'I was just going to say that Dad and Alison are here,' she says, 'and there's a man with a funny accent at the door asking for you.'

The restaurant is filling up rapidly and I crane my neck to look through the crowd. Striding towards me is a familiar dark-haired figure. He gathers me up in his arms and clasps me tightly to his massive chest.

'Soozie! You look bootiful! I have missed you!'

'Darius!' I gasp, when I catch my breath, 'What on earth are you doing here?'

From the corner of my eye, I see Cara and Alicia slinking away. Does this count as an embarrassing experience? Are they leaving already?

'I am here on holiday,' he says. 'I see the ad in the paper, so I decide to come to your launch.' He pronounces it 'lonch' and I'm not sure whether he means launch or lunch.

'That's great,' I say, trying to disentangle myself from his grasp. Jeremy and Alison appear before me. Jeremy sounded genuinely pleased for me when I told him about my book being published. When he asked me what it was about, I told him sex and relationships. He laughed nervously. 'Based on your own experiences of course?'

To which I replied, 'You'll have to buy a copy to find out.' At least I can be sure of one sale.

He and Alison have obviously come straight from work — Jeremy, wearing a suit and tie and Alison a lemon skirt and white blouse. I note with satisfaction that on her short, well-covered frame, it makes her look like a lemon meringue tart.

'Darius, this is my ex-husband, Jeremy and his partner Alison,' I say.

Darius is wearing a woven knit short-sleeved shirt and tight jeans that accentuate his muscular bulges. Despite my best attempts to shake it off, his arm still circles my waist. Jeremy and Alison regard him with the same mixture of suspicion and uncertainty as you would a strange dog, not sure if it's going to bite you.

'Hullo,' Jeremy says, putting out his hand. Darius pumps it up and down, almost wrenching Jeremy's arm out of its socket. The look of alarm on Alison's face as Darius extends his hand towards her soon turns to embarrassment as he gallantly takes her hand and brushes the back of it with his lips.

'She is very bootiful, your wife,' he says to Jeremy. 'And clever.'

'Ex-wife,' I correct him.

'I am taking Soozie out for a drink after,' Darius says. 'Would you like to join us?'

The look of horror on my face would be enough to put them off, even if they were entertaining the thought.

'Er — thank you, but we have to go back to the office afterwards,' Jeremy says. 'Oh look, there's George and Fiona. Nice to meet you, Darius.'

He takes Alison by the hand and they disappear into the crowd.

'What's this about a drink?' I say to Darius.

He looks at me with those brown eyes that are like liquid Tim Tams and gently caresses my arm, sending shivers up my spine.

'It's nice to catch up, don't you think?' he says softly.

I'm pretty sure I know what he means by catching up, and I'm very tempted — at least, my body is tempted; but my head, slightly befuddled as it is by alcohol, is not so sure.

'I don't know. Can you get me another glass of champagne?'

It's more to get rid of him than my need for another drink. The Voice, who's been very subdued lately due to my wholesome, clean-living lifestyle, returns with a vengeance.

Good call, Susan. You know you if you sleep with Darius again it will just be for the sexual gratification and getting drunk is not going to help you make a rational decision. Not only will it ensure that your carnal desires will win out, but you'll be lucky to string two words together when you make your speech.'

Shit, the speech — I'd conveniently pushed it to the back of my mind. Suddenly I feel nauseous. As Darius returns with my glass of champagne, Jules, who is the self-appointed MC, makes his way up to the microphone set up on a makeshift stage at the front of the restaurant. He nods to the pianist and the strains of 'I've Got You Under My Skin' fade away.

'Ladies and gentlemen, may I welcome you all to the launch of the latest literary sensation, *Love Bytes*. I have the privilege of having known the author Susan Hamilton for many years; and may I say that in my unbiased opinion, it's one of the funniest and most moving books I've read in a long time. I'd ask you all to be seated so that lunch can be served, after which the author herself will let us all in on the story behind the story.'

'Thanks, Darius,' I say, grabbing the glass of champagne out of his hand. 'Excuse me, I have to go and confer with my publicity agent.'

Jules is standing near the microphone talking to a stunning blonde woman. She's immaculately dressed in a tailored pantsuit and high heels, her make-up is perfectly applied and every hair on her head sits obediently in place. She emanates that air of elegance and self-confidence common to women who spend a lot of time in the public eye, and she's holding Jules's hand and laughing at something he's saying.

'Susie, I was wondering where you were. This is Victoria.'

Victoria holds out her hand and bestows a smile upon me that would dazzle the Crown Jewels.

'I can't wait to read your book. The title alone is intriguing.'

She raises a seductive eyebrow at Jules and he smiles back. I catch his eye and he gives me a look that says, 'I'll tell you about it later'.

He nods towards my glass of champagne. 'You're looking much more relaxed — you've got a bit of a glow about you now. Just take a few deep breaths and you'll be fine.'

'I'd feel even more relaxed if I could pass out,' I say, 'and if one more person tells me to imagine the audience in their underwear, I'll scream.'

'I wish you were giving a speech,' Victoria purrs to Jules. 'Then you could imagine me sitting here in my underwear.'

'Darling, imagining you in your underwear would be totally counterproductive — it would turn me into a blabbering idiot.'

Victoria smiles smugly and I look at Jules, who's suddenly become absorbed in a pair of engorged breasts bouncing on the wall next to him.

This is a revelation to me. As far as I know, Jules has been a virtual social recluse since Max left; but knowing him as I do, I'm sure that Victoria is just fulfilling the role of emotional putty to fill in the huge void in his life.

Anyway,' I say, 'at last count I have an ex-husband, his partner and an ex-lover present, so perhaps underwear fantasies are not a viable option.'

'Was that Darius I saw you talking to before?' Jules says. 'He's very striking.'

'Yes. I haven't seen him for close on two years and all of a sudden he turns up out of the blue, says he's here on holidays and seems to think we're going out for a drink later, even though he hasn't actually asked me.'

'Oh'. It's Jules's turn to look inquiringly at me, but I bury my face in my champagne glass.

Just as Jules, Victoria and I are seating ourselves at a table with Myf, Annie and Toby, a voice says in my ear, 'Soozie, here you are. Do you have a seat for me?'

There's Darius at my elbow again, looking imploringly at me. He's like a puppy that tries to follow you home and no matter how many times you shoo it away, it won't take the hint.

'There's a seat here next to me,' Toby offers, his gaze travelling up and down Darius's body. Darius takes the seat, obviously disappointed that it's not next to me, and I introduce him to everyone.

'Do tell me,' Toby gushes to Darius, 'how you developed those gorgeous muscles.'

Darius shifts in his seat as far away from Toby as he can, looking exceedingly uncomfortable.

That'll teach you to come back into my life after two years and expect to take up where we left off.

And don't you say a word, I warn The Voice, as I take a final swig of champagne.

During lunch, Amy is passed around the table and we all have a turn at holding her and oohing and aahing. There's something about a baby that transforms normally sensible, articulate adults into babbling idiots.

'Who's a gorgeous, bootiful, cootie dootie little bundle of cuddly duddlyness?' croons Jules, gazing adoringly at Amy as she lies in his lap.

Amy purses her tiny rosebud lips and her sapphire blue eyes stare at Jules with that look of serious consternation that babies are so good at, as if she's saying to herself, 'What the hell is he on about?'

Jules picks her up and passes her to Victoria. Victoria holds her gingerly as if she's just been given a bomb. Amy, with a baby's uncanny radar, senses her unease and starts to wriggle and whinge. Victoria puts her tentatively on her shoulder and pats her back, and Amy promptly spews up on her shoulder.

'Shit!' Victoria shrieks.

'Pass her back to me,' Myf says.

As soon as she's back in her mother's arms, Amy's little body stops wriggling and she buries her face in the crook of Myf's shoulder. Myf rubs Amy's back while she continues her story about Rob's attempts to change Amy's nappy while conducting a phone tutorial from home, resulting in a messy incident and a blast of unprofessional language booming over the conference phone to a room full of astonished students.

I feel a lump in my throat as I watch her. She acts as if it's the most natural thing in the world for her to be sitting at lunch in an exclusive restaurant with a baby contentedly nestled into her shoulder. Not so long ago, she regarded babies as alien, anti-social beings and would have done exactly what Victoria is doing now — dabbing savagely at the white, curd-like epaulet on her two hundred dollar-sleeve — with the same expression of disgust as if a bird had just pooped on her shoulder. I have a flashback to when Cara and Zac were babies, and the rush of maternal love fills me to aching point as it did back then, leaving in its wake a bittersweet sadness that it's a part of my life that's gone forever.

There's a tap on my shoulder and Jules is beside me. 'I thought we'd have your speech before dessert. Are you ready?'

'I'll just do a patch up job on my face and have a final read of my notes.'

And have a quiet panic attack.

I grab my handbag and make a beeline for the Ladies. I shouldn't have worn these high heels; they're making me wobble. I have a long, nervous pee and touch up my make-up, which was probably better left untouched. The restroom is stuffy and I feel as if I'm going to throw up. I take a few deep breaths then open my handbag. No bundle of notes. I unzip all the compartments and grope around inside them. I'm sure I brought them. Panic rising, I park myself on the floor and empty out the entire contents of my handbag. At that moment, the door bursts open and two middle-aged matrons bustle in.

'I always thought I should write a book about my years in the fashion industry,' one is saying.

'I bet you'd have some fascinating stories to tell,' her friend says.

They stop dead in their tracks when they see me, slumped on the floor under the hand dryer, surrounded by pens, tampons, lipstick, tissues and other assorted accoutrements.

'Are you all right?' the first woman says, taking a couple of steps forward.

'Yeah, I'm just looking for something. Needless to say, I didn't find it.' I scramble to my feet, gather up all my personal effects, stuff them into my handbag and make as graceful an exit as I can.

'You always get someone who overdoes it at these functions.' The second woman's voice floats out behind me. 'What book is this for again?'

I find Jules huddled in a corner with the maitre d' of the restaurant discussing the options of cream or ice-cream to be served with the chocolate mud cake.

"Excuse me.' I nod to the maitre d'. 'Jules, have you got my speech?'

'No, I thought you had it.'

'Fuck.' It's out before I can stop it. I've only said that in polite company twice in my life and I can't remember the other occasion, but I'm sure it wasn't as life threatening as this one. The maitre d', one of the old school, purses his lips.

'Sorry,' I say. And then to Jules, 'I must have left it at home.'

An image flashes into my mind of a pile of notes strewn on the table in the courtyard where I was sitting this morning.

'I know exactly where it is. Have I got time to go and get it?'

'Definitely not. You're on in five minutes.'

'I'll apologise in advance this time,' I say to the maitre d'. 'Fuck.'

'Excuse me,' he says to Jules. 'I'll go and attend to your query.' And disappears into the kitchen.

'I hope he remembers it has to be King Island cream,' Jules says.

'Fuck the King Island cream.' I'm warming to the theme now, I feel as if I'm playing a role in an Eddie Murphy movie, where every second word is fuck.

'Susie,' Jules says, taking my hands, 'calm down and take a few deep breaths. I'm sure you can remember most of what's in your notes, anyway. Just single out one person in the audience, someone who looks friendly and receptive, and talk to him or her as if you're in a normal everyday conversation; and forget the rest of the audience.'

'That's fucking easy for you to say.'

'Come on, it's time.' I follow him on to the stage, willing my legs not to buckle under me. The pianist is on a break and is sitting at a table chatting up a couple of purple-haired ladies in frocks and beads who look as if they've wandered in accidentally on their way to bridge. I frantically try to recall my speech — is there anything in it that would offend them? Too late now, I guess.

Jules takes the microphone and starts talking. I'm not taking in what he's saying although occasionally a word or phrase impinges itself on my consciousness — 'well known freelance writer', 'first novel', 'fantastic reviews'. I look around the audience. Mostly women, with the occasional couple, the male half probably enticed by the prospect of food and drink and/or a couple of hours out of the office. The only man seemingly without a partner is sitting at a table with two forty-something couples. I try not to think about Martin's predictions of the male members of the audience imagining me naked. Two of them have already seen me naked, another two wouldn't have the slightest interest (I'm lumping Jules in with Toby), so that leaves how many?

'Here she is, ladies and gentlemen, Susan Hamilton!'

I force my legs to step forward. Jules moves the microphone so that it stands in front of the lectern that I requested to rest my now non-existent notes on. But I'm glad it's there — something to hide behind to lessen the feeling of exposure.

'Good afternoon, ladies and gentlemen,' my mouth says into the microphone, 'and thank you, Julian, for your objective and completely unbiased introduction.'

There are a few titters from the audience. My voice sounds loud and resonant and confident. Is that really me? Cara and Alicia are sitting at a table near the exit, as good as their word, and Cara grins and gives me the thumbs up. I glance at the faces at my table, all looking up at me with an air of encouraging expectancy until my eyes meet those of the two women I encountered in the Ladies, sitting at the next table. They're regarding me with an air of horrified recognition. Ex-fashion industry woman murmurs something to her friend, and I'd place bets on her now thinking twice about becoming an author, with the obvious effects it has on a person's mental health.

The man next to the two couples reminds me of a younger version of Scottish comedian Billy Connolly — in his early forties perhaps, with shoulder-length brown curly hair and the same mischievous twinkle in his eyes. He looks friendly and receptive enough to be my audience target.

'American writer Edna St. Vincent Millay is quoted as saying that publishing a book is like appearing in public with your pants down,' I say into the microphone, looking directly at my Billy Connolly look-alike, 'and as a first-time novelist, that's exactly how I feel. That's why I'm standing behind this lectern.'

Another titter from the audience, and my BC look-alike is laughing as well. Maybe I can do this after all. Somehow the rest of my speech is delivered — the points are not made in the order I originally formulated and I've ad-libbed some extras, but BC look-alike and the rest of the audience have laughed in all the right places. As Jules suggested, I finish by reading a couple of not-so-explicit excerpts from the book, which are well received — even the purple-haired ladies are smiling. Everyone gives me a hearty round of applause and Jules bounds back onto the stage and gives me a hug. 'Well done, I knew you could do it.'

I just got up on stage and made a speech in front of one hundred people, and what's more, I sounded okay. I didn't make a fool of myself and people liked it and thought it was funny. The bubble of exhilaration inside me swells until I think it's going to burst. I am woman, I am invincible, I can do anything. Maybe I'll even join the public speaking circuit.

Jules prises the microphone from my grasp. 'Ladies and gentlemen, I know it's impossible to upstage such an entertaining speech; but there will be a delicious dessert of chocolate mudcake being served shortly, after which you can purchase your own copy of *Love Bytes* which Susan will be happy to autograph for you.'

He switches off the microphone. 'Better go and have some dessert; you'll need all your energy for autographing books. With a bit of luck, we'll sell them all.' He glances over at Darius who is working his charm on Annie, sitting across from him. 'Or maybe we can try strongarm tactics. Get your Darius to stand at the door and look menacing — no one leaves until they've bought your book.'

'Very funny. And he's not *my* Darius.'

On my arrival back at my table, I'm overwhelmed by hugs, kisses and a chorus of congratulations.

'Great stuff,' Annie says. 'I knew you were nervous, but you didn't show it. Everyone loved it.'

'For someone who feared public speaking more than death, you made a stunning debut,' Myf says. 'How did you do it?'

'I wore my best underwear in case you decided to do the old imagining the audience in their underwear trick,' Annie says.

'Ooh, I hope not,' Toby says, with a meaningful look at Darius, 'I'm not wearing any.' Darius shifts uncomfortably in his seat and stares intently at a passing waitress as if willing her to rescue him. Obviously the Polish phrasebook doesn't cater for this type of encounter.

'If you really want to know, I took Jules's advice,' I say in answer to Myf's question, 'I found a cute guy in the audience and addressed my entire speech to him.'

'Sounds promising,' Myf says. 'You'll have to find him and thank him for his help.'

'Not a bad idea.' Particularly as BC look-alike appears to be here without a female companion.

The waitress arrives with a tray laden with dishes of mud cake and cream. Darius has changed position at the table so that the only spare seat is next to him, so I pull out the chair beside him.

'You were wonderful, Soozie,' he says, and pats my leg as I'm sitting down. 'I am very proud of you.'

Darius is becoming too proprietary for my liking. I tuck into my slab of chocolate mud cake. It's heavy and moist, like mud cake should be but often isn't, and garnished with a hug blob of thick cream — King Island, of course. Just as I've shoved the last piece of cake and cream into my mouth, Jules appears beside me.

'I have a surprise for you, Susie.' Standing beside him is my Billy Connolly look-alike. 'This is Martin Pascoe.'

I stare at the man who's much better looking than Billy Connolly close up. His eyes draw me in — they're warm and friendly and brimming with humour, as if we're sharing a secret joke. Although he's about average height and build, I glean a sense of well-developed muscle. I'm not usually attracted to long hair in men but his suits him — it's neat and tidy and makes him look scholarly, but at the same time someone who doesn't take himself too seriously.

He's holding his hand out towards me. Did he just say 'Hi Susan?' I stand up, put my hand in his and he gives it a firm shake.

'What are you doing here?' I blurt out and the second the words are out I realise how rude they sound. A jumble of thoughts tosses around in my mind. So I directed my speech to someone I thought was really cute and it turns out to be my editor. He looks nothing like I imagined. Why didn't he tell me he was coming?

'Sorry,' I say hastily. 'I didn't mean to sound rude. It's just that I'm so surprised to see you.'

'Don't worry about it.' Martin smiles. 'I wanted to surprise you so it has the desired effect. I only decided yesterday that I was going to come, and luckily I was able to get a flight. Congratulations on your speech, it was excellent.'

Did he realise I was addressing it to him? He couldn't possibly have failed to notice all that eye contact. I feel the colour rising in my cheeks. Was he imagining me naked? Even with the lectern in front of me? Maybe that's why he was laughing. My face feels ready to ignite.

Martin has a mischievous glint in his eye as if he's read my thoughts — which is even more embarrassing, if that's possible. Does he have X-ray vision as well?

Darius pipes up from beside me. 'Are you going to introduce me, Soozie?'

For once I'm glad of the diversion. I introduce Darius to Martin, and as Darius stands up to shake Martin's hand, he puts his other arm around my waist. Martin's eyes flicker over him then back up to hold my gaze for what is probably a few seconds, but seems like an eternity.

A sharp jolt rushes through my body. I know this man well, through weeks of emails and phone calls, yet I feel as if I've just met a complete stranger. For some reason, I imagined him to be tall and broad-shouldered with dark hair; and now I have to reconcile my long-distance mentor with this flesh and blood person standing in front of me.

'I suppose you've been told lots of times how much like Billy Connolly you look,' I tell him.

'Let's just say if I had a dollar for every time someone has asked me for my autograph, I'd probably be as rich as he is,' Martin says. 'Anyway, my jokes are better than his.'

'In that case, I'd like to hear some of them. Have you got time for a coffee later before you go back?'

'I'm going to Brisbane this afternoon to catch up with my sister,' Martin says, 'but I'll be up this way again in a couple of days. I'll give you a call and we'll do lunch, if you like.'

Now I know I've made it — I've been invited to 'do lunch' with my editor. 'That'd be great. Now if you'll excuse me, I have to go and do the autograph thing for my adoring fans.'

Chapter 20

Our bodies are sliding together in slippery synchrony. The room is air-conditioned, but we've created our own heat and the sweat is pouring off our bodies. Without warning I climax, and even the tips of my fingers and toes are tingling as I buck wildly against the body underneath me, in an attempt to extract every last bit of pleasure.

The rhythm of our bodies slows down to a standstill, but I'm still trembling with the aftershock. I lean forward and stretch myself out languorously along the warm damp flesh, solid yet so deliciously yielding, feeling the silky chest hairs against my cheeks and drinking in the musky aroma of masculine sweat and aftershave.

'Soozie, Soozie, you are — how you say it — away with the fairies.'

I'm jolted out of my Darius daydream. We're sitting in a licensed cafe on the corner of the Esplanade. He looks at me with reproach as he strokes my hand. It's an unseasonably hot, muggy spring and there's a continuous parade of after-work beachgoers straggling past us. An intense mood of melancholy grips me and I feel very alone in the midst of all these people. Maybe I'm just coming down from the excitement of the day — the launch was far more successful than I'd dared hope.

'Come on,' Darius says. 'Finish your drink and we go to my motel.'

He continues stroking my hand. I'm still aroused from my erotic reverie and that's not helping.

You'll regret it. It's only short-term gratification. Like Chocolate Obsession. In the long term, it will make you hungrier.

Instantly I know it's true. I've known it for a long time, but now I'm admitting it to myself. Sometimes having just some of what you want is fine. But there comes a time when it ceases to satisfy you. I want the total experience — mind, body, and soul. Nothing less.

Darius looks at me and raises one eyebrow — the very same gesture that had me nearly wetting my pants three years ago when I met him at the gym. I retrieve my hand from his grasp and put it in my lap.

'I'm sorry, Darius, I'm tired. I've had a big day; I just want to go home.'

Darius looks at me disbelievingly, as if he thinks I'm making up some ineffectual excuse.

'All right, I stay longer. What about tomorrow?'

I take a deep breath. 'No, not tomorrow or any day. You can't just walk back into my life after two years and expect to take up where we left off.'

'Why not?'

Is he being deliberately obtuse? Before I can answer, Darius says, 'I like making love, you like making love, what's the problem?'

Suddenly I feel weary. It's too hard to explain. 'There's no problem. I just don't want to do it any more.'

Darius's eyes are flashing at me from under his bushy eyebrows. They're not liquid Tim Tams now, more like pools of fiery molten lava. His full sensuous lips, which I imagined only a few minutes ago methodically kissing every inch of my body, are now pursed in a thin line. He pushes back his chair.

'You,' he says through clenched teeth, 'are a stupid fucking bitch.'

And he gets up and strides off along the Esplanade, weaving his way determinedly through the crowd.

I'm stunned, unable to move a muscle. Then I have an overwhelming desire to burst into tears. I've never been called a stupid fucking bitch before — albeit by a man whose ego was severely dented, but that doesn't make it any less hurtful. The Polish phrasebook should be commended for its colloquial authenticity. My melancholic mood settles over me again like a black cloud. I know I'll be glad later; but right now, I feel like shit.

***

My Wonderpants are digging into my stomach, as it tries to expand to accommodate the enormous quantity of food and drink descending upon it. The adrenalin has rushed straight to my hands, and the more I try to stop them, the more they assert their independence by finishing off all the garlic bread, the cheese platter and the bottle of wine.

I don't know why I'm so nervous — this is only a business lunch with my editor and all we've done so far is talk business. Except the bit where he mentioned his partner. Just in passing.

'I'm catching a flight back tonight,' he said in answer to my question about when he was returning to Sydney. 'I'd love to stay in Brisbane longer and see more of my sister, but Simone has a work function on tomorrow night that I promised to attend.'

I assume Simone is his partner or wife. Of course he's taken; all the decent men are. I've railed against this defeatist philosophy for so long, but now I agree wholeheartedly.

You know very well why you're nervous. You're madly attracted to him and he's unattainable. And you don't want him to know.

Okay, I'll admit I love how he seems to understand what I'm saying before I finish saying it, the way his eyes light up and crinkle around the edges when he laughs at my jokes, how he accidentally brushed my hand as he reached for the salt and set off a tribal drum chorus in my chest; but it's not as if I want to take him to bed.

Bullshit. You know you've already imagined the two of you rolling around naked on your bed.

On my bed with the faded quilt cover. I really will have to buy a new one — it spoils the whole ambience of my fantasy. My eyes focus on the scene they've been gazing at through the restaurant window — the Pumicestone Passage spread out before us like a vast quilt of diamonds glittering in the sun, with the soft purple peaks of the Glasshouse Mountains on the horizon. Now that would be a beautiful quilt on which to make love.

'Earth to Susan, where are you?'

Martin is looking at me with a half-quizzical, half-ironic expression. The heat infuses my cheeks, and I hope like crazy he attributes my rosy complexion to post-alcohol glow.

'Sorry, I just drifted away for a minute. Occupational hazard of being a writer and living in your imagination.'

'Especially when that writer has demolished the best part of a bottle of wine,' Martin says, flashing his cute grin. Is that strange feeling my heart doing a somersault in my chest or the beginnings of indigestion?

'I've enjoyed our lunch, but I have to go. Got to head back to Brisbane and get organised for the flight.'

'I guess Simone will be glad to have you back.'

I'm not prying, just making conversation.

'I suspect Emily has missed me more than Simone. She's my daughter,' he adds.

'How old is she?'

'Eight. She's a real Daddy's girl. She sees her mother every weekend but she always wants to come home.'

His tone brims with pride and affection. There's something very endearing about a man who makes no secret of his adoration for his children. So Simone is a stepmother. It can be a tough gig. I almost feel a pang of sympathy for her.

Martin pays the bill and waves away my protests. 'All on the expense account.' Though I'm sure, being self-employed, he doesn't have an expense account.

He offers to give me a lift home in his hire car, even though it's in the opposite direction to where he's going. I lent my car to Cara this morning, which was not a good idea in retrospect, because if I'd had to drive, I'd have limited myself to one glass of wine. I cadged a lift with Jules to the restaurant in Caloundra as he had to see a client nearby, and I'd arranged to phone him when I was ready to go home. But an extra half hour with Martin is a more enticing offer. I send Jules an SMS. 'Getting a lift home with Martin.' Let him think whatever he likes.

As Martin pulls out from the parking bay into the traffic I say, 'I really appreciate you coming all this way for the launch. Do you do that for all your clients?'

'Not at all. Most of my clients take my advice and don't splash out on big, expensive book launches.'

He gives me a sideways glance and grins. 'I did have an ulterior motive though. I've been promising to come up and visit Caroline for ages. Then when Jules rang me and asked if I could come to the launch, I thought, why not? I could kill two birds with one stone.'

'Jules rang you?'

'Yes, he wanted it to be a surprise.'

'It was certainly that.'

The sneaky so-and-so. I remember now Jules asking me Martin's surname. Just out of interest, he said. But obviously so he could look up his phone number.

'Anyway, I guess the surprise was on me. Not only did you sell all your books, you got orders for more. And made a profit from the day.'

'Only fifty dollars. But the main point was that I got a lot of exposure from it. I've already had a couple of radio stations ring me to ask for interviews.'

'That's great. If I wasn't so full from lunch, I'd eat my words. What's the latest on your e-book sales?'

'As of a couple of days ago, fifty-five.'

I try to suppress the disappointment in my voice. Fifty-five is okay, if you add it on to the two hundred and more I sold at the launch. But on its own, not so good. The book's been up for sale for almost two months. I was hoping for at least a few hundred by now.

'Don't be disappointed,' Martin says. 'As I told you before, it takes time. And solid marketing.'

He pauses. 'Just out of interest, how much of your book is based on personal experience?'

He glances at me and grins again. 'Sorry, I know it's such a clichéd question to ask a writer, but you'd better get used to it. Everyone will want to know.'

'I'm used to it already. Do you mean the sex or the internet dating?'

I can't resist calling his bluff even though I know what his answer will be.

'Er … I was referring to the online dating part of it.'

'Quite a bit, actually. I don't think you could write about something like that without personal experience. Which is why I did it, of course.'

'Of course.'

I recount my dating adventures, from my Jules-created profile (I've got him laughing already — is that because he thinks my being Sexyandsultry is so unbelievable?) to my last disaster with Lennie — without the gory sexual details, of course. He is my editor after all. We have a professional relationship.

'So as you can see, I had a lot of raw material to work with. All the men in my book are combinations of the ones I've dated with extra bits added or removed. To protect the guilty parties.'

'And your boyfriend? Did you meet him online?'

'What boyfriend?'

'The guy you were with at the launch. Was it Darian?'

'Darius. He's not my boyfriend. Well, he was, but he isn't any longer although he thinks he still is. Or he thought he was, but I've put him straight.'

Stop garbling, for God's sake.

'And to answer your question, I didn't meet him on the internet, it was at the gym. It was just a fling, really, I needed my ego bolstered after my marriage break-up.'

'I know what you mean. I've been there too. It's tough going.'

Martin's empathy, my alcohol-induced lack of inhibition and the fact that we are by now stuck in a traffic jam and going nowhere, have combined to create an irresistible impulse to keep on gabbling. I tell him the story of my marriage break-up and my self-imposed exile with Tim Tams and Hugh Grant.

'When I look back on our marriage, the signs were there but we ignored them. And sometimes I wonder if we were doomed from the start. Jeremy and I had a fantastic friendship but the sex was pretty ordinary. It didn't worry me at first, I thought it would improve with time but it didn't. We tried, but it didn't happen, the chemistry just wasn't there. Then when I met Darius, it was just the opposite — it was all mind-blowing sex but not much else.'

Stop right there. Professional relationship, remember?

'So now at least I know what I want. A clone made up of the best of Jeremy and Darius. In other words, Perfect Sex.'

Silence. Shit, I've said too much. He thinks I'm a blabbering idiot. I steal a glance at him. He's staring straight ahead and I can't see his expression because of his sunglasses. The cars in front start to move and he puts the car into gear with a slow, deliberate movement.

'That's a tall order. What exactly is perfect sex, if there is such a thing?'

'It's more than just loving someone — it's the whole package. The physical, emotional, intellectual, spiritual even, all blending together, especially during sex, so that you're on another level, another dimension that only the two of you can experience.'

My words echoing in the space between us seem trite and mawkish.

'I know it sounds very Mills and Boonish and maybe you're right. Maybe it's not even attainable. I might spend the rest of my life searching for perfect sex and never find it.'

'I don't think it's unattainable,' Martin says, 'and I think you're right. You shouldn't settle for second best — in anything, but particularly relationships.'

A sombre note has crept into his voice. Time to change the subject. The traffic is moving freely now and we chat about inconsequential things until Martin pulls up in my driveway.

He stops the engine, leaps out and walks around to open my door. I know it's an outdated custom, but he's just gone up another notch on my scale of desirability. We both stand beside the passenger door.

'Thanks so much for lunch and the lift,' I say. 'I'd ask you in but I know you have to get back.'

'Next time,' Martin says. 'Thank you, too. I enjoyed it.'

He looks into my eyes and smiles. 'A lot.'

I smile back into his eyes, but out of the corner of my eye, I'm looking at his mouth and imagining the softness of his lips wrapped around mine. Without warning, an enormous contraction of pain grips my stomach and I groan and bend over.

'What's the matter?' Martin asks, alarmed.

'It's nothing,' I gasp, 'just my stomach protesting because I ate too much at lunch.'

He needs a bit of convincing that I'm not going to collapse at his feet, but finally I wave him off. I climb the stairs to my bedroom, almost bent double with pain. You idiot, you missed a once in a lifetime opportunity. You should have pretended to pass out and he would have carried you up to the bedroom and laid you tenderly on the bed. When you opened your eyes and gazed into his, the violins would start playing and you'd both realise you were meant for each other. You'd make love, and it would be the most fantastic sex ever — in fact, it would be perfect.

Cold hard facts such as Martin having a plane to catch as well as a partner and daughter waiting for him in Sydney are not factored into my fantasy.

Anyway, he'd probably be too shagged out after carrying you up the stairs to do any other sort of shagging. I swear I'm going to kill that Voice.

I kick off my shoes and lift up my dress, a figure-hugging design in purple and black, bought in a last minute panic especially for our lunch. I wedge my fingers into the top of my Wonderpants, an act which defies the laws of spatial physics as they're so tight they've created a seam in my stomach, and yank them down to my feet. My cramps instantly dissipate and my stomach, bottom and thighs settle back into their comfort zones with a collective sigh of relief.

I pick up the Wonderpants and stride out of my bedroom, down the stairs and out the front door to the garbage bin. I open the lid, toss them in and slam the lid down hard, in case they have any ideas about escaping.

***

It's only 7.20 pm but Radio City, as the headquarters of the three local radio stations is called, looks deserted. There are only three cars in the carpark, including mine. The front door of the building is locked, so I press the intercom button as Jodie, the producer, instructed me to do when we organised the interview.

'Come on in, Susan,' her voice peals out, and there's a buzz as the door unlocks.

I enter the foyer, an expanse of soft, lush carpet. A huge sign on the wall, depicting a lone surfer riding the crest of a gigantic wave, welcomes me to Waves 93.1. A slim, blond figure hurries towards me from the end of a long corridor.

'Hi, I'm Jodie.' We shake hands. She'd have to be at least in her twenties, but she doesn't look a day over seventeen.

I follow her down the corridor to a glass door on the right emblazoned with the words 'Studio One'. A neon sign beside it is glowing with the words 'On Air'.

A door beside the studio says 'Producer'. Jodie leads me through her office to a small room with a couch, a couple of chairs and a coffee table, on which sits a carafe of water and two glasses.

'This is our equivalent of the green room,' she smiles. 'Just sit and relax for a couple of minutes. You're not nervous, are you?'

'No. Well, a little.'

'Don't worry, you'll be fine,' she says cheerfully. It's the sort of complacent remark made by someone who's far removed from the experience you're about to undergo.

I glance through the window that looks into the studio. It's a small room filled with a sprawling U-shaped desk. At the far end of the desk sits a woman in headphones talking into a microphone. She looks to be in her late thirties with fair hair pulled back into a bun and dark rimmed glasses, attractive in a schoolmarmish sort of way.

This is Rosie McVeigh, the host of a weekly program called 'Love Matters'. I've heard snippets of it on my car radio — it covers the whole gamut of love/sex/relationships, incorporating guest speakers, talkback and even a 'Dial-a-Date' segment, in which single listeners are invited to ring in, describe themselves and their ideal date on air then sit back and wait for the deluge of offers. Rosie phoned me a couple of days after the launch and invited me to talk on the show, and now, two weeks after sending her a complimentary copy of *Love Bytes*, here I am.

She looks up, spies me peering at her and waves. Jodie appears at my side. 'You're on after this song. Come on through.'

I follow her into the studio. At the opposite end of the desk to Rosie, nearest the door, sit three microphones in a row in front of three chairs. Jodie pulls out the middle chair for me and adjusts the microphone to my height.

Rosie smiles at me. 'Welcome to the show.' She picks up my book from the desk beside her. 'Just finished this. Fantastic — very funny and down to earth. I'm sure our listeners will relate to it.'

'Thank you.'

'I'll just ask you the usual questions about what inspired you to write the book and so on. You don't mind a few candid questions, do you?'

This last question is delivered in the crisp, no-nonsense tone that implies that she's going to ask them regardless. So far I've managed to keep my nerves at bay, but now I start to feel a few stirrings in my stomach.

'What sort of candid?'

'About your own experiences — this is a love and relationships program, after all, which translated means sex and sex.'

She smiles knowingly at me.

'You're on,' Jodie says. 'Just talk normally and be yourself. You'll be great.' Then she disappears.

How can I talk normally and be myself when I'm going to be asked to divulge intimate details about myself to the entire Sunshine Coast? Or even further afield, if I cared to investigate the demographics of this radio station, which I don't.

Rosie's voice booms out over the microphone. 'And now we're going to meet local author Susan Hamilton whose first novel, *Love Bytes*, has been published to rave reviews.'

Rave reviews. Sounds impressive. Admittedly, I've had a lot of four- and five-star reviews on the Amazon and Smashwords book review sites, but there has also been a fair sprinkling of less favourable reviews. But who am I to quibble about semantics?

'I've just finished reading Susan's book myself,' Rosie continues, 'and I've found it a very funny and insightful look at relationships and sex. Good evening, Susan.'

'Good evening, Rosie.' My voice sounds hesitant and there's a slight tremor in it. For some reason, the thought of being listened to by thousands of faceless people is suddenly more nerve-wracking than giving a speech in front of one hundred flesh and blood people. Pull yourself together, Susan. How many people listen to night-time radio anyway? Just the odd shiftworker or business executive working late, and a few lonely and desperate people who listen to a love and relationships program because they don't have any in their own life.

Rosie is looking expectantly at me. Oops, she's asked me a question and I haven't got a clue what it is. I smile my apology and mouth 'Pardon?'

Rosie's low resonant voice echoes around me. 'The story of four middle-aged women who join an internet dating service to find their Mr Right is something that touches a chord in a lot of us. Can you tell us what happens in the book, without giving too much away?'

I draw in a deep breath. 'Briefly, Rosie, it's about...' And I launch into my spiel about the plot of the book, which I could rattle off in my sleep and probably do. Rosie asks me a few more innocuous questions about the process of writing the book and my own experiences of internet dating. I'm feeling quite comfortable now as if the two of us are chatting in my lounge room and I've forgotten about the thousands of people out there hunched over their radios, hanging on to my every word.

'One of the things I enjoyed most about the book,' Rosie says, 'is its very frank and honest portrayal of female sexuality. I presume you have drawn heavily on your own experiences in that regard?'

Here we go. 'That's true, Rosie, in the sense that all writers draw on their own experiences when writing. However, the good thing about writing fiction is that we can also interweave those experiences with a hefty dose of imagination and creativity.'

'But the issues that you explore — promiscuity, sexual boredom in marriage and lack of female sexual satisfaction, for example, are written with such sensitivity and honesty that the reader can't help but feel that you've gone through a lot of these experiences yourself.'

'I think that many women of my generation, who came of age in the free love era then settled down and did the family and kids thing, have gone through similar experiences, so I'm not necessarily speaking entirely from my own perspective.'

I congratulate myself — I'm dodging and weaving like an expert. I should have been a politician.

But Rosie's not giving up. 'Let me give you some examples — scenes such as Amanda keeping a collection of vibrators, one for each day of the week, and looking forward to getting home from her date so she can use it; Jill composing letters to an agony aunt about her lack of sexual satisfaction while her husband is making love to her; and Claire's obsession with having sex in the dark because she's embarrassed about her body. These are the sorts of funny yet poignant situations that really ring true, and it's natural for the reader to assume that the author has experienced them herself.'

Rosie is smiling at me as if she's in a toothpaste ad, pearly white teeth gleaming.

'If you're asking me whether I have a collection of vibrators and whether I have composed letters to agony aunts while making love to my husband in complete darkness, I'll have to leave you in suspense. Some of the book is based on my own experiences, some of it on other people's experiences and some of it completely from my imagination — I'll leave it up to the reader to guess.'

Rosie is still smiling. 'One of the recurring themes in your book is the lack of female sexual fulfillment within relationships. We find on this program that this is a very common theme amongst our callers. From your experience, would you agree that this is a major problem for women today?'

Her teeth have now metamorphosed into werewolf fangs.

'I'm glad you asked me that question, Rosie.' I bare my teeth back at her. This is war, baby. 'If you believe half of what you hear and read in the media, there are a lot of women out there who aren't happy with their sex life. But I think one of the problems these days is that we're suffering from information overload. Back in our parents' day, there wasn't much information about sex. It wasn't discussed, so if you were unhappy with your sex life you just suffered in silence. These days we're saturated with sex. You're made to feel that if you don't have sex every night in a different position and have screaming orgasms every time, there's something wrong with you.'

Rosie opens her mouth, undoubtedly to ask another probing question, but I plough on. I'm on a roll and I'm not going to stop.

'As for my own experience, I find that as I get older, the sex gets better. I'm more relaxed about my body, less inhibited, more able and willing to communicate my needs to my partner. I think you'll find the same with a lot of middle-aged women. Whoever said that youth was wasted on the young was only half right — sex is also wasted on the young. The trouble with today's society and its emphasis on youth and beauty is that no one wants to acknowledge that middle-aged and elderly people are having sex — all those wrinkly, flabby bodies heaving and slapping against each other, and God forbid that they should actually enjoy it as well. And if they do enjoy it then they shouldn't talk about it. They might embarrass the children or make them sick. When was the last time you saw a movie about two middle-aged people falling in love — I mean, real people, not plastic, artificially uplifted people —with a real bedroom scene in it, warts and all?'

I pause for breath. 'Maybe not necessarily warts, but saggy bodies, losing their glasses in the bedclothes, having to get up and go for a pee in the middle of it and the unsurpassed enjoyment of having sex with a man who's been doing it for 40 years and finally got it right! In fact, that might be my next project, writing the script for such a film...'

Rosie sees the potential for a gap and dives in. 'That sounds like a wonderful idea! If there are any movie producers listening tonight, please give Susan a call. Thank you for a very interesting chat and we'll wait with bated breath for the movie version of *Love Bytes*.'

Chapter 21

'I can't believe I said those things. I was so nervous at first I didn't think I was going to be able say anything intelligible, then it all came pouring out.'

'I imagine middle-aged women across the land would have been applauding,' Jules says. 'It's about time someone stood up for us wrinklies who love bonking and who still plan to be bonking up to the minute we drop dead.'

He's on a lunch break from work and I've joined him for sandwiches and takeaway coffee on a seat overlooking the beach. I need respite from an article I'm writing on sex and the over sixties, commissioned by the editor of a seniors magazine. Suddenly I'm an expert on sex for senior citizens. I'm not sure if I should be flattered or not.

I watch Jules wrapping his mouth around a turkey and cranberry sauce panini. He looks at least ten years younger than his forty-two years.

'I hardly think you qualify as a member of the wrinkly set. But I'll make you an honorary member, if you like. Anyway, she was giving me the shits, trying to get me to talk about my own sexual experiences. Serves her right.'

'If you write a book about sex, you have to expect that. They're hardly going to ask you about knitting or twentieth century philosophy,' Jules points out.

'Talking of sex, what's with you and Victoria? Where did you find her?'

'She does some modelling for a client of mine. She made a play for me, so I just went along with the flow.'

'Are you sleeping with her?'

'Of course I am.'

That's one of the fundamental differences between men and women — losing the love of his life doesn't stop a man from having a bonk if the opportunity arises. The last thing a woman wants to do after a relationship break-up is have sex — copious quantities of tears, wine and chocolate are far more therapeutic options.

'At least I *was* sleeping with her,' Jules adds. 'I don't think I am any more. I think she's dumped me.'

'What do you mean, you think? How can you not know if you've been dumped?'

'Put it this way — she hasn't returned any of my phone calls over the past week, and one night I rang her and her flatmate told me she couldn't come to the phone because she was reorganising the pantry.'

'That's not a good sign if she'd rather commune with her herbs and spices than with you.'

'She doesn't have any herbs and spices. Her pantry takes minimalism to the extreme. How long does it take to rearrange a bottle of tomato sauce and four cans of baked beans?'

'What did you do to deserve that?'

A faint pink seeps into his face. I'm intrigued — I can't remember the last time I saw Jules embarrassed.

'You didn't burst into tears and launch into a monologue about how much you miss Max, did you?' I ask.

'If only it were that simple,' he says sheepishly. 'We were having sex and in the middle of it all I accidentally called her Max. I wasn't even aware I'd done it until Victoria nudged me in the ribs — I've still got the bruise — and demanded to know who Max was. What could I say? He's my next-door neighbour? Or my dog?'

I'm trying hard not to laugh because Jules looks so anguished. 'That really takes the cake for sexual faux pas. That would take one hell of an act of imagination to think about Max when you're making love to Victoria.'

'To tell you the truth, it was rather an ordeal. She's got a fantastic body and she's very... let's say, energetic in bed, but my heart wasn't in it, or any of my other organs for that matter, and the only way I could get through it was to fantasise about being with Max. She said, "I suppose you're going to tell me that Max is actually short for Maxine and that she was your first love, who died tragically at a young age and you've never gotten over it." And I thought, wow, what a great story, I wish I'd thought of it first, but it was too late, so I just put my clothes on, which she threw at me and went home. And she hasn't spoken to me since.'

'Much as I didn't take to Victoria, I can see why. Being mistaken for a man in a moment of passion is not something a woman could easily forgive.'

'It's probably for the best anyway.' He sighs. 'I think I'm doomed to a lifetime of embarrassing myself at intimate moments, because I'm always thinking of Max. Anyway, speaking of sex, I noticed a frisson of something happening between you and Martin at the launch. What's going on?'

'Absolutely nothing, he's got a live-in partner in Sydney.'

'That's bad luck. He seems to have all the right qualities — he's cute, funny and intelligent and he obviously likes you. I guess we can always pray for a relationship break-up,' he adds uncharitably.

'You're forgetting one important point. Even if he was available, he lives a thousand kilometres away. Long-distance relationships are doomed from the start.'

***

I'm making myself a cup of coffee when Cara bounds into the kitchen. These days she operates on two speeds — bounding or mooching. Yesterday was mooching.

'Why didn't you tell me?' she demands.

'Tell you what?'

'About the video!'

'What video?'

'Don't come the innocent act. You know what video.'

'You're not an adult yet so you can quit the role reversal. I have no idea what you're talking about.'

'YouTube, that's what I'm talking about! The *Love Bytes* video! Everyone's been talking about it and I knew nothing about it! I feel like a total loser!'

I stare blankly at her. She comes over and gives me a hug. 'Don't worry, Mum, I'm not mad at you. I think it's awesome. How did you do it?'

'Cara,' I say firmly. 'I have no idea what you're talking about. If there's a video on YouTube about *Love Bytes*, I had nothing to do with it!'

Cara looks at me disbelievingly. 'Who else would have done it? I've been taking all the credit for it — on your behalf, of course.'

'Very thoughtful of you. You'd better show me then.'

In my study, Cara fires up my computer and logs onto YouTube. She types Love Bytes into the search bar.

At the top of the list of videos pertaining to Love Bytes is a screenshot of four animated figures standing in a row with arms linked. 'Figures' is a misnomer — they're gross exaggerations, huge heads and torsos over skinny legs and tiny feet. Not to mention their hugely exaggerated assets — the men with biceps bulging Popeye-like from their ripped-off shirts and the crotches of their tight jeans resembling not one banana but a whole bunch. The women look in danger of toppling over by the weight of their mountainous breasts bursting over the top of the sequinned dresses, barely containing their Jessica Rabbit curves. Their huge red lips are parted in a terrifying smile to display gleaming teeth that would do Jaws proud.

Cara clicks on the image and the figures spring to life. A backdrop appears – a huge image of the cover of my book. A rap beat starts up and the words 'Love Bytes by Susan Hamilton' pulsate in time. The figures dance to the beat — intricate rap moves, handstands, twirling, jumping, sliding, chicken legs buckling under the weight, biceps and bulges and boobs bumping and grinding together. A chorus of voices chants the words:

I got a byte

And it's all right

And I said 'love,

How about it, guv?'

I got a book

So have a look

It's called Love Bytes

And it's all right

It's all about chicks

With great big ... smiles

Looking for guys

With great big ... wallets

Then back to verse one. It's all over in less than a minute, with a final screenshot of the *Love Bytes* front cover and the words 'Available now on Amazon and Smashwords', with links to the book on both sites.

'Bloody hell.'

It's the only thing I can say. I'm still reeling with the shock of it.

'So you're telling me you had nothing to do with it?' Cara demands.

'Absolutely.'

I press the play button and watch it again. It makes me cringe but it's funny in a raw, schoolboyish way.

'I had no idea about this, but I'm pretty sure I know who does.'

'Did you happen to notice how many views it's had?' Cara said.

I click back and look at the description. It was uploaded two weeks ago and has had 8,576 views.

'So eight and a half thousand people have seen this?'

'Or else four thousand people have seen it twice.' Cara grinned. 'Seriously, Mum, that's awesome! It took Fo Shizzy three months to get that many views.'

I'm not sure about the merit of being compared to her favourite rap artist, but I'll take it as a compliment. I phone Jules.

'You sneaky sonofabitch.'

'What are you talking about?' It's obvious he knows very well.

'*Love Bytes* in rap. And don't tell me it wasn't you.'

'It's a surprise present. One of the young graduates at work is a whiz at digital animation and he put it together for me. I've been dying for you to discover it. Do you like it?'

'Er ... yes. It's different. I suppose eight and half thousand people can't be wrong.'

'Of course they can't. I thought it would take weeks to get any traction, so you've been incredibly lucky. Obviously a few people with a bit of clout have liked it and it's gone viral. Hopefully it'll translate into lots of sales.'

'Thanks, that was very sweet of you. It's certainly the most unusual present I've ever had.'

First Martin arriving out of the blue at my book launch and turning out to be quite a charmer, now my novel becoming famous on YouTube without my knowing — I'm not sure if I can take any more surprises.

I log into the Amazon site and go to my book sales page. I haven't been there for ages, no reason to. Number of sales so far this month is 6,000. It must be 60. I blink and look again. It's definitely 6,000. And we're only into day 12 of the month. That's how many a day? My brain is too befuddled to think.

I phone Jules again. 'Amazon says I've sold 6,000 books so far this month. That can't be right, surely!'

'That's fantastic! Of course it's right! I wouldn't mind betting it's a direct result of the YouTube video.'

'Really? But 6,000 in 12 days? That's...'

'An average of 500 a day. At the royalty rate of $2.08 per book, that's $12,480 you've earned this month. Not bad for a starving, penniless writer.'

It turns out I can take more surprises, after all. 'That's incredible! Even if I don't sell any more it's still beyond my wildest dreams!'

'Think big, baby. This is just the beginning. You need to do some serious promotion to keep up the momentum. How about I invite myself over for dinner tonight, and we'll brainstorm some new marketing strategies?'

' Does this mean you're now my publicity agent?'

'If you like. But I'll let you keep all your royalties. Just cook me the occasional dinner and let me cry on your shoulder about Max every now and then.'

I can't resist phoning Martin. He gives a whoop of delight. 'That's brilliant! I told you to hang in there, didn't I?' Sometimes all it takes is a lucky break. I'd better get you to autograph me a copy before you become too famous to talk to me!'

'As if that would ever happen. I wouldn't be selling any books at all if it weren't for your judicious editing. And by the way, everything you told me to do that I didn't agree with — I take it all back!'

'Apology gracefully accepted. If I'd known you were going to become a bestselling author I'd have charged twice as much. *Fifty Shades of Grey*, eat your heart out!'

'Just joking,' he adds, before I can think of a suitable rejoinder.

Chapter 22

The domestic terminal at Sunshine Coast Airport is bulging at the seams with the Christmas holiday crowds. I strain my eyes for a glimpse of my parents in the crowd streaming along the walkway from the tarmac. There are joyful family reunions at the arrival gates while other travellers sidestep the hugging clusters with wistful glances or studied nonchalance. I always feel sorry for those who don't have anyone to greet them off the plane; I want to rush up and throw my arms around their neck and cry, 'Lovely to see you again!' I make a mental note that a job as a professional airport greeter would be a novel way for one of my future fictional characters to meet men...

'Hullo, sweetheart!' I'm engulfed in a strong, warm embrace.

'Dad! I was watching for you! Where did you spring from?'

Tears spring to my eyes; it's been over two years since I last saw my parents, and it's not till I see them that I realise how much I miss them.

'Right through the gates with everybody else. You were a million miles away!'

'Hullo, dear.' Mum gives me a quick hug. Without preamble she says, 'I was so embarrassed, the woman sitting next to me on the plane was reading your book. On her Kindle!' An added affront, as Mum doesn't approve of e-readers.

'How did you know it was my book?'

'She kept bursting into laughter and she finally apologised and said "I'm terribly sorry but I'm reading this really funny book. It's called *Love Bytes*".'

'Did you tell her the author was your daughter?'

'Of course not!'

'Why were you embarrassed then?'

'Just thinking of her reading all those sex scenes was enough. I know it's old-fashioned of me, but I happen to believe sex is a private matter between two people, not to be shared with the whole world.'

'It's not *my* sex life in the book,' I point out. 'Anyway, that's why so many of your generation were unhappy with their sex lives. Because sex wasn't talked about, people didn't know what to do about it.'

'Anyway,' Mum says, 'sex is such a small part of life; the way everyone carries on these days you'd think it was the only thing that mattered.'

We wait by the baggage carousel for their luggage. Standing beside us is a curvy young blonde in a low-cut blouse and short skirt. I watch Dad's eyes travel up her long, slim legs to the round buttocks hugged by her skirt and to her breasts, like two firm peaches ready to burst out of their skins.

I catch his glance and we both quickly look away. I'm embarrassed to catch him staring but I also feel a stab of pity. Maybe that's why Dad spends so much time playing lawn bowls and golf — to sublimate his sexual urges.

'There it is,' he says. He leaps over, rescues a brown leather suitcase from its journey around the carousel and bears it back triumphantly.

'That's not ours, Frank,' my mother says, lips tight. 'Ours has a red strap.'

The blonde's breasts bounce over, the rest of her following closely behind. She bestows on Dad a dazzling smile. 'I believe that's mine.'

'Terribly sorry,' Dad stammers, handing her the suitcase. She takes it, treats him to another flash of her pearly whites and wiggles away. Dad gives me and Mum a rueful smile before taking his place again in the front row of the carousel audience. My mother rolls her eyes at me as if to say 'Men! Hopeless, aren't they?'

At dinner, when the subject of my book comes up again, Mum remarks, 'All the ladies at the bridge club know you've written a book. I don't know how, because I didn't tell them. Anyway, when they asked me what it was about I just pretended to be very vague. I couldn't tell them, could I?'

She looks around the table. I shrug. 'I don't see why not. But they probably twigged it was about something racy because you didn't want to talk about it.'

Cara grins. 'And they probably went home and bought it straight away on Amazon.'

Mum gives Cara a sharp look. 'That's exactly what they did. It was so embarrassing — we were in the finals of the competition and I had to try and concentrate on the game knowing full well that the other members of my team were in the middle of reading about your...' she glances at Cara and Zac, eating their dinner in angelic innocence, 'adventures.'

I give an exasperated sigh. 'Not *my* adventures, my characters' adventures.'

'It's all the same,' Mum says impatiently. 'Everyone knows that you don't make up those sorts of adventures from your imagination.'

With all these adventures, my book is starting to sound like the *Boys Own Annual.* Zac has a dangerous glint in his eye — I give him a look that says, 'Don't even think about it', and scoop more apple pie and ice cream into his bowl to shut him up.

'It's called sex, Grandma,' Cara says. 'You can say it if you like — Zac and I have seen the "Where Did I Come From" movie several times.'

'This apple pie is delicious,' Dad butts in before Mum can reply. 'Pat, I think you're making far too much of this. You said yourself that Beryl and Agnes enjoyed the book.'

'I think the word they used was "naughty",' Mum says, 'if you could possibly think that denotes enjoyment.'

I catch Dad's eye and spring up to clear away the dishes before I burst out laughing.

'Perhaps they meant naughty in a nice sort of way,' Zac suggests. 'Like "Ooh, you are naughty but I like you!"' this last bit delivered in a falsetto tone.

'I think that's exactly how they meant it,' Dad agrees solemnly.

Mum folds her napkin into a neat square. 'I know this is what you wanted, so I'm glad you've had a book published. I just wish it was about something less revealing.'

'Like gardening?' Cara suggests, all innocence, but I know she's smirking inside.

Mum nods. 'Exactly.'

***

I sink into the couch with my late night snack of toasted sandwiches. I'm basking in the quietness, having dropped my parents at the airport a few hours ago. I love having them visit and they spoil Cara and Zac rotten, but my mother in particular is exhausting to be around. Although she tries hard not to, she can't help giving me advice on everything from how to organise my cupboards more efficiently to cutting down my grocery bill. I'm thankful she's never likely to read my novel; undoubtedly, she'd come up with a list of things to be changed or expunged.

With Zac spending the night at a friend's house and Cara at a party, I'm also enjoying the rare luxury of sitting in front of a silent, blank TV screen. When it's on, which seems to be most of the time with the children around, it dominates the house like a strident overlord and I much prefer it in its present state — humble and inconspicuous.

A car door bangs and a key scrapes in the front door lock. It's only ten-thirty; I wasn't expecting Cara home so soon. The party was a birthday-do for a distant acquaintance, and she only went because she knew local football hero Byron Hartley, whom she has adored from afar for years, would be there.

The front door bursts open and Cara barges in. One look at her face tells me the night was not a success.

'Your book has affected my whole life!'

She flounces into the kitchen and bangs around getting herself a drink of water. I jump up and follow her in.

'What on earth are you talking about?'

She gulps down her water and slams her glass on the bench. 'Even when I'm being chatted up by a hot guy, your book is there, like a big...' She gestures wildly, lost for words, 'ugly blob!'

'You don't mean to tell me someone had my book at the party!'

'They may as well have. I managed to get a chance to talk to Byron, just the two of us, which wasn't easy because he's always got people hanging around him, and we'd only been talking for a couple of minutes and he said, "Oh, you're the chick whose mother wrote that book about internet dating!" So then he spent forever telling me all about his father, who's just separated from his mother, who'd heard about your book so he bought it on Amazon and read it and raved about it! Apparently he's going through a mid-life crisis — I mean, why else would a man read a book about middle-aged women having sex!'

'But if he was reading a book about young women having sex, you'd think he was sleazy,' I point out. 'At least, it's more realistic for someone of his obviously advanced years.'

She gives me one of her looks. It's clear that the idea of a man of that age thinking about sex with anybody is too gross to consider.

'Anyway Bryon thought it was hilarious that his Dad had read your book and by the time he'd finished carrying on about it, some other chick dragged him away and I didn't see him again!'

Her eyes well up with tears. This is the same girl I overheard yesterday on the phone boasting about her Mum who's a 'bestselling author — have you seen the YouTube video?'

'I'm sorry, honey.' I give her shoulder a squeeze. 'I'm sure you'll get another chance to catch up with him. Next time, tell him straight up you're banning books from the conversation.'

Cara smiles up at me through her tears. 'That shouldn't be too hard for him. He's a footballer, after all.'

She's growing up — not so long ago, she would have dismissed my apology and stomped off to her room. A pang hits me — it's not my fault that Bryon paid more attention to my book than he did to Cara, but I'm taking the rap for it anyway.

***

'I wish I'd written a book on gardening.'

I'm beginning to pant. Annie and Myf, with Amy in her jogging buggy, are setting a cracking pace on our walk. The excesses of Christmas and New Year have taken possession of our thighs — mine and Annie's, anyway. Myf always keeps hers firmly under control when it comes to eating.

'It would be a very short book because you don't know anything about gardening,' Myf says.

Amy gurgles her agreement. Propped up in the buggy with her angelic face peering out from her bonnet, she's a miniature Queen Muck, surveying her adoring subjects as her fawning servant pushes her along.

'That's true, but at least my family wouldn't be complaining all the time about how I've embarrassed them.'

'Is Cara still upset about Byron?' Annie asks.

'No, it's Zac this time. It's only two weeks into the school term and already he's being teased. Apparently his arch-enemy Carl Taylor announced in English class that Zac's mother had written a book called *Love Bytes* and could they study it for their assignment? Of course, that went down like a lead balloon with the teacher, but the kids loved it. Zac was mortified, he hates being the centre of attention, especially coming from Carl.'

'Poor thing,' Annie said. 'It's really hard for kids at that age; they hate being singled out. Any minute now my eldest is going to hit adolescence.'

'And to make matters worse, another student, Angie, piped up and said, "my Mum's read it and she said there's a lot of sex in it". So then the class went wild, and since then Carl has never let a chance go by to tease Zac, saying things like, "has Angie given you any love bites lately?" I suspect Zac has a crush on Angie, though of course he'd rather die than admit it.'

Again the pangs of guilt wash over me, not helped by the fact that Zac thinks I'm completely to blame for his anguish. I've tried to offer suggestions on how to deal with Carl (apart from my initial impulse to wrestle him to the ground and tattoo a love bite on his neck with a very sharp instrument), but he cuts me off mid-sentence with, 'Don't worry about it — you wouldn't understand', before stomping into his bedroom and slamming the door.

What I haven't mentioned is that I recently caught him flicking through the pages of my book, after he'd declared several times he had no intention of reading it. Although he's now fourteen, he's still pretending to have no interest in girls or sex, though I don't know who he thinks he's kidding. When I came into the room, he hurriedly put the book down with a look on his face as if I'd just caught him raiding my secret chocolate supply. I knew in an instant he'd been looking for the sex scenes.

'He'll get over it,' Myf says, with the insensitive bravado of a parent who is yet to undergo the adolescent experience. She overtakes a gaggle of grey-haired wanderers, almost mowing them down. She's lethal with a jogging buggy — Annie and I jog a few paces to catch up.

'I appreciate your empathy,' I pant. 'The funny thing is that the only person who's not embarrassed by my book is Jeremy. And out of everyone, he'd have the most reason.'

Jeremy bought an autographed copy at the launch and I'm sure the first thing he did when he arrived home was to leaf anxiously through it to see if he was in it. He must have come to the happy conclusion that he wasn't or chose to ignore the allusions to boring sex and errant husbands. When he phoned me later, he said, 'It was good, Susan, very entertaining.'

Trying to ignore the note of surprise in his voice, I said, 'What did Alison think?'

He hesitated. 'She hasn't read it.' His tone said it all — she had no intention of reading it, even if you offered her all the older married men in the world on a silver platter.

We've slowed down to a crawl to get through the crowd of surf lifesavers milling around the surf club wielding oars and hauling kayaks, about to head down to the beach for training.

'He probably only read the sexy bits,' Myf says, eyeing off a nylon-clad butt sauntering past her.

'Speaking of sex, I've got something to tell you,' Annie says. 'I'm a lesbian.'

I gape at her. I thought by now I'd cease to be surprised by anything Annie does, but I should have guessed it was coming — testing the sexual boundaries is probably the last frontier. It only remains for her to shave her head, become a Buddhist nun and enroll in pole dancing classes for her mid-life transformation to be complete.

'When did this happen?' Myf enquires. As if you're transformed overnight — you go to sleep heterosexual and wake up a lesbian.

'Since I met Terri — that's Terri with an 'I'.'

'How did you meet this Terri with an 'I'?' I ask.

'We met at the Psychic Fair. She was reading my tarot cards and then the Lovers card came up, and she said I was going to meet a beautiful, exotic person who would change my life, and then she looked into my eyes and we both knew it was her!'

'How romantic.' I'm trying not to sound cynical. 'But if she's a psychic, she already knew it was going to happen.'

'Of course she did, but she thought it would be a man. She's only recently left her husband and she's got three little kids, so we haven't had a chance to, you know, do anything much yet in the sexual sense. But that's the nice thing about being with a woman — it's very gentle and sensual, and we can just take our time. I don't have to worry about beard rash, contraception or who's going to sleep on the wet spot.'

'Have you told Richard and the kids?'

'I haven't told the kids yet. I'm waiting for the right opportunity. I didn't have to tell Richard — he guessed. Don't ask me how. He hasn't even met Terri. When we were married, he wouldn't have noticed if I'd had an orgy on the lounge room floor!'

'What did he say?' Myf asks.

'He just looked sort of sad and said, "You're a complete stranger to me. I don't have a clue who you are — maybe I never did." That's probably the most profound thing he's ever said.'

'How could he know who you were when you didn't know yourself?' Myf says.

'Are you any closer to knowing who you are now?' I ask.

'In an existential sense, no.'

'Existential?'

'Oh, didn't I tell you? I've enrolled in a night course in elementary philosophy.'

Thank God it's not pole dancing.

Chapter 23

My mobile phone rings as I'm sitting in the courtyard tapping away on my laptop, a present to myself from my royalties. It's an interstate number I don't recognise. Should I answer it? On the one hand, it'll be a welcome diversion from novel number two, which is not going at all to plan. But on the other hand, it'll probably be another reporter and I'm not sure if I'm up to it.

In the three and a half months since Jules and I created what he calls my 'enhanced marketing plan', I've been inundated with requests for interviews from newspapers, magazines, radio stations and blogs. I've also done author signings at bookstores and talks at libraries and am at the point now where I only get mild nausea before a public appearance instead of a desire to quaff a whole bottle of wine. It's all been like a chaotic dream, the sort you wake up from feeling exhausted. If anyone had told me a few weeks ago that I'd be baulking at a chance to promote my book, I'd have thought they were crazy. But the interviewers tend to ask the same questions and I'm running out of original and witty things to say about my book. And if one more person compares its success to that of *Fifty Shades of Grey*...

I answer the phone anyway.

'Hullo Susan, this is Letitia Duncan from Channel 7. I'm the producer of 'The Breakfast Show'. How are you?'

TV! Holy shit. I try to engage my brain into Serious Author mode.

'Fine, thanks.'

'I've just finished reading your book and I loved it. I can understand why it's been such a hit. Like *Fifty Shades of Grey* all over again.'

I grit my teeth. I'm not being churlish — I really don't mind my book being compared to *Fifty Shades of Grey* if that's what it takes to sell it. Well, all right, I do. Because it's nothing like *Fifty Shades*.

'But without the bondage,' I reply. 'Or the brooding hero. Or the naive heroine.'

She gives a polite laugh. 'Of course. Yours is a much better book, needless to say. Why I'm phoning is we'd love you to appear on our show to talk about your book and its success. I'm sure your many fans would love to get to know you in person.'

The Breakfast Show. National television. No way can I do TV.

Of course I can do TV. I'm a veteran interviewee now. But it's different doing interviews for radio and print media — people aren't watching you. It's not so hard to sound witty and sophisticated; it's a hell of a job to look it. Although at least with TV they do your hair and make-up, and it would be a good excuse to buy a new outfit.

'I'd be delighted. When were you thinking of?' I try to effect an air of nonchalance as if I'll slot it in my diary in between my hairdressing appointment and my gym workout.

'Next week, probably Friday morning.'

'That soon?' I squeak. Only a week to work myself up to it?

'Is that not convenient?'

'Um … that's fine. Are you flying me to Sydney?'

I picture myself being chauffeured in a limousine from the airport to my luxury hotel suite, and then to the TV studio where I sip champagne with the other guests in the green room. Is the green room really green? Or does that refer to the colour of the guests' faces?

Letitia gives a short laugh. 'Sorry to dash your hopes. Cost-cutting measures, I'm afraid. We have a crew in Brisbane who'll be going up your way to do a story on Friday afternoon, so we thought we'd slot you in for the morning. They'll probably arrive at about eight o'clock to get set up.'

'Arrive where?'

'At your house.'

'My house?' I've worked my way up to a screech.

'It's easiest for everyone. Is there a problem?'

No problem. Apart from the embarrassment of the whole world being able to see the evidence of my abysmal housekeeping and non-existent interior decorating skills. I really will have to buy a new quilt. Not that they'll be holding the interview in the bedroom. Or going in there at all, I hope.

'No, my house is fine.' What am I saying? I'll be spending every spare moment over the next few days armed with a cloth, mop and bucket. I'm exhausted just thinking about it.

Letitia rings off, promising me she'll be in touch again in a couple of days to nut out the finer details. I sit staring at the tiny garden bed in front of me, a bunch of tired daisies wilting in the sun. I can see the TV camera panning around my patchy lawn and my pathetic excuse for a garden. The interviewer asking me the usual questions — my inspiration for the book, my own experiences in internet dating, how much of the book is autobiographical and stopping just short of wanting to know my favourite sexual position. This is worse than appearing in public with my pants down; this is appearing in a million lounge rooms across the nation stark naked.

I ring Jules to break the news, but his phone goes to MessageBank. My hand hovers over Martin's number. Should I phone him? I haven't spoken to him since the day I discovered the YouTube video. I'm not sure of the boundaries — technically our professional relationship has ended, at least until I'm ready for him to edit my second novel, whenever that may be. But we're friends, aren't we? At least, I consider we are. But on the other hand I don't want him to think that I'm coming on too strong, that I want something more out of the relationship.

But you do.

All right, in a perfect world, he wouldn't have a partner, and would find me irresistibly sexy and intelligent and warm and funny and all those other relationship buzz words, and would move up from New South Wales to be closer to me ... But as we don't live in a perfect world, I don't fancy him.

My hand is still hovering. I feel as if I'm back in high school, this 'should I' or 'shouldn't I' angst. Isn't it supposed to be easier when you're an adult?

Adult. Of course. Adults ring their friends when they have good news. And they don't automatically assume that their friends have a secret desire to race them off.

My finger taps on 'Martin mobile' before I can change my mind. It rings a few times and I'm just about to hang up when he answers.

'Hi! Did I catch you at a bad time?'

'No, not really.' He sounds distracted. Oh shit, I've interrupted him and Simone doing the deed. Or having an intimate coffee. I knew this was a bad idea.

'It's nothing important. I can ring back later.'

'It's fine, really. You caught me unawares. We're on holidays, lying on a beautiful secluded beach soaking up the sun.'

'Lucky you.'

I was right. About the nookie. But would he have answered the phone? Maybe they were just thinking about it.

'I'll just quickly tell you my news. I've been asked to appear on "The Breakfast Show".'

'Way to go! There's no stopping you now!'

'I think there'll be plenty stopping me when I'm in the hot seat with the TV cameras panning in on me.'

'You'll be fine. Just pretend you're having a cosy chat in your lounge room with an old friend. When's the big day?'

I tell him the details, briefly. 'Anyway, I'll let you get back to slaving away under a hot sun. And apologise to Simone for me for the interruption.'

A slight pause. 'She's not here. She couldn't get away from work. It's just Emily and me.'

'Oh. Well, I hope you two have a wonderful holiday.'

He sounded different, with a distance that had nothing to do with kilometres. Did I overstep the mark after all?

Chapter 24

Tony Benveneto, national TV interviewer, is sitting in my courtyard. Clean-cut and dark-haired with rimless glasses that give him an earnest air, he leans back in one of my plastic outdoor chairs with his legs crossed, sipping a cup of coffee and looking as if he's just popped in for morning tea.

If I'd known they were going to film the interview outside, I would have bought a new outdoor setting — a frosted glass-topped table with modern chrome chairs and colourful cushions, something appropriate for national television. I've spent the past week cleaning every inch of the house and have even bought a new leather lounge suite for the living room. Then when the technicians called around yesterday afternoon to do a reconnaissance, they informed me they'd be filming in the courtyard. At four-thirty it was too late to rush out and buy new furniture.

Looking on the bright side, I guess the green plastic furniture, minus the two amputee chairs shoved hurriedly into the garden shed, will lend an air of homely ordinariness to the scene. 'She's a successful author,' my readers will say admiringly, 'but still so down to earth.'

Cameraman Mike and sound technician Andy are setting up the equipment. Tony's darting nervous glances through the glass sliding doors into the house. I can't say I blame him.

My small lounge room is overflowing with people and commotion — it's just as well the interview is being prerecorded, as they'll probably need to do some judicious editing. As soon as I told Jules about my exposure on national television, he sent out invitations to everyone to come and witness the spectacle, like the throwing of the Christians to the lions.

'Everyone' constitutes himself and Victoria ('we've kissed and made up,' Jules whispers to me, 'she's bored with her pantry.'), Myf and Amy, Annie and Terri, and Terri's eldest child, a four-year-old boy burdened with the name of Joachim. The other two are in day care, but Joachim wasn't able to go due to his runny nose. Myf, having already denied his request to 'pat the baby', is doing everything in her power, apart from putting a gas mask on Amy, to prevent her being anywhere in the vicinity of him.

The TV is blaring through the hum of incessant chattering, and woven through the texture of noise is a single dominant thread of childish voice. 'Mummy, I *have* to have a Chupa Chups!'

'Mummy doesn't have any Chupa Chups, Joachim.' Terri's low, husky voice drifts out into the courtyard. 'You can have some natural, no- sugar snakes.'

Terri is tall and willowy with long auburn hair, green eyes that remind me spookily of a cat and a flawless complexion. With her long peasant skirt, cheesecloth blouse and beaded headband around her forehead, she appears to be suspended in a seventies time warp. A time warp in another galaxy — maybe it's to do with being a psychic, but she seems to be in a permanent out-of-body state. She floats rather than walks, and exudes an aura of calm serenity, totally unperturbed by her surroundings, including the antics of her child. Whatever she's on, I want some — desperately.

Joachim's whining is revving up — any four-year-old worth his salt knows that natural, no-sugar snakes are a fob-off. It's drowned out by a sudden ear-splitting shout — 'You'll love the new Ab Sculptor — rock hard abs in just 30 days! Two monthly payments of $49.95!'

'Joachim, please give Mummy the remote control,' Terri says, in the same tone of voice as if asking him to pass the butter.

I dart a glance at Tony. 'I'll go and tell them to keep the noise down.'

I totter over to the doorway, my heels sinking into the grass. 'Hey guys, can you keep it down to a dull roar?'

Someone's managed to wrestle the remote control from Joachim and muted the TV, where the Ab Man is silently flexing his admirable torso. Amy, who's been asleep in her pram, is startled awake by the silence. She opens her mouth and lets forth a most un-Amy-like bellow. Jules, who's fussing about in my kitchen organising morning tea for the audience, nearly drops the coffee pot. Victoria is slicing bun loaf with an expression that says, 'I'm destined for higher pursuits and only doing this under sufferance'.

Jules comes over and pats me on the shoulder. He's wearing my 'Mother Knows Best' apron, depicting a 1950s housewife brandishing a wooden spoon with a glint in her eye, as if anticipating other uses for it apart from cooking. 'I've got it all under control. You go and get yourself ready for your big moment.'

'I *am* ready,' I reply indignantly. I check myself out in the hall mirror. It's only nine am but on this unseasonably hot March day I'm already perspiring in my black and cream pantsuit. I've decided the long pants and high-heeled sandals (borrowed from Myf — she calls them her 'skin flick shoes') are necessary in case the camera does a full body pan. I wear so much black now I've thrown my Wonderpants away that I'm in danger of being mistaken for a middle-aged Goth.

I've slapped on my red 'kiss-me-if-you-dare' lipstick and lots of mascara in case I decide to do the eyelash fluttering bit. My hair wasn't behaving itself until Annie arrived, and with some mousse and a few flicks of the comb, it's been blow-dried into submission. Forget the feminist principles today. When it comes to selling my book, I'll do whatever is necessary even if it means pouting and fluttering my eyelashes at Tony Whatshisname.

Who am I kidding? There'll be a million people watching me but there's only one person I want to impress, and he'll be sitting at the breakfast table playing happy families with Simone and Emily.

From behind me, an arm wraps itself around my neck. 'Good luck, Mum.'

Cara has skipped a university tutorial to watch the filming, and has been viewing the preliminary proceedings with an air of bemused superiority. It's definitely a step up from eye-rolling disdain.

I turn around and give her a hug. 'Thanks. I appreciate you taking the morning off uni.'

She shrugs. 'It was only Basic Constructs of Sociology Theory. And Mum, please don't say anything embarrassing about sex. Some of my friends might see it.'

'I'll bear that in mind. Before I open my mouth, I'll apply the "Would Cara's Friends Approve" test.'

She smiles. 'Thanks.' Her jeans pocket tinkles and she whips out her phone. 'Gotta take this call.'

I totter back outside. I'm not used to heels as high as these and I feel like a circus act on stilts. Zac has wandered out from the refuge of his bedroom and is watching Mike set up his camera. He's ecstatic about being given a day off school, so the occasion is irrelevant — I could be demonstrating Origami for Beginners for all he cares. I'm sure he'll be keeping his fingers crossed that none of his classmates will be watching 'The Breakfast Show' on the day my interview is shown.

Tony beckons me over. 'We're nearly ready to start.'

'Am I able to see the list of questions first?'

Tony gives me a look that says, 'Who do you think you are? Julia Roberts?'

'I don't have a list. There're no trick questions — just the usual ones you've probably been asked dozens of times already. It's very informal — just relax and pretend we're having a friendly chat.'

'You'll be okay, Mum,' Zac pipes up. 'Just don't crack any jokes, especially the one about the priest and the stripper.'

'That sounds like good advice,' Tony says gravely.

Final Lesson from Mother to Son. Take note of the title of this book — lessons from mother to son, not vice versa. If you can't resist the urge to give advice to your mother, at least base it on some semblance of reality, not on some spurious joke she told once when she was slightly tipsy (even if it was at a christening) and which has no relevance to the current situation.

At my request, Zac goes inside to inform everyone that shooting is about to begin. I take my seat in a plastic chair opposite Tony. We're both sitting at an angle to the sun so we don't have to squint into it, with a backdrop consisting of my only tree, a tall eucalypt, a few straggly ferns and my clothes line folded back against the fence.

Mike is standing beside Tony with his camera pointing towards me, and Andy is standing beside me holding a long pole with an arm attached, on the end of which is a large blob of fur. It's a microphone, dangled above my head in my peripheral vision, so that as I sit there waiting for the action to begin, I have the disconcerting impression of an oversize hairy centipede hovering above me.

'Okay, we're ready to roll,' Tony says. 'The intro will be done in the studio, so we'll get straight into the interview.'

I cross my legs demurely, put my hands in my lap, and lean back slightly in my chair, trying to emulate a relaxed, I've-done-this-a-million-times-before air.

Tony leans forward and bestows on me a brilliant smile, with an expression that says 'I'm ready to be enthralled'.

'Susan, your book has been described not so much as Mommy porn, as *Fifty Shades of Grey* was, but Mommy erotica. Would you agree with that?'

I look over at him then to the camera, then over to the sliding glass doors, where Jules, Victoria, Myf, Annie and Terri are standing, — crowded together in the doorway — smiling encouragement at me. Cara is hovering in the background looking anxious and Zac has retreated to a corner of the courtyard, out of the line of fire of my priest/stripper jokes.

There's an expectant hush as everyone waits for my answer, and as I open my mouth, a plaintive cry from inside the house pierces the silence. 'Mummy, I need to do a wee-wee!'

My mind goes completely blank and I look helplessly at Tony, but he is too busy trying not to look annoyed at the interruption to realise my predicament. He smiles encouragingly at me and after an embarrassing silence, I murmur, 'I'm sorry, I've forgotten the question.' I look at Mike. 'Can we cut this?'

Tony stifles a sigh. 'This isn't the movies; we don't do cuts. Just keep going— we'll edit it later. I'll ask the question again.'

He does.

'That's an interesting question, Tony,' I reply earnestly, as if I've never heard it before in my life. I rack my brains to think of an original answer but draw a blank. 'I think that like pornography, erotica is in the eye of the beholder. I didn't set out to write an erotic book, I just tried to be truthful about sex, but if readers find it erotic, I'll take it as a compliment.'

Not exactly mind-blowing stuff, but Tony is nodding sagely as if I've just revealed the meaning of life. This gives me confidence to make a reasonably good fist of the next few questions. As I'm in the middle of explaining that my book is only loosely based on my own experiences of internet dating and that indeed the four main characters have far more interesting sex lives than mine, the front gate of the courtyard clicks open and the lawn mowing man strolls in. He's brandishing his whipper snipper and whistling at the top of his tuneless voice. I've completely forgotten he's due today and of course this would have to be the one day he arrives on time. He stops dead in his tracks when he sees the TV cameras.

'Oops, sorry!' he says cheerfully. 'Is this one of them reality TV shows?'

Tony is giving the appearance of keeping his cool, though I notice a light sheen of perspiration has appeared on his smooth face.

'Sorry to disappoint you,' I say. 'And we're not doing "Backyard Blitz" either, otherwise you could stay. Can you come back on Monday?'

'No worries, guvnor,' he says, saluting me with his whipper snipper. He strides out the front gate, still whistling. Why do some people have to put on a silly accent the minute they see a TV camera?

Tony draws a deep breath. 'Only one more question.' I can see the 'Thank God' think bubble above his head. He fixes me with a dazzling smile. 'And the question I'm sure all your fans are asking — will there be a sequel?'

I give what I hope is an inviting yet enigmatic smile. 'Well, Tony, they'll just have to wait and see.'

'Don't keep us all in suspense for too long. It's been a pleasure talking to you today, Susan Hamilton, author of bestselling novel *Love Bytes*.' He picks up a copy of the book from the table beside him and holds it up in front of him, beaming.

'That's it,' he says with an almost audible sigh of relief. He switches off his smile, digs a handkerchief out of his pocket and mops his brow. 'You can wait there while we do the noddy,' he tells me.

'Noddy?'

The first thing that springs to my mind is Big Ears, and I'm wondering whether the stress and the heat have got the better of both Tony and me.

Mike explains it to me. 'We only have one TV camera and it was filming you during the interview. But when we show the segment we also need footage of the interviewer as well, so now we're going to do a shoot of Tony asking the questions again.'

'Don't worry,' he adds hastily, seeing the expression on my face, 'you don't have to answer them again.'

That still doesn't explain where Noddy comes into it, but I decide not to pursue it any further. Mike moves his camera next to me, and angles it in Tony's direction and Andy moves his pole next to Tony and dangles the hairy centipede above his head.

'Shoot,' says Mike.

Tony leans forward in his chair, looks me straight in the eye and says, 'Susan, your book has been described not so much as Mommy porn, as *Fifty Shades of Grey* was, but Mommy erotica. Would you agree with that?'

I know I'm not supposed to answer, but he's looking straight at me and I feel rude just staring back at him. After a few seconds, he nods and after staring at me intently for a few more seconds, he nods again. Now I know why they call it the 'noddy' and I can feel the giggles rising up inside me.

He proceeds to question two, repeated word for word, and again nods at me periodically during the ensuing silence. I notice that he varies his nods — sometimes it might be quite an emphatic nod, other times a subtle inclination of the head, all the time staring into my eyes with a 'gosh this is so fascinating' expression. I feel a sudden desire to poke my tongue out at him or make a face just to see his reaction.

By question four, I can't contain my giggles any more and they surface as a kind of snort. Tony falters for just a moment and then continues his question — I can't help but admire such single-minded self-control. I have to look away because if I'm forced to continue watching him nodding sagely to my replies of utter silence, I'm going to end up with a serious case of hysterics.

I give an inward sigh of relief as he asks the final question, 'Is there going to be a sequel?' Before I can give my usual non-reply, a voice from inside the house says, 'That's *so* typical, you're doing a shoot for *Better Homes and Gardens* and you don't invite me.'

In the doorway leading out onto the courtyard, standing head and shoulders above everyone else, is a gorgeous man who looks awfully like Max, but it can't be, because Max is in Sydney making love to his Porsche.

Jules whips around and turns so white that he not only looks as if he's seen a ghost, he *is* the ghost.

'You absolute fucking bitch,' he says in a low voice. But the tremor in it gives him away and the next thing he and Max are clasped together and hugging so tightly you can see the muscles flexing in their arms. Everyone is spellbound — Tony, Mike and Andy are frozen in a tableau of astonishment and I have a lump in my throat the size of a small boulder.

'Mummy,' Joachim says in high, piercing tones, 'that man just said a rude word.'

Chapter 25

My face is warm and I'm sticky with perspiration. I wrench open my eyes and am almost blinded by the sunlight streaming in through my bedroom window. I focus on my bedside clock — 9.15. Better get up, I've got a hell of a mess to clean up from the after-filming-welcome-home-Max party yesterday.

I throw off the bedcovers and ease myself out of bed. I'm exhausted, as if I've just gone ten rounds in the boxing ring. Face up to it, Susan, you're too old for parties. But this was a special occasion — it's not every day you become a TV star and your best friend is reunited with his lover. Trust Max to choose that particular moment to turn up, like a long-lost character making his dramatic reappearance in a soap opera. Max had gone to Jules's work first, then to his apartment and then had logically assumed he would find him at my house.

I throw on a sarong and proceed gingerly down the stairs. The kitchen and living room are spotless — all the empty bottles and half-eaten dishes of food have been cleared away, the dishes are washed and drying on the rack, and all surfaces are sparkling clean. It looks like the 'after' picture for Spray 'n' Wipe. The only thing that looks out of place is Zac in the kitchen making toast.

'Have the cleaning fairies been here?' I enquire.

'Jules and Max did it,' Zac informs me. 'I helped too.'

Seeing the incredulous look on my face, he adds, 'Sort of. I showed them where the garbage bin is.'

There's a note propped up against the electric jug.

'Morning, beautiful. How's your head? Thanks for the loan of your couch. Max and I are off to Sydney this afternoon — will call around before we leave. Love, Jules.'

My heart sinks slowly like an elevator going down, until it lands at my feet. The scene last night comes flooding back to me – Max sobbing into his champagne with happiness and Jules saying, 'Don't think for one second that you're ever going anywhere without me again.'

'No way,' Max hiccupped. 'I'm taking you back to Sydney with me – tomorrow!'

Jules looked like a kid who's just been promised a trip to Disneyland. 'Really? What will your father say?'

'He'll probably set the Rottweilers on you,' sniffled Max, 'but I don't care!'

The day isn't going to get any better. I throw a couple of Panadol down my throat and make myself a cup of coffee.

'Mum,' Zac says, muffled by a mouthful of toast. I look daggers at him, daring him to mention anything about a hangover.

'Are you upset that Jules is going to Sydney with Max?'

The question takes me by surprise — Zac has never shown any interest in my emotions before.

'Yes, I am upset, and surprised too. It was such a spur-of-the-moment decision. I'll miss him.' A lot.

Zac gets up, leaving his dirty plate and a puddle of milk on the table. 'Don't worry, you've still got me,' he says cheerfully as he disappears up the stairs.

I take my coffee out to the courtyard and sit in the shade of my solitary tree. Disjointed fragments from yesterday flash through my mind like movie trailers. The TV crew made a quick getaway despite my invitation to stay for a drink, obviously not wishing to spend a moment longer with this crazy bunch of people. I remember Victoria's face as Jules did the introductions — 'Victoria, this is Max' — and her small, firm buttocks wiggling furiously within the confines of her tight red miniskirt as she stormed out. Myf hugging Amy close to her as she bopped away to Credence Clearwater, and my realisation that she's finally found the love of her life. Terri doing everyone's Tarot card readings and Max becoming even more emotional when his cards revealed The Fool, until Terri explained that this is a good card and he is about to make a new start in life. Annie sitting on the floor with Joachim fast asleep on her lap, drifting back into the motherhood role despite her concerted efforts to add other dimensions to her life. Cara returning later from the movies to the party fallout and instead of the usual eye rolling and attitude, coming over and wrapping her arms around me and whispering in my ear, 'Congratulations, Mum, I'm proud of you', causing my throat to swell and my eyes to water.

And the phone call. How could I forget the phone call? We were well into the celebrations when my mobile phone rang. It was in the kitchen and Max, who was closest to it, answered it and brought it over to me.

'It's a man,' he hissed dramatically, 'I didn't catch the caller ID.'

I took the phone and headed outside to the early evening coolness, away from the noise. After three glasses of the expensive French champagne Jules had insisted on buying, I was feeling very relaxed.

'Sounds like a fun party,' Martin said. My heart did a high jump right up to my throat and back again. "I was ringing to see how you fared in your few moments of stardom, but obviously everything went well.'

After our last strained phone conversation, his tone was more relaxed though still with an air of reserve.

'It did, apart from the odd disaster. Max turned up unexpectedly and Jules is absolutely over the moon, and now we're celebrating. I wish you were here.'

'So do I — it's a long time since I've been to a party.'

'I don't mean I wish you were here because you're missing out on a great party, I wish you were here because ... it would be even more fun with you.'

The words were out of my mouth before I could stop them. You idiot, why did you say that? I wanted to pluck the words right out of the air and stuff them back down my throat. There was silence at the other end of the phone, and my insides knotted together with embarrassment.

'Yes, it would be fun,' Martin said softly. Did I discern a note of wistfulness in his voice? Probably not. There was another silence then I said, 'Well, I'd better get back....' and Martin said at the same time, 'I'll let you get back' and we both laughed awkwardly.

'Go and do your hostess thing,' Martin said. 'I'm glad it went well. I'll wait with bated breath for your TV debut.'

A wave of embarrassment floods over me again as I recall the conversation. Martin must think I'm dumb or desperate, or both, to practically throw myself at him when I know he's got a partner. I go back inside and clatter around in the kitchen making a batch of muffins — anything to take my mind off it.

***

At two o'clock, Jules and Max turn up on my doorstep, both looking fresh and bright in their jeans and colourful shirts — Max in daffodil yellow and Jules as usual in hot pink. As I survey the sleek, curvaceous symmetry of Max's black Porsche parked in my driveway, I can almost understand his passion for it.

I persuade them to come in for coffee and muffins before they leave. I watch Jules as he and Max chat excitedly about their trip and his plans to break into the advertising industry in Sydney. His hair is flattened down with mousse and his eyes are shining. He's leaving behind his whole life — his job, his friends, his immaculate designer apartment with ocean views and everything in it he cherishes, his Waterford crystal, Picasso prints, antique chairs, silk cushions — to go and live with Max in a one-bedroom apartment in the heart of Sydney, with views of lots of other one-bedroom apartments. I want to say something sensible like 'don't you think you should wait a while and think it through?' but I don't want to spoil his excitement.

Jules reaches over and puts his hand over mine. 'Don't look so sad. I'm coming back in a few weeks to collect my stuff and put my unit on the market.'

I can't help myself. 'Isn't that a bit rash? The market's not so good at the moment. Why don't you just rent it out for a while?'

Jules shrugs. 'Maybe. But I've been feeling like a change of scenery, anyhow.'

First I've heard of it. But I smile and blink away my tears. And far too soon we're standing on the doorstep saying our goodbyes. He wraps his arms tightly around me. His body, with all its familiar curves and angles, presses into my embrace, his freshly shaven cheeks smooth against mine. 'I love you, Susie,' he says in my ear, 'I'll miss you.'

'I love you, too.' A hot stream of tears spills out. I squeeze my eyes shut to try and stop them but they have a will of their own. In another time and place things could have been different.

Then they're driving off, grinning as they wave back at me with the breeze ruffling their hair. They look like two young boys setting off on an adventure. I guess they are, in a way.

I wander back inside. I need something to fill the enormous chasm that has just appeared in my life. I can feel a Tim Tam binge coming on. I grab the packet out of my secret chocolate supply, go up to my bedroom and turn on the TV. There's an old Chuck Norris western on, typical Saturday afternoon fare. Instead of Chuck Norris, I see images of Jules. Jules and I drinking cocktails at the Blue Note Bar, with me fending off aggressive women who want to take him home because 'he's so sweet', the two of us plunging fully dressed into the surf in an August westerly wind because we dared each other, lunching at the Surf Club and checking out the lifesavers in their skimpy trunks, Jules cooking me his special secret recipe omelette, he and I laughing till we cried over some pointless joke that tickled our fancy, and crying until we laughed over broken hearts and shattered dreams.

At five o'clock Cara arrives home. She bursts into my bedroom shouting 'Guess what, Mum?' and stops when she sees my face.

'What's wrong?'

'Nothing — I'm just feeling sad because of Jules leaving.'

'Oh.' She's dying to tell me her news but doesn't want to appear unsympathetic.

'Well, come on, what's so exciting? Has Byron finally asked you out?'

She looks crestfallen. Oops, I've guessed it and spoilt her moment.

'He has, actually. He's taking me out to dinner tonight. I can't believe that I'm finally going out with him — it's taken him two years to even notice me!'

"I think he's a total loser.'

Cara looks at me with astonishment.

'To have waited two years before asking you out! I hope you let him know how lucky he is to be taking you out at all.'

'That's such a mother thing to say. But thanks anyway,' she adds. After spending almost an hour in the bathroom doing multiple clothes changes that would put any supermodel to shame, she opts for the classic hipster jeans and midriff top look. When Byron arrives to pick her up, she yells out, 'Bye, I'm going!' and disappears out the front door in a cloud of perfume and hair gel.

I look out my bedroom window and see Byron getting out of his car as Cara goes out to meet him. He's tall, with sandy hair and plenty of muscle — 'buff', as Cara calls it. Not bad. He kisses Cara then opens the car door for her. Nice manners as well — even better. I could go for this Byron myself.

God, what am I thinking — lusting after my daughter's boyfriend! Get a grip! The car roars off into the distance and the silence wraps itself around me once more. It's 6 pm and I'm alone again. Zac has already gone to his father's place for the weekend. Alone again, naturally. Isn't that a song? Gilbert O'Sullivan, I think.

There are few things worse than being alone on a Saturday night when you don't want to be. I know that if I ring Annie or Myf they'd gladly invite me to join in with whatever they're doing, but they both have partners and families (or at least Myf has a part-time partner in Rob, who lives alone but asks her to marry him at least twice a week), and I don't want to intrude on their lives. It's too late to arrange coffee or drinks with any of my casual acquaintances and anyway, I'm not in the mood for superficial chit-chat.

I'm tempted to phone Martin, just to hear the sound of his voice, but what ostensible reason could I have for ringing him at home on a Saturday night? And after my last outburst, I feel I should redeem myself by keeping our conversation purely on a business level. I go upstairs to my office and activate my computer screen, which is in stand-by mode. Page 100 of *Love Hurts,* the sequel to *Love Bytes,* springs to life, glowing mockingly at me. After several false starts, I'm finally into the flow; but it's the last thing I feel like doing at the moment.

I have to get out of the house before I go crazy. I drive down to the Mooloolaba Spit and get into the queue at the fish and chips shop. A teenage boy and girl in front of me are mauling each other like a pair of playful cubs. I feel like throwing a bucket of cold water over them. When the girl with the greasy hair and flushed face yells out 'Number sixty-nine!' (please God, stop it — the irony is killing me!) I take my packet of fish and chips for one to a seat overlooking the beach. As I absorb myself in the comfort of ingesting large quantities of fat and salt, I watch the darkness spread over the sky like a huge ink stain and listen to the slapping of the waves on the sand.

There's a young couple lying on the beach in front of me entwined around each other like vines. He's got one hand up the back of her shirt and she's giggling. They're oblivious to the world around them. This was a bad idea — everywhere I go people are in pairs. Jules has Max, Annie has Terri, Myf has Rob, if and when she decides she wants him, this couple have each other. A conspiracy of coupledom. Maybe I'll make that the title of my next book.

The trouble with self-pity is that it becomes boring after a while, particularly when you have no one to share it with. I need to do something to cheer myself up. On the way home I call into the DVD rental store and hire out *When Harry Met Sally*, with Meg Ryan and Billy Crystal, which never ceases to make me cry.

I slot it into my DVD player and prop myself up in bed with pillows, the packet of Tim Tams beside me. At 10 pm, I wake up with a sore neck, an unhappy stomach and an almost empty packet of Tim Tams. But worst of all, I fell asleep before my favourite scene in the movie where Meg Ryan fakes an orgasm in the restaurant.

Speaking of orgasms, it's been a while since I've had one. Maybe that's what I need. Fred has been languishing in the back of my cupboard, probably sulking from lack of attention. I haul him out, strip off and get to work. But it's hard going and I'm not feeling any sensations. I fantasise that I'm Meg Ryan and Fred is Billy Crystal but that doesn't do it for me — Fred lacks a certain je ne sais quoi. So I try George Clooney, then Johnny Depp, but still nothing.

Then I picture Martin seducing me on my beautiful new quilt with candlelight, incense and Frank Sinatra crooning in the background, slowly undressing me, caressing me from my toes to the top of my head with his fingers and his tongue, finding every little crevice and hollow in my body ... and then it happens. Sharp and intense, then it's over and I'm limp with exhaustion. I look at Fred, whom I've cast aside on the bed now that I'm finished with him. He's looking quite unmoved by the whole experience.

'The problem is,' I tell him, 'you're like a slice of Chocolate Obsession — delicious at the time but still leaves me feeling unsatisfied. Let's face it, Fred, you're just a big prick.'

Chapter 26

Who turned the toaster setting to eight? Cursing loudly, I pluck the two slices of charcoal toast from the toaster and rush around opening doors and windows before the fire alarm goes off. To me, it's perfectly reasonable to expect that when I stumble into the kitchen in the morning, still half-asleep, the setting on the toaster will be where I left it last time. But with two teenagers in the house, there's no such thing as reasonable expectations.

I fling the toast into the kitchen bin on top of the broken pieces of the coffee plunger that I dropped on the floor and smashed a few minutes ago. The day's not off to a good start, and I've only been out of bed for half an hour. I make myself a cup of tea, a poor substitute for coffee as it doesn't give me the necessary caffeine hit, and trudge upstairs to the study to read through the final draft of my article for *Health and Beauty* magazine, which is due tomorrow.

The funny thing is, I don't need to continue freelance writing — from a financial point of view. After my appearance on 'The Breakfast Show' (which I watched, cringing all the way through), the sales were even more frenzied and I've now officially hit the 5 million mark. It's unbelievable that 5 million people worldwide have read my book. It also means that I've earned over 10 million dollars.

It still seems like a dream that I'll wake up from any minute – the zeros on paper haven't translated into reality yet. Most of the money is still in the bank, despite Cara and Zac's pleas for a red Lotus, a penthouse apartment with a pool table and a jacuzzi, and Baskin Robbins ice-cream every day. Admittedly, I've paid off the mortgage on my town house and bought Cara and myself each a new car — practical, economical Mazdas. It's true that old habits die hard. The only luxury I've promised the children is a trip to Europe when I can find the time from the endless rounds of interviews, dodging people I don't want to speak to and writing my next novel.

Despite the fact that I could live comfortably off my earnings for the rest of my life even if I never sold another book, I keep thinking the bubble will burst, and I'll wake up one morning and find it's all just been a wonderful dream — and that I'm still a freelance hack trying to make a living. I don't want to cut off all my ties with my contacts in case I need them in the future. So I continue to write, albeit now I can be a lot more selective about the articles I write. Besides, what else can I do? Writing fulfills me in a way that nothing else does.

After perusing my article 'Fifty Ways to Look Sexy When You're Fifty', for which I had to do a mountain of research, I'm still not happy with it. And in a few years I'll undoubtedly be searching for it so I can take my own advice. To give my mind a break, I log into Amazon to read my latest reviews. I've got hundreds now, most of them rated four or five stars, saying things like 'sexy, hilarious romp', ' makes you laugh and cry at the same time,' 'a must for anyone who's ever done online dating' and 'the sort of book you can curl up with a glass of wine and a box of chocolates'.

The most recent review is someone called 'Lit Lover' who gives it 2 stars, with the comment, 'Ms Hamilton's characters are sketchy, her plot is thin and her humour is sometimes laboured. But who am I to judge, I'm a male under forty. This is chick lit for the over forties, and all the women in my office loved it.'

I've had a few similar reviews and they do hurt even though I try desperately not to let them.

'The more reviews you get, the better your ranking,' Martin told me over the phone, months ago, when I first moaned to him about it. 'Don't worry about the negative reviews — everyone gets them. They won't stop people from buying your book. And it also goes towards proving the credibility of your reviews — that you're not paying people to say good things about your book.'

For God's sake, harden up, I tell myself. You've sold 5 million copies of your book and you're upset about a 2-star review? Obviously he's in the minority. I log out of Amazon and check my emails. I've had to create a new email address specifically for *Love Bytes* correspondence as my normal inbox was becoming too clogged with the hundreds of emails landing there every day. Fans, bloggers, journalists, people asking me the weirdest things, from budding writers begging me to read their manuscripts to the owner of an online sex aids business asking me if I'd endorse a new range of S & M accessories.

And men! Hundreds of them— wanting to take me out, wine and dine me, marry me — even offering me financial advice. Some of them are much more down to earth in their requests. I've offered Myf my rejects (which is all of them), but she wasn't amused. She's lost her sense of humour since she's become a mother. I wait for my emails to finish downloading. Four hundred and sixty since yesterday. Groan. I'm definitely hiring a personal assistant.

I check my eMatch emails. Not that I've had any promising prospects lately and my enthusiasm for the internet dating scene has waned considerably. But there's always that small ray of hope glimmering faintly on the horizon. Lose sight of that and I may as well join a nunnery.

Sure enough, Support@eMatch tells me I have two admirers who have sent me kisses. The first is Callmebigboy — undoubtedly another case of exaggeration of assets. I click into his profile, and find he is a 50-year-old engineer, not bad looking, but he's used no punctuation whatsoever — I'm sure it's from ignorance and not a desire to be avant-garde — and the only books he reads are Westerns and comics. Two big crosses.

The second one is from Lovebytes, which immediately intrigues me. This is either an unbelievable coincidence or it's from someone I know. I haven't changed anything on my profile. I'm still the passionate, epicurean skinny-dipping babe with the undulating hips, and there is no mention of my book. Maybe this is Jules's idea of a joke.

I click into the profile of Lovebytes.

Body type: average

Eye colour: brown

Hair colour: light Brown

Smoke: no

Drink: social

Have children: one — 8 years

Want children: no

Ethnic background: Australian

Religion: none

Occupation: professional

Education level: degree/diploma

Political persuasion: not stated

Vegetarian: no

Personality type: social

Sign of the Zodiac: Sagittarius

Music: I love all kinds of music, from rock'n'roll to jazz to contemporary rock, but most of all, I like music you can slow dance to in a darkened room when there's just the two of you.

Reading: I enjoy a wide variety of books, particularly contemporary literature. One of my favourite contemporary novels is *Love Bytes*, by Susan Hamilton, which I found very funny and moving. My favourite pastime is to relax in the spa bath with that special someone, a glass of champagne, and a funny, sexy book, although how much reading I'd do is debatable...

Movies: I admit to being a movie fanatic and love nothing more than a night out at the movies with my lady, sitting in the back row holding hands and munching on Jaffas together. I love Billy Connolly (I've been told I look like him but also that I'm better looking) and I also enjoy romantic comedies — anything with Meg Ryan is a winner.

Sport: I don't have a lot of time for organised sport, however I do enjoy swimming in the surf, even a spot of skinny dipping with my lover, although I don't mind at all if she's not skinny. I also love long walks on the beach together, and sitting on the sand dunes eating fish and chips and watching the sun go down. I'm always keen to try new sports, particularly contact sports, both outdoor and indoor...

I'm recently separated with an 8-year-old daughter. I have a good sense of humour and I love women, the first quality being a necessary pre-requisite for the second.

(joking, of course). I am looking for a woman with passion and energy who loves music and dancing, and if she does belly dancing, even better. She also has to possess intelligence and humour, and if she wants to cook up a storm for me that's fine, however if she would prefer a gourmet meal to be lovingly prepared for her while she relaxes with a mango daiquiri, I do a very passable imitation of the Naked Chef.

If you'd like to get to know me better, I'd love to hear from you.

There's no photo but I don't need one. I re-read the profile at least six more times, savouring each sentence as I try to make it sink into my befuddled brain. A warm glow slowly suffuses my body, starting from my toes, lingering in certain areas along the way, right up to my head. God, I hope this is not a menopausal hot flush.

'Yes! Yes!! YES!!!!' I jump up from my chair, bound down the stairs to the living room, whack my Peter Allen CD into the player and fast forward to 'I Go to Rio'. Then I pick up the nearest available thing to hug — my happy plant, which has been looking a little sad lately, due to lack of water and attention.

'When my baby, when my baby smiles at me, I go to Rio!' I yell at 100 decibels, to make myself heard over Peter Allen. I hug the plant close to me as I swing it around, dancing in circles and swinging my hips suggestively, clasping it more tightly against me to avert dirt spillage as I execute the occasional dip and turn.

As the last vibrant piano chords fade away, I turn around to see Cara and Byron standing in the front doorway. I have no idea how long they've been there. Cara is looking as if she's just discovered me having it off on the floor with the postman. Byron is sporting a huge grin.

Cara nudges him. 'Come on.'

As they turn and walk out, I hear Byron saying, 'Your Mum is so cool.'

Chapter 27

This is undoubtedly the craziest and most irrational thing I've ever done in my life. And when I think back over some of the things I've done, that's saying something. The tarmac rushes past my window as the plane gathers speed. It gives a jolt as it leaves the ground and rises in the air and I feel a corresponding jolt of excitement in my stomach.

I'm going to Sydney to meet a man who sent me a virtual kiss by email, who doesn't even know I'm coming. I'm going to surprise him, and I only hope it's a welcome surprise.

It wasn't my idea. After my performance with the pot plant, I phoned Jules in a lather of nervousness and exhilaration.

'That's great news! I always said you two were a good match. When did he break up with his partner?'

'I don't know. But it's obviously fairly recent. The last couple of times I've rung him he's been a bit strange, not his usual self.'

I think back to the time I phoned him when he was on holidays. He'd said Simone couldn't get away from work. Maybe that was true. Or maybe they'd already separated.

'Have you replied to his email?' Jules asked.

'Not yet, I don't know what to say.'

'Don't say anything. Book yourself on the first available flight and get down here. Just burst into his office and surprise him.'

'I can't do that,' I said.

'Why not?'

I tried to think of a reason.

'Because it's spontaneous and exciting?' Jules asked.

'Because it's something that Meg Ryan would do in a movie and it would end happily ever after for her.'

'Why wouldn't it be the same for you? You deserve a happy ending just as much as Meg Ryan. Take a risk, Susie — he's worth it. Book a flight on Friday, and if you need a place to stay I'll reserve my couch for you.'

When I told Annie and Myf about the virtual kiss, and that I was thinking of making a surprise visit to Sydney, they pounced on the idea with delight.

'Fantastic! Go for it!' Annie said. 'I'd love to see his face when you walk in the door.'

'Me too,' Myf said. 'He's an attractive man — I'd get down there ASAP before some other woman gets her claws into him. Have a weekend of wild sex with him and get him hooked, so when you come back he won't be able to think of anything else except seeing you again.'

Spoken like a true femme fatale.

So there I was, with the help of my support group/send-off party waving at me as I went through the departure gate at the Sunshine Coast Airport — Myf and Amy, Annie and Terri (thankfully, minus her children), Cara and Byron and

Zac who, after much begging, was allowed to have the day off school again.

'You owe me,' he said. 'Leaving me at home all weekend with Cara and Lover Boy. I'll probably be living on chips and ice-cream.'

An exclusive diet of chips and ice-cream is Zac's idea of gourmet dining, but he knows that the prospect fills me with maternal fears of obesity and scurvy. Why, I don't know, because at fifteen, Zac has, as if by time lapse photography, suddenly become taller than me, considerably thinner, and in the bloom of health.

He spent the morning at the airport with his mobile phone glued to his hand, his fingers dancing over the buttons as he sent a continuous stream of text messages. His eloquence in text messaging is far superior to his verbal skills — perhaps I should try messaging him to see how he grunts by SMS. He wouldn't tell me who he was messaging, but I suspect it was Angie, the girl in his class he's had a crush on and who's been phoning Zac a lot lately for help with her homework. As this would be akin to attending sex therapy with the Pope, I can only conclude that she must be smitten as well.

Over coffee at the airport cafe, Myf announced that she was going to put Amy into childcare for a couple of days a week next semester and go back to uni to do her honours in psychology.

'You're actually going to make a career out of this?' I asked incredulously.

Myf shrugged. 'Maybe. I'm thinking of getting into the academic side and tutoring and then later lecturing.'

'Did Rob have anything to do with this decision?' Annie enquired.

'Of course not,' Myf said curtly. 'Just because I'm moving in with the head of the Psychology Department doesn't mean I get special treatment — not academically, anyway.'

'You're moving in with Rob?' We chorused. People at the surrounding tables swung around and looked at us curiously.

'What's the big deal?' Myf said. 'People do it all the time.'

'People do,' Annie said, 'but you don't. This is the big C, do you realise? Are you ready for it?'

'Of course I am. If this little angel hadn't come along,' — she looked dotingly at Amy, who was sitting up in her pram gurgling and charming the pants off the businessmen at the next table —'it might never have happened, but now that it has, I'm quite okay with it.'

'It's all out of your control anyway,' Terri put in. 'It's up to the planets and how they align themselves — you just have to go with the flow.'

'That's all every well until the flow takes you somewhere you don't want to be,' Annie said.

She was decked out in a self-designed outfit of classic black straight skirt teamed with a psychedelic diaphanous blouse — a sort of career girl on acid look. Lately she's had a restless, frustrated energy about her, as if she's still searching for something and what she's found so far doesn't meet her expectations. She's told me that she and Richard are now on speaking terms and are getting on quite well now that they don't have to contend with the day-to-day issues of their marriage. Richard wants them both to go to counselling, a big step forward for someone who used to be of the opinion that only women and crazy people went to counsellors. Annie wavers in her decision from day to day, and to complicate matters, Terri is still in the equation. If Annie and Richard decide to give their marriage another go, Terri will have to take her own advice about going with the flow.

'Aren't you going to start your own fashion design business and boutique when you finish your course?' I asked. 'That sounds pretty exciting to me.'

'We're going to do it together,' Terri said. 'I've got the financial backing and I'm going to help with the planning.'

Stunned silence. Who would have thought that underneath Terri's ethereal aura was a knack for business?

'Perhaps you could offer Tarot card readings to customers to help them choose the right outfits,' I suggested. 'As in, "you'll be going on an island cruise next year so I'd suggest something in a tropical design".'

'I was thinking that myself actually,' Terri said seriously.

*****

As I queued up to go through the departure gate, Annie said, 'I don't know why you didn't hire your own Learjet and turn up in style. That would really knock his socks off.'

'It's not his socks she wants off,' Myf said. 'It's just as well you met him before you became rich and famous. At least you know he's not a gold digger.'

'I still wouldn't trust him,' Cara said. 'Make sure he pays for dinner, Mum.'

As I shuffled forward in the queue, Myf leaned over and whispered in my ear, 'Got your sexy lingerie packed?'

'Won't need it,' I said mysteriously, winking at her and leaving her to ponder why. Because we won't be progressing that far? Or because we'll be spending the whole weekend in bed anyway?

I don't know the answer to that myself yet and I haven't got as far as thinking about the sex. I'm still trying to think of how to orchestrate my arrival. Pascoe Editing and Consulting is on the fourth floor of an office block in George Street, in the heart of Sydney. Should I phone first and announce 'I'm down in the lobby'? Or just take the lift up and sashay into his office — eyelashes fluttering and a here-I-am-take-me smile, with just a hint of demureness. That's what Meg Ryan would do, and Martin would jump up out of his chair, sweep her into his arms and onto the top of the desk, sending manuscripts flying. But there's always the chance that he's stepped out for a coffee or in the middle of a meeting, which would put a damper on the grand entrance.

The plane is cruising now, the flight attendants have done their spiel, and we've been given permission to undo our seatbelts. All I can see out the window is acres of blue sky dotted with fluffy white clouds. The initial adrenalin rush has faded away and left me with a cold, clammy feeling.

What do I really know about this man anyway, apart from the fact that I feel as if I've known him all my life, he makes me laugh and he's incredibly sexy? I've only met him for a total of about four hours, and for at least half of that time I was under the influence of alcohol. I don't know his favourite colour, his favourite food or who Emily's mother is and how long they were together, or if he really likes Meg Ryan movies or he's just saying that because he knows I do.

And what about sex? Okay, I lied before, I *have* thought about it. Lots. What if we find we're sexually incompatible? That no matter how hard we try, it just doesn't happen? Maybe there really isn't such a thing as perfect sex. Experts are always quoted as saying you have to work at a great sex life, but I maintain that if you have to work at it, the relationship's not right. I work all day — I don't want to have to work when I'm having sex as well.

And there's another big unknown — I imagine Martin is still getting over his separation from Simone and the last thing I want is to be a rebound lover. And what if we got into a relationship and it didn't work out? Who would edit my next book?

How do you know he didn't send kisses to twenty other women? And that he's not having coffee with one of them at this very moment?

For God's sake, shut up. To divert my thoughts, I scrabble around in my handbag and dig out my smartphone. I scroll through my emails until I find the one I want. Sent last night at 8.15pm.

To SusieH@gmail.com

From: JulesYoung4ever@gmail.com

Hi Susie,

I guess you're packing for your big weekend away. I really hope it works out for you and if Martin gives you the flick, he's not as smart as I gave him credit for.

When you rang to tell me about getting the kiss from him, I was in the middle of packing my bags. Things haven't worked out with Max and me here and I've moved into my own apartment until I decide what I'm going to do. I wanted to tell you before but didn't want to spoil your excitement. The reason I'm writing to you now is I'm hoping we can catch up while you're here. I promise I won't cry — well, maybe just a little, but it will be out of happiness at seeing you again.

What happened between Max and me? Nothing big, just lots of differences that hadn't been apparent until we started to build a life together. One of the main reasons is that I've discovered I don't like the big city lifestyle. I really thought I would, but I've found it very difficult to settle in Sydney and find my niche. I'm earning a lot more money in my job here; but the hours are long and there's a lot more pressure, and I'm really yearning for the laid-back lifestyle of the Coast. I've given it six months, and I don't know whether I should keep trying or just give it up and come home. The worst part is that Max and I still love each other, and we don't want to let go of the relationship. I don't know how we'd go with a commuting relationship, though if you and Martin end up in a relationship, you and I could fly to Sydney together to visit our respective lovers. Or you could move to Sydney — I could probably tolerate it if you were here.

What I didn't bank on was how much I was going to miss you. You're not only my best friend, you're my soul mate — you've always said I was the sister you never had, and that's how I feel about you. Over the last six months I've thought a lot about all the things we've done together. There's been nobody else in my life that I've felt so comfortable with and that I've had so much fun with — and that includes lovers.

I have often wondered whether we could have made a go of being in a relationship — I have come perilously close a few times to overstepping the line. Remember that night a couple of years ago when I took you out for dinner on your birthday? You wore that black dress you'd borrowed from Myf, and your hair was out and you had a flower in it, and you looked so soft and feminine. And afterwards at The Blue Note when that big ugly woman tried to drag me onto the dance floor, you whacked her with your handbag and then we had to make a quick getaway before she reported it to the security guard. We ran like crazy all the way back to my place, laughing so much we almost threw up. And then when we were sitting on my couch having coffee and your eyes were shining and your face was still flushed from running, I wanted so badly to take you in my arms and kiss you that I had to sit on my hands to stop myself.

So why did I stop myself? Love. It sounds strange, but loving you was what stopped me from making love to you. It's too big a risk to take — maybe we could live happily ever after, as in *When Harry Met Sally*, maybe we're both missing the opportunity of a lifetime to experience lasting happiness, but I'm a bit more mixed up than Billy Crystal and not as good-looking and it could be disastrous. And that I couldn't handle, because it might mean the end of the most beautiful friendship I will ever have.

Anyway, who knows what the future will bring? Nothing in this life is certain, least of all relationships. Whatever happens, you know I'll always love you. Let's make a pact that if we're both still single when we're 80, we'll check into the nursing home together and I'll have great fun chasing after you on my Zimmer frame.

Give me a call when you get into the airport.

Love, Jules xxx.

I have re-read his email numerous times, and each time it's made me cry. I don't know if I'm happy or sad or both. I start to sniffle and the elderly woman sitting beside me glances at me.

'Are you all right, dear?'

'Yeah, I'm fine,' I sniffle some more. 'Why do relationships have to be so complicated?'

I don't expect an answer and fortunately she doesn't try, just smiles sympathetically and passes me a tissue. I've brought my Kindle with me, but I can't concentrate on reading. I lean back and close my eyes and drift into that delirious half-awake, half-dream state. I'm back at The Blue Note with Jules, and Martin is there as well. Max is performing on stage in drag, then a huge Rottweiler springs through the air towards us, teeth snapping, but it turns out to be Darius in disguise, and he throws us all out. Then Jules appears brandishing Fred and chases Martin down the street, waving Fred at him threateningly.

I'm jolted back to dream-drugged reality by the dulcet tones of the flight attendant. 'Ladies and gentlemen, we've started our descent in preparation for landing. Please make sure your seat backs and tray tables are in their full upright position. Make sure your seatbelt is securely fastened and all carry-on luggage is stowed underneath the seat in front of you or in the overhead lockers.'

I look out my window but there's still only sky and cloud. Soon the vast sprawl of Sydney surrounding its jewel of a harbour will appear below me.

This is it. I'm stowing my fears in the overhead lockers, putting my heart on the line in an upright position and tightening my seatbelt. I'm coming in for touchdown.

THE END

ACKNOWLEDGMENTS

This novel was originally written in 2003 and filed away in the online equivalent of my bottom drawer. When I resurrected it 9 years later, it underwent massive reconstructive surgery, with invaluable input and advice from my team of specialist consultants.

I'm indebted to fellow writer Pam Mariko for her appraisal and critiques, and rising to the challenge of 'can you finish reading this novel before next week?' Many thanks also to my beta readers Genene Reuben, Jill Moffat and Angela Tidy for their time and comments. My copyeditor Christine Cranney did an excellent job of pulling it all into shape and smoothing off the rough edges.

As always, my family has given me lots of encouragement and support, although I think the title has guaranteed my children won't read this book. And last but not least, my deepest thanks and love to my partner Aaron Parker, to whom this book is dedicated, who does all the necessary left brain tasks for which I have little inclination or talent.

Thank-you for buying Perfect Sex. I hope you enjoyed it.

I would appreciate it very much if you would take a few minutes to leave an honest review on Amazon or whichever site you bought it from. Reviews help other readers to decide whether they will enjoy the book, as well as helping it to gain more visibility and ultimately, more sales.

Nothing is more rewarding for me than people reading and enjoying my books.

I would love to connect with you on the following media sites:

Facebook http://www.facebook.com/RobinStoreywriter

Twitter https://twitter.com/RobinStorey1

Pinterest http://pinterest.com/robinstorey

LinkedIn http://www.linkedin.com/in/robinstoreyauthor

Instagram https://instagram.com/robinstorey55/

YouTube https://www.youtube.com/user/RobinStoreyAuthor

Smashwords author page https://www.smashwords.com/profile/view/RobinStorey

Goodreads http://www.goodreads.com/author/show/7057008.Robin_Storey

Other Books by Robin Storey

For books in the Noir Nights crime/suspense series and Robin's stand-alone novels, please visit Storey-Lines http://storey-lines.com or find Robin Storey on Amazon or IngramSpark.

E-books are available at all major e-book retailers.

ABOUT THE AUTHOR

Robin Storey is an indie author who lives on the picturesque Sunshine Coast in Queensland, Australia. She's a former freelance writer who is hooked on writing novels – it's the most challenging, but also the most satisfying thing she's done.

Robin is a certified book nerd and when she is not writing or reading, she enjoys getting out into nature – hiking and chilling out at the beach.

www.ingramcontent.com/pod-product-compliance
Lightning Source LLC
Chambersburg PA
CBHW050143120726
47903CB00002B/478